S0-ABS-408

BEING HERE

BEING HERE
Modern Short Stories from Southern Africa

COMPILED BY ROBIN MALAN

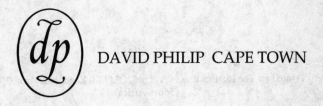

DAVID PHILIP CAPE TOWN

First published in 1994 in Southern Africa by David Philip Publishers (Pty) Ltd, 208 Werdmuller Centre, Claremont 7700, South Africa

© This selection Robin Malan 1994

All rights reserved

ISBN 0 86486 272 5

Cover design by Kim Siebert

Printed by The Rustica Press (Pty) Ltd, Old Mill Road, N'Dabeni 7405, South Africa

D2877

v

CONTENTS

INTRODUCTION

'Before we look forward into the twenty-first century we have the right to assess what we have come through. Being here; the particular time and place that has been twentieth-century Africa.'[1] – Nadine Gordimer, Winner of the Nobel Prize for Literature 1991

The stories collected here are about or come from South Africa, Botswana, Zimbabwe, Swaziland, Mozambique. There is a huge and hugely valuable storehouse of experience formalized in fiction of all sorts – novels, poems, plays and short prose – which comes from this region. There are some very particular conditions applying in Southern Africa which make it a seedbed of real, lived experience.

In South Africa the history of apartheid, of resistance to apartheid and the liberation of the people of South Africa have all created that 'life-giving drop' that Nadine Gordimer believed would 'spread an intensity on the page, burn a hole in it' (see quotation page x).

Zimbabwe went through the experience of Ian Smith's UDI minority white rule and then the trauma of the Chimurenga War before attaining Independence in 1980. For Botswana and Swaziland there has been a British colonial era giving way to two very different kinds of Independence. Mozambique has had to emerge from its Portuguese colonial past only to be plunged into a terrible civil war.

Njabulo Ndebele says:

We cannot wish away evil; but genuine art makes us understand it. Only then can we purposefully deal with it.[2]

Over all of these situations sits the amazing presence, or ambience, of Africa. Doris Lessing had this to say:

I believe that the chief gift from Africa to writers, white and black, is the continent itself, its presence which for some people is like an old fever, latent always in their blood; or like an old wound throbbing in the bones as the air changes. That is not a place to visit unless one chooses to be an exile ever afterwards from an inexplicable majestic silence lying just over the border of memory or of thought. Africa gives you the knowledge that man is a small creature, among other creatures, in a large landscape.[3]

In 1981 in a radio interview for 'Africa Week' Nadine Gordimer was asked why she remained in South Africa, why she did not go into exile. She replied:

One must look at the world *from Africa*, to be an African writer, not look *upon Africa* from the world.

In 1961 she observed:

In South Africa ... the reader knows perilously little about himself or his feelings. We have a great deal to learn about ourselves, and the novelist, along with the poet, playwright, composer and painter, must teach us.[4]

So, too, do we, in the 1990s, need Southern African literature to undo what apartheid education has done. We need it to help us get to know one another, to find our commonality, our samenesses; and, because of our samenesses, to see our differences as strengths to be sought after, shared and valued.

WHY 1960 ONWARDS?

I have dated the stories according to their first appearance in book form. Some, it is true, were published in magazines or journals prior to being collected in a volume. I have found it convenient to use the first volume publication date.

The oldest of these stories comes from 1960. Why the last 'thirtysomething' years? It has been a conscious decision, made not so much because of what is in the book as because of what is missing from it. I decided to start after the great *Drum* era. I must explain. For black writers the only real outlet for creative writing until the 1970s was the magazine *Drum*. Apart from its journalistic articles and features, it served as the only effective channel for the publishing of short fiction by black writers.

In his compilation *The Drum Decade* (University of Natal Press 1989) Michael Chapman tells us that between 1951 and 1958 *Drum* published over ninety short stories. And these were by a 'roll of honour' of writers such as Bloke Modisane, Henry Nxumalo, Arthur Maimane, Can Themba, Ezekiel (now Es'kia)

Mphahlele, Richard Rive, Nat Nakasa, Alex la Guma, Casey Motsisi … To have had that whole era represented in this collection would have doubled its length.

The reader is urged to look beyond this collection, to seek out compilations such as Chapman's *The Drum Decade*, Can Themba's *The Will to Die* and *The World of Can Themba*, Casey Motsisi's *Casey & Co.*, Es'kia Mphahlele's *Afrika my Music*, and *The World of Nat Nakasa*; as well as the autobiographies Todd Matshikiza's *Chocolates for my Wife*, Bloke Modisane's *Blame Me on History* and Es'kia Mphahlele's *Down Second Avenue*.

With 1960 came Sharpeville, the banning of the African National Congress and the Pan Africanist Congress; and the banning or banishment or exiling or death or suicide of virtually all of the *Drum* writers mentioned above. And so, in many ways, the 1960s became 'The Decade of Silence'.

Therefore the decision to devote this collection to stories published since 1960. As is clear from looking at the dates of the stories, some extremely enterprising publishing houses in the 70s and 80s (they have tended to be grouped together as 'the oppositional publishers') started to provide the way in which Southern African writers could be widely read.

WHAT IS A SHORT STORY?

Let's hear what Nadine Gordimer has to say about the short story:

> Nobody has ever succeeded in defining a short story in a manner to satisfy all who write or read them, and I shall not, here. I sometimes wonder if one shouldn't simply state flatly: a short story is a piece of fiction short enough to be read at one sitting? No, that will satisfy no one, least myself. But for me certainly there is a clue, there, to the choice of the short story by writers, as a form: whether or not it has a narrative in the external or internal sense, whether it sprawls or neatly bites its own tail, a short story is a concept that the writer can 'hold', fully realised, in his imagination, at one time. A novel is, by comparison, staked out, and must be taken possession of stage by stage; it is impossible to contain, all at once, the proliferation of concepts it ultimately may use. … A short story *occurs*, in the

imaginative sense. To write one is to express from a situation in the exterior or interior world the life-giving drop –
sweat, tear, semen, saliva – that will spread an intensity on
the page; burn a hole in it.[5]

What has that given us?

* First, there's the famous definition/non-definition of: 'A
short story is a piece of fiction short enough to be read at one sitting.' There are any number of implications and ramifications to
that definition.

* The next element Nadine Gordimer offers is: 'a narrative'.
The word suggests there must be a series of events, a storyline, a
plot. The British theatre critic Kenneth Tynan gave this neat
definition: 'The King died. Then the Queen died.' – That is a
story. 'The King died. Then the Queen died of a broken heart.' –
That is a plot. In other words, there must be causation, cause and
effect in the series of events.

* This narrative, Gordimer says, can be 'in the external or
internal sense'. This opens up the possibility that the story can be
reflective, introspective; it is not necessary that Anything Happens in the story – in the concrete, physical sense. Perhaps the
'events' that occur do so inside the mind, the psyche, of a character, or in fantasy.

* The story can be quite long ('it sprawls') or short and neat
enough to be snappy and clever and come full circle ('bite its
own tail').

* Then, at the heart of what Gordimer is saying is the idea that
the writer's imagination must be able to hold the concept, fully
realised, at one time, and she suggests that this is very different
from the conceiving and writing of a novel.

* Gordimer's final point concerns the intensity of the short
story, that it is a refined, concentrated expression of a new
insight into life or a new view of the world.

Doris Lessing makes a couple of interesting sidelong com-
ments on the short story when writing about 'long stories',
stories which are almost novels:

> A most enjoyable form this, to write, the long story ...
> There is space in them to take one's time, to think aloud, to
> follow, for a paragraph or two, on a side-trail – none of
> which is possible in a real short story.[6]

* So there it is again: the short story condenses, compresses,

contains, and does not allow any 'side-trails'. It is focused, and, generally, has only one focus.

Njabulo Ndebele points to the technical aspects of writing short stories:

> The world of fiction demands that the writer grapple with some of the following problems which are basic to his art: setting, conflict, credible characterisation, consistent narrative point of view, the complexities of fictional language and time.[7]

* The short story must have a 'setting', it must take place somewhere. In the case of the short stories collected in this volume, that somewhere is Southern Africa. Inside that geographical context, the settings are many and various. And, of course, the setting could be 'internalised', the story could 'take place' in a character's mind.

* For there to be any drama, there has to be a conflict of some kind. A clash of wills, of personalities, of ideas, of ideologies, will lead to conflict. That conflict will develop to a climax of some sort. That will be followed by a resolution. That's the 'classic' pattern; and there is a seemingly infinite number of variations. The word 'conflict' usually implies something serious, but, of course, the conflict could lead equally to comedy.

* Next Ndebele mentions 'credible characterisation'. The Points for Discussion raise a number of issues concerning characterisation. Here let me just draw your attention to Ndebele's qualifier, the word 'credible'. The point of any story will be weakened sadly if we do not find the characters believable – in speech, behaviour and actions.

* With the words 'consistent narrative point of view' Njabulo Ndebele brings us to the crucial issue of how the narration is carried. Is there a narrator? How do we identify the narrator? Is it the author? Is it a first-person narrator, the 'I' of the story? Does she or he take an active role in the story? Is it a third-person, omniscient, neutral narrator offering a supposedly objective point of view? These questions are important because, of course, it is through the narrator that we receive the story, and, if the narrator is a participant in the events she or he is describing, then we have to take her or his involvement, prejudices, biases, personality into account. The point Ndebele is making is that, whatever the point of view of the narration, it must be consistent

and carried through.

* 'The complexities of fictional language': Ndebele is referring to the way in which language operates in a particular context, and, to function successfully in fiction, it has to be true, accurate and appropriate to that context. It has to be authentic. This is despite the fact that the author has had to select and shape and 'arrange' the language. There could be a number of other issues involved in what Ndebele has called 'fictional language'. See also the section in this Introduction sub-titled Name-calling.

* By using the words 'fictional ... time', Ndebele raises the issue of manipulating historical or chronological time to suit the author's purpose. A decade can easily pass in the course of one short paragraph; equally, an entire 10-page story can cover no more than a moment in time. This issue is intimately related to the structure of a short story, the way in which the author builds it. She or he may present the events that make up the story chronologically, or may move backwards and forwards in time in order to tell the story from different perspectives. This issue is raised in some of the Points for Discussion that follow individual stories, especially 'The Homecoming'.

The following observations of Nadine Gordimer's open out from the realm of the short story only to all fiction, to all writing:

> ... any individual writer attempts to build the pattern of his own perception out of chaos ... my own constantly changing effort to teach myself how to make out of words a total form for whatever content I seize upon ... the revelation of new perceptions through the different techniques these demanded.[8]

* 'The pattern of his own perception out of chaos': All writing, all art, is an attempt to see and to create order or pattern out of the apparent chaos of living, and to do this personally, individually, singularly, in one's own perception of things.

* 'To make out of words a total form for whatever content...': A real work of art happens where the artist has found exactly the right form for what she or he wants to say; the form should match the content exactly. It should not be possible to add anything or to take anything away. The work of art should have 'integrity', wholeness, completeness.

* 'The revelation of new perceptions through the different techniques these demanded': There is little or no point in the

writer continuing to write unless her or his perceptions of life alter or are affected and re-shaped and re-formed. And there is no point in continuing to read unless one is going to have new perceptions revealed to one. And these new ways of looking at things will require new ways of expressing them.

To round off this section without further comment from me, have the following statement by Njabulo Ndebele in mind as you read these stories:

> I have learned, in the craft of fiction for example, that the difference between writers is not so much in the subjects of their writings: the range of subject matter is relatively limited. Rather, it is in the inventiveness of treatment, in the sharpening of insight, and in the deepening of consciousness.[9]

NAME-CALLING

Reading through these stories, mainly the South African ones, you will be amazed at the names some South Africans have called other South Africans. Black people have been called 'Kaffirs' and 'natives', so-called 'Coloured' people have been called 'Bushies' and 'hotnots', white people have been called 'blooming Jews' and 'whiteys'. And a lot more besides.

In the 1990s, as race classification becomes irrelevant and unacceptable and South Africans eventually grow into the state of 'colour-blindness' that is enjoyed in most international communities, you may need an historical/literary perspective on this, in order to cope with it.

An interesting insight comes from Nadine Gordimer while she was reading through collections of her short stories that spanned thirty years:

> Even the language changes from book to book: 'native' becomes first 'African' then 'Black', because these usages have been adopted (*), over three decades, by South Africans of various opinions, often at different stages. For example, the old Afrikaner in 'Abroad' (a recent story) still speaks quite naturally of 'natives', whereas for English-speaking whites the use of the term 'African' is now general, no longer even indicating, as it would have ten years ago, that the speaker was showing his political colours as

liberal if not leftist. The use of the blunt term 'Black' is now the reverse of pejorative or insulting: indeed it is the only one, of all generic words used to denote them, that has not been imposed upon but has been chosen by blacks themselves.

(*) There is a fourth, roughly concurrent with 'African', but I don't think it occurs in any of these stories: 'Bantu'. The word means 'people', and so, used in conjunction with the English word, as it often is – 'Bantu people' – it produces the idiotic term 'People people'. The use of 'Bantu' is official government *politesse*, adopted to replace the more offensive appellations with a term almost as negative – and revealing, so far as the user is concerned – as 'non-white'.[10]

Richard Rive was also interesting on the business of name-calling:

My birth certificate says that my parentage is mixed; that is, that I come from Black and White stock. By official decree I have been variously labelled 'Coloured', 'Non-European', and 'Non-White'. The first appellation is meaningless, since everyone is coloured. Some are coloured pink, others brown, others black. … 'Non-European' and 'Non-White' are highly insulting labels. They imply that the persons described are negative entities, non-somethings. … There must be few precedents in world history of an indigenous people being called by so negative an appellation.[11]

From the literary point of view, it is important to put the use of these various words into context. Be careful not to assume that the *writer* is using the word. It could be a *character* using it. It could be the *narrator* using it. And each of them would use the word for *her or his* own reasons, not the writer's.

So, when the two small girls in 'Traitors' refer to 'natives' they do so because that was the word for black people that they knew and heard their parents and their parents' friends use. They probably mean nothing more than 'black people'.

When someone in the Soweto crowd calls Johnny a 'Bushie' in Don Mattera's story 'Die Bushie is Dood …', that black character is using the derogatory term 'Bushman' for a so-called 'Coloured' person; it appears from the context to be used casually rather than insultingly. It is not Don Mattera, who himself had an Italian grandfather and a grandmother of Xhosa, Dutch and Griqua extraction, using the word.

So, be sure to examine who is using these words, and why. To quote Njabulo Ndebele in a slightly different context: 'Only then can we purposefully deal with it.'

RM
Cape Town
1994

REFERENCES

[1] Nadine Gordimer: Paper delivered at 'Symposium on the Main Issues in African Fiction and Poetry on the Threshold of the 21st Century', Harare, February 1992

[2] Njabulo Ndebele: in 'Turkish Tales and Some Thoughts On South African Fiction' from *Rediscovery of the Ordinary* (COSAW) Fordsburg 1991 p 31

[3] Doris Lessing: 'Preface for the 1964 Collection' in *Collected African Stories* Volume 1 *This Was The Old Chief's Country* (Paladin HarperCollins) London 1992 p 8

[4] Both Nadine Gordimer quotations are taken from Charlotte H Bruner (ed): *Unwinding Threads,* Writing by Women in Africa (Heinemann) London 1983 p 118

[5] Nadine Gordimer: Introduction to *Selected Stories* (Penguin) Harmondsworth 1983 p 15

[6] Doris Lessing: op cit p 8

[7] Njabulo Ndebele: ibid p 28

[8] Nadine Gordimer: op cit p 10

[9] Njabulo Ndebele: in 'Noma Award Acceptance Speech' op cit p 160

[10] Nadine Gordimer: op cit p 14

[11] Richard Rive: *Writing Black* (David Philip) Cape Town 1981 p 2

NADINE GORDIMER

The Bridegroom

He came into his road camp that afternoon for the last time. It was neater than any house would ever be; the sand raked smooth in the clearing, the water drums under the tarpaulin, the flaps of his tent closed against the heat. Thirty yards away a black woman knelt, pounding mealies, and two or three children, grey with Kalahari dust, played with a skinny dog. Their shrillness was no more than a bird's piping in the great spaces in which the camp was lost.

Inside his tent, something of the chill of the night before always remained, stale but cool, like the air of a church. There was his iron bed, with its clean pillowcase and big kaross. There was his table, his folding chair with the red canvas seat, and the chest in which his clothes were put away. Standing on the chest was the alarm clock that woke him at five every morning and the photographs of the seventeen-year-old girl from Francistown whom he was going to marry. They had been there a long time, the girl and the alarm clock; in the morning when he opened his eyes, in the afternoon when he come off the job. But now this was the last time. He was leaving for Francistown in the Roads Department ten-tonner, in the morning; when he came back, the next week, he would be married and he would have with him the girl, and the caravan which the department provided for married men. He had his eye on her as he sat down on the bed and took off his boots; the smiling girl was like one of those faces cut out of a magazine. He began to shed his working overalls, a rind of khaki stiff with dust that held his shape as he discarded it, and he called, easily and softly, *'Ou Piet, ek wag.'* But the bony black man with his eyebrows raised like a clown's, in effort, and his bare feet shuffling under the weight, was already at the tent with a tin bath in which hot water made a twanging tune as it slopped from side to side.

When he had washed and put on a clean khaki shirt and a pair of worn grey trousers, and streaked back his hair with sweet-smelling pomade, he stepped out of his tent just as the lid of the horizon closed on the bloody eye of the sun. It was winter and the sun set shortly after five; the grey sand turned a fading pink, the low thorn scrub gave out spreading stains of lilac shadow that presently all ran together; then the surface of the desert showed pocked and pored, for a minute or two, like the surface of the moon through a telescope, while the sky remained light over the darkened earth and the clean crystal pebble of the evening star shone. The campfires — his own and the black men's, over there — changed from near-invisible flickers of liquid colour to brilliant focuses of leaping tongues of light; it was dark. Every evening he sat like this through the short ceremony of the closing of the day, slowly filling his pipe, slowly easing his back round to the fire, yawning off the stiffness of his labour. Suddenly he gave a smothered giggle, to himself, of excitement. Her existence became real to him; he saw the face of the photograph, posed against a caravan door. He got up and began to pace about the camp, alert to promise. He kicked a log farther into the fire, he called an order to Piet, he walked up towards the tent and then changed his mind and strolled away again. In their own encampment at the edge of his, the road gang had taken up the exchange of laughing, talking, yelling, and arguing that never failed them when their work was done. Black arms gestured under a thick foam of white soap, there was a gasp and splutter as a head broke the cold force of a bucketful of water, the gleaming bellies of iron cooking-pots were carried here and there in the talkative preparation of food. He did not understand much of what they were saying — he knew just enough Tswana to give them his orders, with help from Piet and one or two others who understood his own tongue, Afrikaans — but the sound of their voices belonged to this time of the evening. One of the babies who always cried was keeping up a thin, ignored wail; the naked children were playing the chasing game that made the dog bark. He came back and sat down again at the fire, to finish his pipe.

After a certain interval (it was exact, though it was not timed by a watch, but by the long habit that had established the appropriate lapse of time between his bath, his pipe, and his food) he called out, in Afrikaans, 'Have you forgotten my dinner, man?'

From across the patch of distorted darkness where the light of the two fires did not meet, but flung wobbling shapes and opaque, overlapping radiances, came the hoarse, protesting laugh that was, better than the tribute to a new joke, the pleasure in constancy of an old one.

Then a few minutes later; 'Piet! I suppose you've burned everything, eh?'

'Baas?'

'Where's the food, man?'

In his own time, the black man appeared with the folding table and an oil lamp. He went back and forth between the dark and light, bringing pots and dishes and food, and nagging with deep satisfaction, in a mixture of English and Afrikaans. 'You want *koeksusters*, so I make *koeksusters*. You ask me this morning. So I got to make the oil nice and hot, I got to get everything ready … It's a little bit slow. Yes, I know. But I can't get everything quick, quick. You hurry, tonight, you don't want wait, then it's better you have *koeksusters* on Saturday, then I'm got time in the afternoon, I do it nice … Yes, I think next time it's better … '

Piet was a good cook. 'I've taught my boy how to make everything', the young man always told people, back in Francistown. 'He can even make *koeksusters*', he had told the girl's mother, in one of those silences of the woman's disapproval that it was so difficult to fill. He had had a hard time, trying to overcome the prejudice of the girl's parents against the sort of life he could offer her. He had managed to convince them that the life was not impossible, and they had given their consent to the marriage, but they still felt that the life was unsuitable, and his desire to please and reassure them had made him anxious to see it with their eyes and so forestall, by changes, their objections. The girl was a farm girl, and would not pine for town life, but, at the same time, he could not deny to her parents that living on a farm with her family around her, and neighbours only thirty or forty miles away, would be very different from living two hundred and twenty miles from a town or village, alone with him in a road camp 'surrounded by a gang of kaffirs all day', as her mother had said. He himself simply did not think at all about what the girl would do while he was out on the road; and as for the girl, until it was over, nothing could exist for her but the wedding, with her two little sisters in pink walking behind her, and her

dress that she didn't recognise herself in, being made at the
dressmaker's, and the cake that was ordered with a tiny china
bride and groom in evening dress, on the top.

He looked at the scored table, and the rim of the open jam tin,
and the salt cellar with a piece of brown paper tied neatly over
the broken top, and said to Piet, 'You must do everything nice
when the missus comes.'

'*Baas?*'

They looked at each other and it was not really necessary to
say anything.

'You must make the table properly and do everything clean.'

'Always I make everything clean. Why you say now I must
make clean.'

The young man bent his head over his food, dismissing him.

While he ate his mind went automatically over the changes
that would have to be made for the girl. He was not used to
visualizing situations, but to dealing with what existed. It was
like a lesson learned by rote; he knew the totality of what was
needed, but if he found himself confronted by one of the com-
ponent details, he foundered: he did not recognise it or know
how to deal with it. The boys must keep out of the way. That
was the main thing. Piet would have to come to the caravan
quite a lot, to cook and clean. The boys – especially the boys who
were responsible for the maintenance of the lorries and the road-
making equipment – were always coming with questions, what
to do about this and that. They'd mess things up, otherwise. He
spat out a piece of gristle he could not swallow; his mind went to
something else. The women over there – they could do the
washing for the girl. They were such a raw bunch of kaffirs,
would they ever be able to do anything right? Twenty boys and
about five of their women – you couldn't hide them under a
thorn bush. They just mustn't hang around, that's all. They must
just understand that they mustn't hang around. He looked
round keenly through the shadow-puppets of the half-dark on
the margin of the fire's light; the voices, companionably quieter,
now intermittent over food, the echoing *chut!* of wood being
chopped, the thin film of a baby's wail through which all these
sounded – they were on their own side. Yet he felt an odd, rank-
ling suspicion.

His thoughts shuttled, as he ate, in a slow and painstaking

way that he had never experienced before in his life — he was worrying. He sucked on a tooth; Piet, Piet, that kaffir talks such a hell of a lot. How's Piet going to stop talking, talking every time he comes near? If he talks to her … Man, it's sure he'll talk to her. He thought, in actual words, what he would say to Piet about this; the words were like those unsayable things that people write on walls for others to see in private moments, but that are never spoken in their mouths.

Piet brought coffee and *koeksusters* and the young man did not look at him.

But the *koeksusters* were delicious, crisp, sticky, and sweet, and as he felt the familiar substance and taste on his tongue, alternating with the hot bite of the coffee, he at once became occupied with the pure happiness of eating as a child is fully occupied with a bag of sweets. *Koeksusters* never failed to give him this innocent, total pleasure. When first he had taken the job of overseer to the road gang, he had had strange, restless hours at night and on Sundays. It seemed that he was hungry. He ate but never felt satisfied. He walked about all the time, like a hungry creature. One Sunday he actually set out to walk (the Roads Department was very strict about the use of the ten-tonner for private purposes) the fourteen miles across the sand to the cattle-dipping post where the government cattle officer and his wife, Afrikaners like himself and the only other white people between the road camp and Francistown, lived in their corrugated-iron house. By a coincidence, they had decided to drive over and see him, that day, and they had met him a little less than halfway, when he was already slowed and dazed by heat. But shortly after that Piet had taken over the cooking of his meals and the care of his person, and Piet had even learned to make *koeksusters*, according to instructions given to the young man by the cattle officer's wife. The *koeksusters*, a childhood treat that he could indulge in whenever he liked, seemed to mark his settling down; the solitary camp became a personal way of life, with its own special arrangements and indulgences.

'Ou Piet! *Kêrel!* What did you do to the *koeksusters*, hey?' he called out joyously.

A shout came that meant 'Right away'. The black man appeared, drying his hands on a rag, with the diffident, kidding manner of someone who knows he has excelled himself.

'Whatsa matter with the *koeksusters*, man?'

'Here, bring me some more, man.' The young man shoved the empty plate at him, with a grin. And as the other went off, laughing, the young man called. 'You must always make them like that, see?'

He liked to drink at celebrations, at weddings or Christmas, but he wasn't a man who drank on a Saturday afternoon, when the week's work was over, and for the rest of the time, the bottle that he brought from Francistown when he went to collect stores lay in the chest in his tent. But on this last night he got up from the fire on impulse and went over to the tent to fetch the bottle (one thing he didn't do, he didn't expect a kaffir to handle his drink for him; it was too much of a temptation to put in their way). He brought a glass with him, too, one of a set of six made of tinted imitation cut glass, and he poured himself a tot and stretched out his legs where he could feel the warmth of the fire through the soles of his boots. The nights were not cold, until the wind came up at two or three in the morning, but there was a clarifying chill to the air; now and then a figure came over from the black men's camp to put another log on the fire whose flames had dropped and become blue. The young man felt inside himself a similar low incandescence; he poured himself another brandy. The long yelping of the jackals prowled the sky without, like the wind about a house; there was no house, but the sounds beyond the light his fire tremblingly inflated into the dark – that jumble of meaningless voices, crying babies, coughs, and hawking – had built walls to enclose and a roof to shelter. He was exposed, turning naked to space on the sphere of the world as the speck that is a fly plastered on the window of an aeroplane, but he was not aware of it.

The lilt of various kinds of small music began and died in the dark; threads of notes, blown and plucked, that disappeared under the voices. Presently a huge man whose thick black body had strained apart every seam in his ragged pants and shirt loped silently into the light and dropped just within it, not too near the fire. His feet, intimately crossed, were cracked and weathered like driftwood. He held to his mouth a one-stringed instrument shaped like a lyre, made out of a half-moon of bent wood with a ribbon of dried palm leaf tied from tip to tip. His big lips rested gently on the strip and while he blew, his one hand, by controlling the vibration of the palm leaf, made of his breath a small, faint, perfect music. It was caught by the very limits of the capacity of the human ear; it was almost out of range. The first music men every heard, when they began to stand upright among the rushes at the river, might have been like it. When it died away it was difficult to notice at what point it really had gone.

'Play that other one,' said the young man, in Tswana. Only the smoke from his pipe moved.

The pink-palmed hands settled down round the instrument. The thick, tender lips were wet once. The faint desolate voice spoke again, so lonely a music that it came to the player and listener as if they heard it inside themselves. This time the player took a short stick in his other hand and, while he blew, scratched it back and forth inside the curve of the lyre, where the notches cut there produced a dry, shaking, slithering sound, like the far-off movements of dancers' feet. There were two or three figures with more substance than the shadows, where the firelight merged with the darkness. They came and squatted. One of them had half a paraffin tin, with a wooden neck and other attachments of gut and wire. When the lyre-player paused, lowering his piece of stick and leaf slowly, in ebb, from his mouth, and wiping his lips on the back of his hand, the other began to play. It was a thrumming, repetitive banjo tune. The young man's boot patted the sand in time to it and he took it up with hand-claps once or twice. A thin, yellowing man in an old hat pushed his way to the front past sarcastic remarks and twit-tings and sat on his haunches with a little clay bowl between his feet. Over its mouth there was a keyboard of metal tongues. After some exchange, he played it and the others sang low and nasally, bringing a few more strollers to the fire. The music came to an end, pleasantly, and started up again, like a breath drawn. In one of the intervals the young man said, 'Let's have a look at that contraption of yours, isn't it a new one?' and the man to whom he signalled did not understand what was being said to him but handed over his paraffin-tin mandolin with pride and also with amusement at his own handiwork.

The young man turned it over, twanged it once, grinning and shaking his head. Two bits of string and an old jam tin and they'll make a whole band, man. He'd heard them playing some crazy-looking things. The circle of faces watched him with pleasure; they laughed and lazily remarked to each other; it was a funny-looking thing, all right, but it worked. The owner took it back and played it, clowning a little. The audience laughed and joked appreciatively; they were sitting close in to the fire now, painted by it. 'Next week,' the young man raised his voice gaily, 'next week when I come back, I bring radio with me, plenty real music. All the big white bands play over it – ' Someone who had once worked in Johannesburg said 'Satchmo', and the others took it up, understanding that this was the word for what the white man was going to bring from town. Satchmo. Satch-mo. They tried it out, politely. 'Music, just like at a big white dance in town. Next week.' A friendly appreciative silence fell, with them all resting back in the warmth of the fire and looking at him indulgently. A strange thing happened to him. He felt hot, over first his neck, then his ears and his face. It didn't matter, of course; by next week they would have forgotten. They wouldn't expect it. He shut down his mind on a picture of them, hanging round the caravan to listen, and him coming out on the steps to tell them –

He thought for a moment that he would give them the rest of the bottle of brandy. Hell, no, man, it was mad. If they got the taste for the stuff, they'd be pinching it all the time. He'd give Piet some sugar and yeast and things from the stores, for them to make beer tomorrow when he was gone. He put his hands deep in his pockets and stretched out to the fire with his head sunk on his chest. The lyre-player picked up his flimsy piece of wood again, and slowly what the young man was feeling inside him- self seemed to find a voice; up into the night beyond the fire, it went, uncoiling from his breast and bringing ease. As if it had been made audible out of infinity and could be returned to infinity at any point, the lonely voice of the lyre went on and on. Nobody spoke. The barriers of tongues fell with silence. The whole dirty tide of worry and planning had gone out of the young man. The small high moon, outshone by a spiky spread of cold stars, repeated the shape of the lyre. He sat for he was not aware how long, just as he had for so many other nights, with the stars at his head and the fire at his feet.

But at last the music stopped and time began again. There was tonight; there was tomorrow, when he was going to drive to

Francistown. He stood up; the company fragmented. The lyre-player blew his nose into his fingers. Dusty feet took their accustomed weight. They went off to their tents and he went off to his. Faint plangencies followed them. The young man gave a loud, ugly, animal yawn, the sort of unashamed personal noise a man can make when he lives alone. He walked very slowly across the sand; it was dark but he knew the way more surely than with his eyes. 'Piet! Hey!' he bawled as he reached his tent. 'You get up early tomorrow, eh? And I don't want to hear the lorry won't start. You get it going and you call me. D' you hear?'

He was lighting the oil lamp that Piet had left ready on the chest and as it came up softly it brought the whole interior of the tent with it: the chest, the bed, the clock, and the coy smiling face of the seventeen-year-old girl. He sat down on the bed, sliding his palms through the silky fur of the kaross. He drew a breath and held it for a moment, looking round purposefully. And then he picked up the photograph, folded the cardboard support back flat to the frame, and put it in the chest with all his other things, ready for the journey.

Rain

Rain poured down, blotting out all sound with its sharp and vibrant tattoo. Dripping neon signs reflecting lurid reds and yellows in mirror-wet streets. Swollen gutters. Water over-flowing and squelching on to pavements. Gurgling and sucking at storm-water drains. Table Mountain cut off by a grey film of mist and rain. A lost City Hall clock trying manfully to chime nine over an indifferent Cape Town. Baleful reverberations through a spluttering all-consuming drizzle.

Yellow light filters through from Solly's 'Grand Fish and Chips Palace'. Door tightshut against the weather. Inside stuffy with heat, hot bodies, steaming clothes, and the nauseating smell of stale fish oil. Misty patterns on the plate-glass windows and a messy pool where rain has filtered beneath the door and mixed with the sawdust.

Solly himself in shirt sleeves, sweating, vulgar, and moody. Bellowing at a dripping woman who has just come in.

'Shut 'e damn door. Think you live in a tent?'

'Ag, Solly.'

'Don' ag me. You coloured people can never shut blarry doors.'

'Don't you bloomingwell swear at me.'

'I bloomingwell swear at you, yes.'

'Come. Gimme two pieces o' fish. Tail cut.'

'Two pieces o' fish.'

'Raining like hell outside,' the woman said to no one.

'Mmmmmm. Raining like hell,' a thin befezzed Malay cut in.

'One an' six. Thank you. An' close 'e door behin' you.'

'Thanks. Think you got 'e on'y door in Hanover Street?'

'Go to hell!' Solly cut the conversation short and turned to another customer.

The northwester sobbed heavy rain squalls against the windowpanes. The Hanover Street bus screeched to a slithery stop and passengers darted for shelter in a cinema entrance. The street lamps shone blurredly.

Solly sweated as he wrapped parcels of fish and chips in a newspaper. Fish and chips. Vinegar? Wrap? One an' six please. Thank you! Next. Fish and Chips. No? Two fish. No chips? Salt? Vinegar? One an' six please. Thank you! Next. Fish an' chips.

'Close 'e blarry door!' Solly glared daggers at a woman who had just come in. She half smiled apologetically at him.

'You also live in a blarry tent?'

She struggled with the door and then stood dripping in a pool of wet sawdust. Solly left the counter to add two presto logs to the furnace. She moved out of the way. Another customer showed indignation at Solly's remark.

Fish an' chips. Vinegar? Salt? One an' six. Thank you. Yes, madam?'

'Could you tell me when the bioscope comes out?'

'Am I the blooming manager?'

'Please.'

'Half pas' ten, tonight,' the Muslim offered helpfully.

'Thank you. Can I stay here till then? It's raining outside.'

'I know it's blarrywell raining, but this is not a Salvation Army.'

'Please, baas!'

This caught Solly unawares. He had had his shop in that corner of District Six since most could remember and had been called a great many unsavoury things in the years. Solly didn't mind. But this caught him unawares. *Please baas*. This felt good. His imagination adjusted a black bow tie to an evening suit. *Please, Baas*.

'Okay, stay for a short while. But when 'e rain stops you go.'

She nodded dumbly and tried to make out the blurred name of the cinema opposite, through the misted windows.

'Waitin' for somebody?' Solly asked. No response.

'I ask if yer waitin' fer somebody?' The figure continued to stare.

'Oh go to hell,' said Solly, turning to another customer.

Through the rain blur Siena stared at nothing in particular. Dim visions of slippery wet cars. Honking and wheezing in the rain. Spluttering buses. Heavy, drowsy voices in the Grand Fish and Chips Palace. Her eyes travelled beyond the street and the water cascades of Table Mountain, beyond the winter of Cape

Town to the summer of the Boland. Past the green grapelands of
Stellenbosch and Paarl and the stuffy wheat district of Malmes-
bury to the sun and laughter of Teslaarsdal. A tired sun here. An
uninterested sun. Now it seemed that the sun was weary of the
physical effort of having to rise, to shine, to comfort, and to set.

Inside the nineteenth-century, gabled mission church she had
first met Joseph. The church is still there, and beautiful, and the
ivy climbs over it and makes it more beautiful. Huge silver oil
lamps suspended from the roof, polished and shining. It was in
the flicker of the lamps that she had first become aware of him.
He was visiting from Cape Town. She sang that night like she
had never sung before. Her favourite psalm.

'*Al ging ik ook in een dal der schaduw des doods* ... Though I walk
through the valley of the shadow of death ... *der schaduw des
doods.*' And then he had looked at her. Everyone had looked at
her, for she was good in solos.

'*Ik zoude geen kwaad vreezen* ... I will fear no evil.' And she had
not feared but loved. Had loved him. Had sung for him. For the
wide eyes, the yellow skin, the high cheekbones. She had sung
for a creator who could create a man like Joseph. '*Want gij zijt
met mij; Uw stok and Uw staf, die vertroosten mij.*'

Those were black-and-white polka-dot nights when the moon
did a golliwog cakewalk across a banjo-strung sky. Nights of
sweet remembrances when he had whispered love to her and
told her of Cape Town. She had giggled coyly at his obscenities.
It was fashionable, she hoped, to giggle coyly at obscenities. He
lived in one of those streets off District Six, it sounded like
Horsburg Lane, and was, he boasted, quite a one among the
girls. She heard of Molly and Miena and Sophia and a sophisticated Charmaine, who was almost a schoolteacher and always
spoke English. But he told her that he had only found love in
Teslaarsdal. She wasn't sure whether to believe him. And then
he had felt her richness and the moon darted behind a cloud.

The loud screeching of the train to Cape Town. Screeching
loud enough to drown the protest of her family. The wrath of her
father. The icy stares of Teslaarsdal matrons. Loud and confused
screechings to drown her hysteria, her ecstasy. Drowned and
confused in the roar of a thousand cars and a hundred thousand
lights and a summer of carnival evenings that is Cape Town.
Passion in a tiny room off District Six.

And the agony of the nights when he came home later and later and sometimes not at all. The waning of his passion and whispered names of others. Molly and Miena and Sophia. Charmaine. The helpless knowledge that he was slipping from her. Faster and Faster. Gathering momentum.

'Not that I'm saying so but I only heard …'

'Why don't you go to bioscope one night and see for yourself …?'

'Marian's man is searching for Joseph …' Searching for Joseph. Looking for Joseph. Knifing for Joseph. Joseph. Joseph. *Joseph.* Molly! Miena! Sophia! Names! Names! Names! Gossip. One-sided desire. Go to bioscope and see. See what? See why? When! Where!

And after he had been away a week she decided to see. Decided to go through the rain and stand in a sweating fish and chips shop owned by a blaspheming Jew. And wait for the cinema to come out.

The rain had stopped sobbing against the plate-glass window. A skin-soaking drizzle now set in. Continuous. Unending. Filming everything with dark depression. A shivering, weeping neon sign flickered convulsively on and off. A tired Solly shot a quick glance at a cheap alarm clock.

'Half pas' ten, bioscope out soon.'

Siena looked more intently through the misty screen. No movement whatsoever in the deserted cinema foyer.

'Time it was bloomingwell out.' Solly braced himself for the wave of after-show customers who would invade his Palace.

'Comin' out late tonight, missus.'

'Thank you, baas.'

Solly rubbed sweat out of his eyes and took in her neat and plain figure. Tired face but good legs. A few late stragglers catching colds in the streets. Wet and squally outside.

'Your man in bioscope, missus?'

She was intent on a khaki-uniformed usher struggling to open the door.

'Man in bioscope, missus?'

The cinema had to come out some time or other. An usher opening the door, adjusting the outside gate. Preparing for the crowds to pour out. Vomited and spilled out.

'Man in bioscope?'

No response.

'Oh, go to hell!'

They would be out now. Joseph would be out. She rushed for the door, throwing words of thanks to Solly.

'Close 'e blarry door!'

She never heard him. The drizzle had stopped. An unnatural calm hung over the empty foyer, over the deserted street. Over her empty heart. She took up her stand on the bottom step. Expectantly. Her heart pounding.

Then they came. Pouring, laughing, pushing, jostling. She stared with fierce intensity, but faces passed too fast. Laughing, roaring, gay. Wide-eyed, yellow-skinned, high cheekboned. Black, brown, ivory, yellow. Black-eyed, laughing-eyed, gay, bouncing. No Joseph. Palpitating heart that felt like bursting into a thousand pieces. If she should miss him. She found herself searching for the wrong face. Solly's face. Ridiculously searching for hard blue eyes and a sharp white skin in a sea of ebony and brown. Solly's face. Missing half a hundred faces and then again searching for the familiar high cheekbones. Solly. Joseph. Molly. Miena. Charmaine.

The drizzle restarted. Studying overcoats instead of faces. Longing for the pale blue shirt she had seen in the shop at Solitaire. A bargain at £1.5s. She had scraped and scrounged to buy it for him. A week's wages. Collecting her thoughts and continuing the search for Joseph. And then the thinning out of the crowd and the last few stragglers. The ushers shutting the iron gates. They might be shutting Joseph in. Herself out. Only the ushers left.

'Please, is Joseph inside?'

'Who's Joseph?'

'Is Joseph still inside?'

'Joseph who?'

They were teasing her. Laughing behind her back. Preventing her from finding him.

'Joseph is inside!' she shouted frenziedly.

'Look, merrim, it's raining cats an' dogs. Go home.'

Go home. To whom? To what? An empty room? An empty bed?

And then she was aware of the crowd on the corner. Maybe he was there. Running and peering into every face. Joseph. The crowd in the drizzle. Two battling figures. Joseph. Figures locked in struggle slithering in the wet gutter. Muck streaking down clothes through which wet bodies were silhouetted. Joseph. A blue shirt. And then she wiped the rain out of her eyes and saw him. Fighting for his life. Desperately kicking in the gutter. Joseph. The blast of a police whistle. A pickup van screeching to a stop.

'Please, sir, it wasn't him. They all ran away. Please, sir, he's Joseph. He done nothing. He done nothing, my baas. Please, sir, he's my Joseph. Please, baas!'

'*Maak dat jy weg kom. Get away. Voetsak!*'

'Please, sir, it wasn't him. They ran away!'

Alone. An empty bed. An empty room.

Solly's Grand Fish and Chips Palace crowded out. People milling inside. Rain once more squalling and sobbing against the door and windows. Swollen gutters unable to cope with the giddy rush of water. Solly sweating to deal with the after-cinema rush.

Fish an' chips. Vinegar? Salt? One an' six. Thank you. Sorry, no fish. Wait five minutes. Chips on'y. Vinegar? Ninepence. Tickey change. Thank you. Sorry, no fish. Five minutes time. Chips? Ninepence. Thank you. Solly paused for breath and stirred the fish.

'What's 'e trouble outside?'

'Real bioscope, Solly.'

'No man, outside!'

'I say, real bioscope.'

'What were 'e police doin'? Sorry, no fish yet, sir. Five minutes' time. What were 'e police doin'?.

'A fight in 'e blooming rain.'

'Jeeesus, in 'e rain?'

'Ja.'

'Who was fightin'?

'Joseph an' somebody.'

'Joseph?'

'Ja, a fellow in Horsburg Lane.'

'Yes, I know Joseph. Always in trouble. Chucked him outta here a'reddy.

'Well, that chap.'

'An' who?'

'Dinno.'

'Police got them?'

'Got Joseph.'

'Why were 'ey fightin'? Fish in a minute, sir.'

'Over a dame.'

'Who?'

'You know Miena who works by Patel? Now she. Her boyfriend caught 'em.'

'In bioscope'

'Ja.'

Solly chuckled deeply, suggestively.

'See that woman an' 'e police?'

'What woman?'

'One cryin' to 'e police. They says it's Joseph's girl from 'e country.'

'Joseph always got plenty dames from 'e town and country. F-I-S-H R-E-A-D-Y!!! Two pieces for you, sir? One an' six. Shilling change. Fish an' chips? One an' six. Thank you. Fish on'y? Vinegar? Salt? Ninepence. Tickey change. Thank you. What you say about 'e woman?'

'They say Joseph's girl was crying to 'e police.'

'Oh, he got plenty 'e girls.'

'This one was living with him.'

'Oh, what she look like? Fish, sir?'

'Okay. Nice legs.'

'Hmmmmm,' said Solly, 'Hey, close 'e damn door. Oh, you again.' Siena came in. A momentary silence. Then a buzzing and whispering.

'Oh,' said Solly, nodding as someone whispered over the counter to him. 'I see. She was waiting here. Musta been waitin' for him.' A young girl in jeans giggled.

'Fish an' chips costs one an' six, madam.'

'Wasn't it one an' three before?.

'Before the Boer war, madam. Price of fish go up. Potatoes go up an' you expect me to charge one an' three?'

'Why not?'

'Oh, go to hell! Next please!'

'Yes, that's 'e one, Solly.'

'Mmmm. Excuse me, madam' — turning to Siena — 'like some fish an' chips. Free of charge, never min' 'e money.'

'Thank you, my baas.'

The rain now sobbed wildly as the shop emptied, and Solly counted the cash in his till. Thousands of watery horses charging down the street. Rain drilling into cobbles and pavings. Miniature waterfalls down the sides of buildings. Blurred lights through unending streams. Siena listlessly holding the newspaper parcel of fish and chips.

'You can stay here till it clears up,' said Solly.

She looked up tearfully.

Solly grinned, showing his yellow teeth. 'It's OK.'

A smile flickered across her face for a second.

'It's quite OK by me.'

She looked down and hesitated for a moment. Then she struggled against the door. It yielded with a crash and the northwester howled into Solly's Palace.

'Close 'e blarry door!' he said grinning.

'Thank you, my baas,' she said as she shivered out into the rain.

ALEX LA GUMA

Nocturne

There were three of them sitting at the table near the window. At that time of the afternoon The Duke's Head was quiet. The plump barman wiped the smooth, stained teak in front of him. At the end of the bar a haggard man sat like a lone penitent in a cathedral and slowly sipped his flat beer. Somewhere across the street somebody was playing a piano. The three at the table were drinking beer and port and talking quietly.

'It's easy,' Moos was saying. 'Frog will be outside holding candle. You and I, Harry, will get in and floor the watchman. Hell, Harry, you aren't listening.'

Harry was listening to the piano across the street. The music came through the open window, now tinkling like water dripping into a fine china bowl, now throbbing and booming with the sound of many beautifully tuned gongs, rippling away and rising again in great waves.

'God, what playing,' Harry said, as the piece ebbed to a gentle finish. 'Did you rookers hear that?'

'—,' Moos said. 'Classical stuff. Just a helluva noise. Give me a wakker jol anytime.' He dismissed the subject by taking a swallow of beer. 'Now listen. We'll go over it again …'

'I know, I know,' Harry said. 'Frog is outside keeping watch. We'll be inside fixing the watchman. Now what time do we meet?'

'Nine,' Moos answered. 'I'll pick Frog up and we'll get you outside the Modern.'

'How much you think we'll pick up?' Frog asked, drinking some of his port. The piano started again, the music drifting cautiously into the barroom.

'About a hundred and forty or fifty,' Moos said. He was aware of the sound again, but ignored it. Only Harry continued to listen. He sipped his port and let his mind lap at the music. The gentle, perfect notes touched something inside him, and he got a strange feeling, but did not try to fathom it. He kept listen-

ing. He tried the air under his breath, struggling with it like a
terrier with an expensive slipper, and gave it up to listen again.
The piano music quivered and undulated. Once a car passed and
drowned it momentarily, but it emerged again, gentle as the
drop of tears. It was the Nocturne No. 2, in E flat major, by
Chopin, but Harry did not know that.

Moos and Frog began talking about other things as the piano
drifted in to the 'Fantasie-Impromptu'. Harry was completely
absorbed in the music now. It held him in its spell, tying him to
itself with wires of throbbing sound, drugging his mind into a
coma of swelling and fading rhythm. The music went on,
seemingly inexhaustible: Liszt's 'Hungarian Rhapsody' pounded
and crashed, the theme from Tchaikovsky's 'Pathétique' wept
quietly, waltzes and minuets pranced and cavorted, pieces of
Beethoven marched sombrely, and Spanish gypsy dances
whirled and stamped. Schubert's 'Serenade' called longingly to
some unknown lover in a darkened room. The Nocturne came
again, drifting with the step of fairies on moonlit grass.

The Duke's Head began to fill up steadily with the six o'clock
crowd, until the music was lost in the steady hum of voices.
Harry got up and wandered to the bar. The spell was broken. He
whistled softly through his teeth, trying to capture a tune, but
his mind had not drunk deeply enough of the music. He joined
the three-deep line at the bar and shouldered his way through
until he could order half-a-pint of white wine. He leaned against
the wet teakwood and drank quietly, still trying to remember.
Around him men discussed every topic imaginable: work, races,
politics, women, wine, bioscope, religion. A dirty and dis-
hevelled man came in, selling pickles and curry pies. At one end
of the bar an argument developed, and for a few moments there
was uproar, until the plump barman broke it up.

Somebody tapped Harry on the shoulder and he turned his
head. It was Moos.

'Nine o'clock. Don't forget.'

'Okay. Okay. See you later.'

Harry did not watch Moos and Frog go out. He finished the
white wine and then extricated himself from the jam at the bar
and pushed past the swinging doors into the street. He paused
on the pavement. It was growing dark, and the street lamps
were on. From diagonally across the way the piano music was

still going on, a little louder now that he was outside. It came
from an old two-storey building, one of a row that formed one
side of the grimy street.

He stood for a while and listened, and then strolled down the
pavement, looking across at the house, drawn by the music like
an alley cat drawn by the scent of fresh and tender meat.

Drab and haunted-looking people sat in doorways looking
like scarred saints among the ruins of abandoned churches, half
listening, gossiping idly, while the pinched children shot at each
other with wooden guns from behind overflowing dustbins in
the dusk. Harry crossed the street and paused, hesitating, outside the house.

The music gripped him again. It came from a half-open
window on the first floor, bubbling out like a spring of cool
water in a wasteland. Then he made up his mind suddenly and
climbed the chipped front steps and edged into the house. The
hallway was dim and smelled of stale cooking and carbolic
water. The sound came from the upper landing, slipping down
the worn staircase, echoing from the gloomy corners and the
high stained ceiling. He climbed the stairs slowly, advancing
into the crescendo of Ravel's 'Bolero'.

Outside the door he stopped, nervous now, a little afraid, but
soaked in the music. He stood there while the 'Bolero' ended in
its crashing chords. Sounds came again, tirelessly, gently, moon-
beam quivering on quiet waters, on trees and grass along a
lonely river bank, sighing for love; and he placed his hand on the
doorknob and turned it.

The music faded away like a cataract in a little mountain nook
quietly running dry, and the girl at the piano looked at him with
sudden surprise.

'I'm sorry if I scared you,' he said, holding the door open. 'I've
been listening to you playing from across the way. Real good
music.'

'Thank you. Do you like it?'

'Don't know anything about it. But it sounds pretty.'

'Come in and sit down if you want to,' she said. 'People
around here often come in to listen.'

'Thanks, miss.'

He entered, awkward as a tramp being admitted to a parish
tea, and was suddenly conscious of the port-wine smell on his

breath. He sat down on a straight chair as if he expected it to collapse under his weight. The room was neat, dustless, polished, the little tables cluttered with bric-à-brac, framed music-school certificates hanging with Queen Victoria, wedding groups, and *God is Love* along the papered walls. Another door led to an adjoining room. The whole place seemed to struggle for survival with the surrounding dilapidation, like a Siamese cat caught in a sewer.

'You learn to play by yourself?' he asked, scarcely daring to speak aloud.

'Oh, no. I studied in a convent.'

'What's it bring you? It's pretty, but what's it bring you? Money?'

'Money's not everything. People come up here to listen.'
She smiled at him and ran her fingers along the keys. Her face was dark and fine and delicate as a costly violin. 'What do you want me to play?'

Harry cleared his throat and said: 'That piece you were playing when I came in. It sounded good.'

'The "Moonlight Sonata".' And the music swelled up again, falling on him like a gentle rain. He sat straight up, listening, and his muscles relaxed and his mind forgot the nervousness and he sank back in the chair.

'I never had a chance to listen to this kind of stuff,' he said, when it had ended. 'High bugs go to the City Hall to hear it.' He wiped his mouth on the back of his hand and went on. 'There's another piece I heard you play. Goes like this.' He pursed his lips and struggled with the tune and managed a few notes while she listened. He tried again and managed a few jumbled bars this time. Then he gave it up, shaking his head and grinning shyly.

But she had caught it and her hands moved again, gently as the fall of a hair, and the music poured from her fingertips. 'You mean Chopin's "Nocturne".'

'Is that what it's called? Yes, that's it.'

He leaned back and shut his eyes and whistled soundlessly with the music, taking it in completely. She played it twice and his head nodded in time.

After that the old-fashioned clock on the sideboard caught his eye and he remembered with a little start that Moos and Frog would be waiting for him. He got up quickly and said: 'I won't keep you any longer. I've got to be going, anyhow.'

'Did you enjoy it?'

'Really. I'd like to come again, some other time.'

'Of course. Come any evening.'

'Thanks, miss. Well, good luck.'

'Good-bye. Thanks for coming in to listen.'

He was out in the dark street again and hurried up it. The doorstep sitters had withdrawn now and the windows of the tenements were yellow with lamplight. Babies wailed here and there, hangers-on lounged against walls, couples made furtive love in doorways. Somewhere beyond, neon signs made a glare against the sky, like a city after a bombardment.

Moos and Frog were waiting impatiently in the light of a shopfront, smoking and cursing fretfully.

'Where the — you been?' Moos asked angrily. 'We been waiting.'

'Awright, awright. I'm here now,' Harry said. 'Let's go.'

They walked down the street together. Harry was still thinking about the girl who played the piano, and that he didn't even know her name. He whistled quietly. Knock something, she had said it was. Funny name. He thought, sentimentally, that it would be real smart to have a goose that played the piano like that.

Traitors

We had discovered the Thompsons' old house long before their first visit.

At the back of our house the ground sloped up to where the bush began, an acre of trailing pumpkin vines, ash-heaps where pawpaw trees sprouted, and lines draped with washing where the wind slapped and jiggled. The bush was dense and frightening, and the grass there higher than a tall man. There were not even paths.

When we had tired of our familiar acre we explored the rest of the farm: but this particular stretch of bush was avoided. Sometimes we stood at its edge, and peered in at the tangled granite outcrops and great ant-heaps curtained with Christmas fern. Sometimes we pushed our way a few feet, till the grass closed behind us, leaving overhead a small space of blue. Then we lost our heads and ran back again.

Later, when we were given our first rifle and a new sense of bravery, we realised we had to challenge that bush. For several days we hesitated, listening to the guinea-fowl calling only a hundred yards away, and making excuses for cowardice. Then, one morning, at sunrise, when the trees were pink and gold, and the grass-stems were running bright drops of dew, we looked at each other, smiling weakly, and slipped into the bushes with our hearts beating.

At once we were alone, closed in by grass, and we had to reach out for the other's dress and cling together. Slowly, heads down, eyes half closed against the sharp grass-seeds, two small girls pushed their way past ant-heap and outcrop, past thorn and gully and thick clumps of cactus where any wild animal might lurk.

Suddenly, after only five minutes of terror, we emerged in a space where the red earth was scored with cattle tracks. The guinea-fowl were clinking ahead of us in the grass, and we caught a glimpse of a shapely dark bird speeding along a path.

We followed, shouting with joy because the forbidding patch of bush was as easily conquered and made our own as the rest of the farm.

We were stopped again where the ground dropped suddenly to the vlei, a twenty-foot shelf of flattened grass where the cattle went to water. Sitting, we lifted our dresses and coasted downhill on the slippery swathes, landing with torn knickers and scratched knees in a donga of red dust scattered with dried cowpats and bits of glistening quartz. The guinea-fowl stood in a file and watched us, their heads tilted with apprehension; but my sister said with bravado: 'I am going to shoot a buck!'

She waved her arms at the birds and they scuttled off. We looked at each other and laughed, feeling too grown-up for guinea-fowl now.

Here, down on the verges of the vlei, it was a different kind of bush. The grass was thinned by cattle, and red dust spurted as we walked. There were sparse thorn trees, and everywhere the poison-apple bush, covered with small fruit like yellow plums. Patches of wild marigold filled the air with a rank, hot smell.

Moving with exaggerated care, our bodies tensed, our eyes fixed half a mile off, we did not notice that a duiker stood watching us, ten paces away. We yelled with excitement and the buck vanished. Then we ran like maniacs, screaming at the top of our voices, while the bushes whipped our faces and the thorns tore our legs.

Ten minutes later we came slap against a barbed fence. 'The boundary,' we whispered, awed. This was a legend; we had imagined it as a sort of Wall of China, for beyond were thousands and thousands of miles of unused Government land where there were leopards and baboons and herds of koodoo. But we were disappointed: even the famous boundary was only a bit of wire after all, and the duiker was nowhere in sight.

Whistling casually to show we didn't care, we marched along by the wire, twanging it so that it reverberated half a mile away down in the vlei. Around us the bush was strange; this part of the farm was quite new to us. There was still nothing but thorn trees and grass; and fat wood-pigeons cooed from every branch. We swung on the fence stanchions and wished that Father would suddenly appear and take us home to breakfast. We were hopelessly lost.

It was then that I saw the pawpaw tree. I must have been staring at it for some minutes before it grew in on my sight; for it was such an odd place for a pawpaw tree to be. On it were three heavy yellow pawpaws.

'There's our breakfast,' I said.

We shook them down, sat on the ground, and ate. The insipid creamy flesh soon filled us, and we lay down, staring at the sky, half asleep. The sun blazed down; we were melted through with heat and tiredness. But it was very hard. Turning over, staring, we saw worn bricks set into the ground. All round us were stretches of brick, stretches of cement.

'The old Thompson house,' we whispered.

And all at once the pigeons seemed to grow still and the bush became hostile. We sat up, frightened. How was it we hadn't noticed it before? There was a double file of pawpaws among the thorns; a purple bougainvillaea tumbled over the bushes; a rose tree scattered white petals at our feet; and our shoes were scrunching in broken glass.

It was desolate, lonely, despairing; and we remembered the way our parents had talked about Mr Thompson who had lived here for years before he married. Their hushed, disapproving voices seemed to echo out of the trees; and in a violent panic we picked up the gun and fled back in the direction of the house. We had imagined we were lost; but we were back in the gully in no time, climbed up it, half sobbing with breathlessness, and fled through that barrier of bush so fast we hardly noticed it was there.

It was not even breakfast-time.

'We found the Thompsons' old house,' we said at last, feeling hurt that no one had noticed from our proud faces that we had found a whole new world that morning.

'Did you?' said Father absently. 'Can't be much left of it now.'

Our fear vanished. We hardly dared look at each other for shame. And later that day we went back and counted the pawpaws and trailed the bougainvillaea over a tree and staked the white rosebush.

In a week we had made the place entirely our own. We were there all day, sweeping the debris from the floor and carrying away loose bricks into the bush. We were not surprised to find dozens of empty bottles scattered in the grass. We washed them in a pothole in the vlei, dried them in the wind, and marked out the rooms of the house with them, making walls of shining bottles. In our imagination the Thompson house was built again, a small brick-walled place with a thatched roof.

We sat under a blazing sun, and said in our Mother's voice: 'It is always cool under thatch, no matter how hot it is outside.' And then, when the walls and the roof had grown into our minds and we took them for granted, we played other games, taking it in turn to be Mr Thompson.

Whoever was Mr Thompson had to stagger in from the bush, with a bottle in her hand, tripping over the lintel and falling on the floor. There she lay and groaned, while the other fanned her and put handkerchiefs soaked in vlei water on her head. Or she reeled about among the bottles, shouting abusive gibberish at an invisible audience of natives.

It was while we were engaged thus, one day, that a black woman came out of the thorn trees and stood watching us. We waited for her to go, drawing together: but she came close and stared in a way that made us afraid. She was old and fat, and she wore a red print dress from the store. She said in a soft, wheedling voice: 'When is Boss Thompson coming back?'

'Go away!' we shouted. And then she began to laugh. She sauntered off into the bush, swinging her hips and looking back over her shoulder and laughing. We heard that taunting laugh away among the trees; and that was the second time we ran away from the ruined house, though we made ourselves walk slowly and with dignity until we knew she could no longer see us.

For a few days we didn't go back to the house. When we did we stopped playing Mr Thompson. We no longer knew him: that laugh, that slow insulting stare had meant something outside our knowledge and experience. The house was not ours now. It was some broken bricks on the ground marked out with bottles. We couldn't pretend to ourselves we were not afraid of the place; and we continually glanced over our shoulders to see if the old black woman was standing silently there, watching us.

Idling along the fence, we threw stones at the pawpaws fifteen feet over our heads till they squashed at our feet. Then we kicked them into the bush.

'Why have you stopped going to the old house?' asked Mother cautiously, thinking that we didn't know how pleased she was. She had instinctively disliked our being there so much.

'Oh, I dunno ...'

A few days later we heard that the Thompsons were coming to see us; and we knew, without anyone saying, that this was no ordinary visit. It was the first time; they wouldn't be coming after all these years without some reason. Besides, our parents didn't like them coming. They were at odds with each other over it.

Mr Thompson had lived on our farm for ten years before we had it, when there was no one else near for miles and miles. Then, suddenly, he went home to England and brought a wife back with him. The wife never came to this farm. Mr Thompson sold the farm to us and bought another one. People said: 'Poor girl! Just out from home, too.' She was angry about the house burning down, because it meant she had to live with friends for nearly a year while Mr Thompson built a new house on his new farm.

The night before they came, Mother said several times in a strange, sorrowful voice, 'Poor little thing; poor, poor little thing.'

Father said: 'Oh, I don't know. After all, be just. He was here alone all those years.'

It was no good; she disliked not only Mr Thompson but Father too, that evening, and we were on her side. She put her arms round us, and looked accusingly at Father. 'Women get all the worst of everything,' she said.

He said angrily, 'Look here, it's not my fault these people are coming.'

'Who said it was?' she answered.

Next day, when the car came in sight, we vanished into the bush. We felt guilty, not because we were running away, a thing we often did when visitors came we didn't like, but because we had made Mr Thompson's house our own, and because we were afraid if he saw our faces he would know we were letting Mother down by going.

We climbed into the tree that was our refuge on these occasions, and lay along branches twenty feet from the ground, and played at Mowgli, thinking all the time about the Thompsons.

As usual, we lost all sense of time; and when we eventually returned, thinking the coast must be clear, the car was still there. Curiosity got the better of us.

We slunk on to the veranda, smiling bashfully, while Mother gave us a reproachful look. Then, at last, we lifted our heads and looked at Mrs Thompson. I don't know how we had imagined her; but we had felt for her a passionate, protective pity.

She was a large, blonde, brilliantly coloured lady with a voice like a go-away bird's. It was a horrible voice. Father, who could not stand loud voices, was holding the arms of his chair, and gazing at her with exasperated dislike.

As for Mr Thompson, that villain whom we had hated and feared, he was a shaggy and shambling man, who looked at the ground while his wife talked, with a small apologetic smile. He was not in the least as we had pictured him. He looked like our old dog. For a moment we were confused; then, in a rush, our allegiance shifted. The profound and dangerous pity, aroused in us earlier than we could remember by the worlds of loneliness inhabited by our parents, which they could not share with each other but which each shared with us, settled now on Mr Thompson. Now we hated Mrs Thompson. The outward sign of it was that we left Mother's chair and went to Father's.

'Don't fidget, there's good kids,' he said.

Mrs Thompson was asking to be shown the old house. We understood, from the insistent sound of her voice, that she had been talking about nothing else all afternoon; or that, at any rate if she had, it was only with the intention of getting round to the house as soon as she could. She kept saying, smiling ferociously at Mr Thompson: 'I have heard such *interesting* things about that old place. I really must see for myself where it was that my husband lived before I came out ...' And she looked at Mother for approval.

But Mother said dubiously: 'It will soon be dark. And there is no path.'

As for Father, he said bluntly: 'There's nothing to be seen. There's nothing left.'

'Yes, I heard it had been burnt down,' said Mrs Thompson with another look at her husband.

'It was a hurricane lamp ...,' he muttered.

'I want to see for myself.'

At this point my sister slipped off the arm of my Father's chair, and said, with a bright, false smile at Mrs Thompson, 'We know where it is. We'll take you.' She dug me in the ribs and sped off before anyone could speak.

At last they all decided to come. I took them the hardest, longest way I knew. We had made a path of our own long ago, but that would have been too quick. I made Mrs Thompson climb over rocks, push through grass, bend under bushes. I made her scramble down the gully so that she fell on her knees in the sharp pebbles and the dust. I walked her so fast, finally, in a wide circle through the thorn trees that I could hear her panting behind me. But she wasn't complaining: she wanted to see the place too badly.

When we came to where the house had been it was nearly dark and the tufts of long grass were shivering in the night breeze, and the pawpaw trees were silhouetted high and dark against a red sky. Guinea-fowl were clinking softly all around us.

My sister leaned against a tree, breathing hard, trying to look natural. Mrs Thompson had lost her confidence. She stood quite still, looking about her, and we knew the silence and the desolation had got her, as it got us that first morning.

'But *where* is the house?' she asked at last, unconsciously softening her voice, staring as if she expected to see it rise out of the ground in front of her.

'I told you, it was burnt down. *Now* will you believe me?' said Mr Thompson.

'I *know* it was burnt down ... Well, where was it then?'

She sounded as if she were going to cry. This was not at all what she had expected.

Mr Thompson pointed at the bricks on the ground. He did not move. He stood staring over the fence down to the vlei, where the mist was gathering in long, white folds. The light faded out of the sky, and it began to get cold. For a while no one spoke.

'What a god-forsaken place for a house,' said Mrs Thompson, very irritably, at last. 'Just as well it was burnt down. Do you mean to say you kids play here?'

That was our cue. 'We like it,' we said dutifully, knowing very well that the two of us standing on the bricks, hand in hand, beside the ghostly rosebush, made a picture that took all the harm out of the place for her. 'We play here all day,' we lied.

'Odd taste you've got,' she said, speaking at us, but meaning Mr Thompson.

Mr Thompson did not hear her. He was looking around with a lost, remembering expression. 'Ten years,' he said at last. 'Ten years, I was here.'

'More fool you,' she snapped. And that closed the subject as far as she was concerned.

We began to trail home. Now the two women went in front; then came Father and Mr Thompson; we followed at the back. As we passed a small donga under a cactus tree, my sister called in a whisper, 'Mr Thompson, Mr Thompson, look here.'

Father and Mr Thompson came back. 'Look,' we said pointing to the hole that was filled to the brim with empty bottles.

'I came quickly by a way of my own and hid them,' said my sister proudly, looking at the two men like a conspirator.

Father was very uncomfortable. 'I wonder how they got down here?' he said politely at last.

'We found them. They were at the house. We hid them for you,' said my sister, dancing with excitement.

Mr Thompson looked at us sharply and uneasily. 'You are an odd pair of kids,' he said.

That was all the thanks we got from him; for then we heard Mother calling from ahead: 'What are you all doing there?' And at once we went forward.

After the Thompsons had left we hung around Father, waiting for him to say something.

At last, when Mother wasn't there, he scratched his head in an irritable way and said: 'What in the world did you do that for?'

We were bitterly hurt. '*She* might have seen them,' I said.

'Nothing would make much difference to that lady,' he said at last. 'Still I suppose you meant well.'

In the corner of the veranda, in the dark, sat Mother, gazing into the dark bush. On her face was a grim look of disapproval and distaste and unhappiness. We were included in it, we knew that.

She looked at us crossly and said, 'I don't like you wandering over the farm the way you do. Even with a gun.'

But she had said that so often, and it wasn't what we were waiting for. At last it came.

'My two little girls,' she said, 'out in the bush by themselves, with no one to play with ...'

It wasn't the bush she minded. We flung ourselves on her. Once again we were swung dizzily from one camp to the other. 'Poor Mother,' we said. 'Poor, poor Mother.'

That was what she needed. 'It's no life for a woman, this,' she said, her voice breaking, gathering us close.

But she sounded comforted.

LUIS BERNARDO HONWANA
The Hands of the Blacks

I don't remember now how we got onto the subject, but one day
Teacher said that the palms of the blacks' hands were much
lighter than the rest of their bodies because only a few centuries
ago they walked around on all fours, like wild animals, so their
palms weren't exposed to the sun, which made the rest of their
bodies darker and darker. I thought of this when Father
Christiano told us after catechism that we were absolutely hopeless, and that even the blacks were better than us, and he went
back to this thing about their hands being lighter, and said it was
like that because they always went about with their hands
folded together, praying in secret. I thought this was so funny,
this thing of the blacks' hands being lighter, that you should just
see me now – I don't let go of anyone, whoever they are, until
they tell why they think that the palms of the blacks' hands are
lighter. Dona Dores, for instance, told me that God made their
hands lighter like that so they couldn't dirty the food they made
for their masters, or anything else they were ordered to do that
had to be kept quite clean.

Senhor Antunes, the Coca Cola man, who only comes to the
village now and again when the Cokes in the cantinas have been
sold, said to me that everything I had been told was a lot of
baloney. Of course I don't know if it was really, but he assured
me it was. After I said yes, all right, it was baloney, then he told
me what he knew about this thing of the blacks' hands. It was
like this: 'Long ago, many years ago, God, Our Lord Jesus Christ,
the Virgin Mary, St Peter, many other saints, all the angels that
were in Heaven then, and some of the people who had died and
gone to Heaven – they all had a meeting and decided to make
blacks. Do you know how? They got hold of some clay and
pressed it into some second-hand moulds. And to bake the clay
of the creatures they took them to the Heavenly kilns. Because
they were in a hurry and there was no room next to the fire, they
hung them in the chimneys. Smoke, smoke, smoke – and there

you have them, black as coals. And now do you want to know why their hands stayed white? Well, didn't they have to hold on while their clay baked?'

When he had told me this Senhor Antunes and the other men who were around us were very pleased and they all burst out laughing. That very same day Senhor Frias called me after Senhor Antunes had gone away, and told me that everything I had heard from them there had been just one big pack of lies. Really and truly, what he knew about the blacks' hands was right – that God finished making men and told them to bathe in a lake in Heaven. After bathing the people were nice and white. The blacks, well, they were made very early in the morning, and at this hour the water in the lake was very cold, so they only wet the palms of their hands and the soles of their feet before dressing and coming into the world.

But I read in a book that happened to mention it, that the blacks have hands lighter like this because they spent their lives bent over, gathering the white cotton of Virginia and I don't know where else. Of course Dona Estefánia didn't agree when I told her this. According to her it's only because their hands became bleached with all that washing.

Well, I don't know what to think about all this, but the truth is that however calloused and cracked they may be, a black's hands are always lighter than all the rest of him. And that's that!

My mother is the only one who must be right about this question of a black's hands being lighter than the rest of his body. On the day that we were talking about it, us two, I was telling her what I already knew about the question, and she just couldn't stop laughing. What I thought was strange was that she didn't tell me at once what she thought about all this and she only answered me when she was sure that I wouldn't get tired of bothering her about it. And even then she was crying and clutching herself around the stomach like someone who had laughed so much that it was unbearable. What she said was more or less this:

God made blacks because they had to be. They had to be, my son. He thought they really had to be ... Afterwards he regretted having made them because the other men laughed at them and took them off to their homes and put them to serve like slaves or not much better. But because he couldn't make them all be

white, for those who were used to seeing them black would complain, He made it so that the palms of their hands would be
exactly like the palms of the hands of other men. And do you
know why that was? Of course you don't know, and it's not surprising, because many, many people don't know. Well listen: it
was to show that what men do is only the work of men ... That
what men do is done by hands that are the same ... hands of
people who, if they had any sense, would know that before
everything else they are men. He must have been thinking of this
when He made the hands of the blacks to be the same as the
hands of those men who thank God they are not black!'

After telling me this, my mother kissed my hands. As I ran off
into the yard to play ball, I thought that I have never seen a person cry so much when nobody had hit them.

Translated by Dorothy Guedes

CHARLES MUNGOSHI

Shadows on the Wall

Father is sitting just inside the hut near the door and I am sitting far across the hut near the opposite wall, playing with the shadows on the wall. Bright sunlight comes in through the doorway now, and father, who blocks most of it, is reproduced in caricature on the floor and half-way up the wall. The wall and floor are bare, so he looks like a black scarecrow in a deserted field after the harvest.

Outside, the sun drops lower and other shadows start creeping into the hut. Father's shadow grows vaguer and climbs further up the wall like a ghost going up to heaven. His shadow moves behind sharper wriggling shadows like the presence of a tired old woman in a room full of young people, or like that creepy nameless feeling in a house of mourning.

He has tried five times to talk to me but I don't know what he wants. Now he talks about his other wife. He wants me to call her 'mother' but I can't because something in me cries each time I say it. She isn't my mother and my real mother is not dead. This other woman has run away. It is now the fourth time she has run away and tomorrow he is going to cycle fifty miles to her home to collect her. This will be the fourth time he has had to cycle after her. He is talking. I am not listening. He gives up.

Now the sun shines brilliantly before going down. The shadows of bushes and grass at the edge of the yard look as if they are on fire and father's features are cut more sharply and exaggerated. His nose becomes longer each time he nods because now he is sleeping while sitting, tired of the silence.

Father dozes, wakes up; dozes, wakes up and the sun goes down. His shadow expands and fades. Now it seems all over the wall, behind the other shadows, moving silently like a cold wind in a bare field. I look at him. There is still enough light for me to see the grey stubble sticking up untidily all over his face. His stubble, I know, is as stiff as a porcupine's, but as the light wanes now, it looks fleecy and soft like the down on a dove's nestling.

I was in the bush, long ago, and I came upon two dove nestlings. They were still clumsy and blind, with soft pink vulnerable flesh planted with short scattered grey feathers, their mouths open, waiting for their mother. I wished I had corn to give them. As it was, I consoled myself with the thought that their mother was somewhere nearby, coming home through the bush in the falling dark with food in her mouth for her children.

Next day I found the nestlings dead in their nest. Somewhere out in the bush or in the yellow ripe unharvested fields, someone had shot their mother in mid-flight home.

Not long after that, I was on my father's shoulders coming home from the fields at dusk. Mother was still with us then, and father carried me because she had asked him to. I had a sore foot and couldn't walk and mother couldn't carry me because she was carrying a basket of mealies for our supper on her head and pieces of firewood in her arms. At first father grumbled. He didn't like to carry me and he didn't like receiving orders from mother: she was there to listen to him always, he said. He carried me all the same although he didn't like to, and worse, I didn't like him to carry me. His hands were hard and pinchy and his arms felt as rough and barky as logs. I preferred mother's soft warm back. He knew, too, that I didn't want him to carry me because I made my body stiff and didn't relax when he rubbed his hard chin against my cheek. His breath was harsh and foul. He wore his battered hat that stank of dirt, sweat and soil. He was trying to talk to me but I was not listening to him. That was when I noticed that his stubble looked as vulnerable as the unprotected feathers on a dove's nestling. Tears filled my eyes then and I tried to respond to his teasing, but I gave it up because he immediately began picking on mother and made her tense and tight and this tension I could feel in me also.

After this he always wanted me to be near him and he made me ignore mother. He taught me to avoid mother. It was hard for me but he had a terrible way of making mother look despicable and mean. She noticed this and fought hard to make me cheerful, but I always saw father's threatening shadow hunched hawkishly over me. Instead of talking to either of them I became silent. I was no longer happy in either's presence. And this was when I began to notice the shadows on the wall of our hut.

One day the eternal quarrel between mother and father flared up to an unbelievable blaze. Mother went away to her people. After an unsuccessful night full of nightmares with father in the hut, he had to follow her. There had been a hailstorm in the night and everything looked sad in the dripping chill of the next day. The small mealie plants in the yard had been destroyed by the storm; all the leaves torn off except the small hard piths which now stood about in the puddles like nails in a skull. Father went away without a word and I was alone.

I lay under the blankets for a long time with the door of the hut open. One by one, our chickens began to come in out of the cold.

There is something in a cold chicken's voice that asks for something you don't know how to give, something more than corn.

I watched them come into the hut and I felt sorry for them. Their feathers were still wet and they looked smaller and sicklier than normal. I couldn't shoo them out. They came and crowded by the fire, their little bird voices scarcely rising above the merest whisper. My eyes left them and wandered up and down the walls.

At first I couldn't see them but when one chicken made a slight move I noticed that there were shadows on the wall.

These shadows fascinated me. There were hundreds of them. I spent the whole day trying to separate them, to isolate them, but they were as elusive and liquid as water in a jar. After a long time looking at them, I felt that they were talking to me. I held my breath and heard their words distinctly, a lullaby in harmony: sleep, sleep, you are all alone, sleep and don't wake up, ever again.

I must have fallen asleep because I remember seeing later on that the sky had turned all dark and a thin chilly drizzle was falling. The chickens, which must have gone out feeling hungry, were coming in again, wet, their forlorn voices hardly audible above the sound of the rain. I knew by the multitude of shadows on the wall that night was falling. I felt too weak to wake up and for a long time watched the shadows multiply and fade, multiply, mingle and fade, and listened to their talk. Again I must have fallen asleep because when I woke up I was well tucked in and warm. The shadows were now brilliant and clear on the wall because there was a fire on the hearth.

Mother and father had come in and they were silent. Seeing them, I felt as if I were coming from a long journey in a strange country. Mother noticed that I was awake and said,

'How do you feel?'

'He's just lazy,' father said.

'He is ill,' mother said. 'His body is all on fire.' She felt me.

'Lies. He is a man and you want to turn him into a woman.'

After this I realized how ill I was. I couldn't eat anything: there was no appetite and I wasn't hungry,

I don't know how many days I was in bed. There seemed to be nothing. No light, no sun, to show it was day or darkness to show it was night. Mother was constantly in but I couldn't recognize her as a person. There were only shadows, the voices of the shadows, the lonely cries of the dripping wet fowls shaking the cold out of their feathers by the hearth, and the vague warm shadow that must have been mother. She spoke to me often but I don't remember if I answered anything. I was afraid to answer because I was alone on a solitary plain with the dark crashing of thunder and lightning always in my ears, and there was a big frightening shadow hovering above me so that I couldn't answer her without it hearing me. That must have been father.

They might have had quarrels — I am sure they had lots of them — but I didn't hear them. Everything had been flattened to a dim depthless grey landscape and the only movement on it was of the singing shadows. I could see the shadows and hear them speak to me, so I wasn't dead. If mother talked to me at all, her voice got lost in the vast expanse of emptiness between me and the shadows. Later when I was beginning to be aware of the change of night into day, her voice was the soft pink intrusion like cream on the hard darkness of the wall. This turned later into a clear urgent sound like the lapping of water against boulders in the morning before sunrise. I noticed too that she was often alone with me. Father was away and must have been coming in late after I had fallen asleep.

The day I saw father, a chill set in in the hut.

There was another hailstorm and a big quarrel that night. It was the last quarrel.

When I could wake up again mother was gone and a strange

woman had taken her place in the house.

This woman had a shrill voice like a cicada's that jarred my nerves. She did all the talking and father became silent and morose. Instead of the frightful silences and sudden bursts of anger I used to know, he now tried to talk softly to me. He preferred to talk to me rather than to his new wife.

But he was too late. He had taught me silence and in that long journey between mother's time and this other woman's, I had given myself to the shadows.

So today he sits just inside the hut with sun playing with him: cartooning him on the bare cold floor and the bare dark walls of the hut, and me watching and listening to the images on the wall. He cannot talk to me because I don't know how to answer him, his language is too difficult for me. All I can think of, the nearest I can come to him, is when I see that his tough grey stubble looks like the soft unprotected feathers on a dove's nestling: and when I remember that the next morning the nestlings were dead in their nest because somebody had unknowingly killed their mother in the bush on her way home, I feel the tears in my eyes.

It is all — all that I feel for my father; but I cannot talk to him. I don't know how I should talk to him. He has denied me the gift of language.

BESSIE HEAD

The Wind and a Boy

Like all the village boys, Friedman had a long wind blowing for him, but perhaps the enchanted wind that blew for him, filled the whole world with magic.

Until they became ordinary, dull grown men, who drank beer and made babies, the village boys were a special set all on their own. They were kings whom no one ruled. They wandered where they willed from dawn to dusk and only condescended to come home at dusk because they were afraid of the horrible things in the dark that might pounce on them. Unlike the little girls who adored household chores and drawing water, it was only now and then that the boys showed themselves as useful attachments to any household. When the first hard rains of summer fell, small dark shapes, quite naked except for their loincloths, sped out of the village into the bush. They knew that the first downpour had drowned all the wild rabbits, moles, and porcupines in their burrows in the earth. As they crouched down near the entrances of the burrows, they would see a small drowned nose of an animal peeping out; they knew it had struggled to emerge from its burrow, flooded by the sudden rush of storm water and as they pulled out the animal, they would say, pityingly:

'Birds have more sense than rabbits, moles and porcupines. They build their homes in trees.' But it was hunting made easy, for no matter how hard a boy and his dog ran, a wild rabbit ran ten times faster; a porcupine hurled his poisonous quills into the body; and a mole stayed where he thought it was safe – deep under the ground. So it was with inordinate pride that the boys carried home armfuls of dead animals for their families to feast on for many days. Apart from that, the boys lived very much as they pleased, with the wind and their own games.

Now and then, the activities of a single family could captivate the imagination and hearts of all the people of their surroundings; for years and years, the combination of the boy, Friedman, and his grandmother, Sejosenye, made the people of Ga-Sefete-Molemo ward smile, laugh, then cry.

They smiled at his first two phases. Friedman came home as a small bundle from the hospital, a bundle his grandmother nursed carefully near her bosom and crooned to day and night with extravagant care and tenderness.

'She is like that,' people remarked, 'because he may be the last child she will ever nurse. Sejosenye is old now and will die one of these days; the child is a gift to keep her heart warm.'

Indeed, all Sejosenye's children were grown, married, and had left home. Of all her children, only her last-born daughter was unmarried and Friedman was the result of some casual mating she had indulged in, in a town a hundred miles away where she had a job as a typist. She wanted to return to her job almost immediately, so she handed the child over to her mother and that was that; she could afford to forget him as he had a real mother now. During all the time that Sejosenye haunted the hospital, awaiting her bundle, a friendly foreign doctor named Friedman took a fancy to her maternal, grandmotherly ways. He made a habit of walking out of his path to talk to her. She never forgot it and on receiving her bundle she called the baby, Friedman.

They smiled at his second phase, a small dark shadow who toddled silently and gravely beside a very tall grandmother; wherever the grandmother went, there went Friedman. Most women found this phase of the restless, troublesome toddler tedious; they dumped the toddler onto one of their younger girls and were off to weddings and visits on their own.

'Why can't you leave your handbag at home some times, granny?' they said.

'Oh, he's no trouble,' Sejosenye would reply.

They began to laugh at his third phase. Almost overnight he turned into a tall, spindly-legged, graceful gazelle with large, grave eyes. There was an odd, musical lilt to his speech and when he teased, or was up to mischief, he moved his head on his long thin neck from side to side like a cobra. It was he who became the king of kings of all the boys in his area; he could turn his hand to anything and made the best wire cars with their wheels of shoe polish tins. All his movements were neat, compact, decisive, and for his age he was a boy who knew his own mind. They laughed at his knowingness and certainty of all things, for he was like the grandmother who had had a flaming youth all her own too. Sejosenye had scandalized the whole village in her days of good morals by leaving her own village ward to live with a married man in Ga-Sefete-Molemo ward. She had won him from his wife and married him and then lived down the scandal in the way only natural queens can. Even in old age, she was still impressive. She sailed through the village, head in the air, with a quiet, almost expressionless face. She had developed large buttocks as time went by and they announced their presence firmly in rhythm with her walk.

Another of Sejosenye's certainties was that she was a woman who could plough, but it was like a special gift. Each season, in drought or hail or sun, she removed herself to her lands. She not only ploughed but nursed and brooded over her crops. She was there all the time till the corn ripened and the birds had to be chased off the land, till harvesting and threshing were done; so that even in drought years with their scanty rain, she came home with some crops. She was the envy of all the women of the surroundings.

'Sejosenye always eats fine things in her house,' they said. 'She ploughs and then sits down for many months and enjoys the fruits of her labour.'

The women also envied her beautiful grandson. There was something special there, so that even when Friedman moved into his bad phase, they forgave him crimes other boys received a sound thrashing for. The small boys were terrible thieves who harassed people by stealing their food and money. It was all part of the games they played but one which people did not like. Of them all, Friedman was the worst thief, so that his name was mentioned more and more in any thieving that had been uncovered.

'But Friedman showed us how to open the window with a knife and string,' the sobbing, lashed boys would protest.

'Friedman isn't as bad as you,' the parents would reply, irrationally. They were hypnotised by a beautiful creature. The boy Friedman, who had become a real nuisance by then, also walked around as though he were special. He couldn't possibly be a thief and he added an aloof, offended, disdainful expression to his pretty face. He wasn't an ordinary sort of boy in Ga-Sefete-

Molemo ward. He was …

It happened, quite accidentally, that his grandmother told him all those stories about the hunters, warriors, and emissaries of old. She was normally a quiet, absent-minded woman, given to dreaming by herself but she liked to sing the boy a little song now and then as they sat by the outdoor fire. A lot of them were church songs and rather sad; they more or less passed as her bed-time prayer at night — she was one of the old church-goers. Now and then she added a quaint little song to her repertoire and as the night-time, fire-light flames flickered between them, she never failed to note that this particular song was always well received by the boy. A little light would awaken in his eyes and he would bend forward and listen attentively.

'Welcome, Robinson Crusoe, welcome,' she would sing, in clear, sweet tones. 'How could you stay, so long away, Robinson, how could you do so?'

When she was very young, Sejosenye had attended the mission school of the village for about a year; made a slight acquaintance with the ABC and one, two, three, four, five, and the little song about Robinson Crusoe. But girls didn't need an education in those days when ploughing and marriage made up their whole world. Yet Robinson Crusoe lived on as a gay and out-of-context memory of her school-days. One evening the boy leaned forward and asked:

'Is that a special praise-poem song for Robinson Crusoe, grandmother?'

'Oh yes,' she said smiling.

'What great things did he do?' the boy asked pointedly.

'They say he was a hunter who went by Gweta side and killed an elephant all by himself,' she said making up a story on the spot. 'Oh! In those days, no man could kill an elephant by himself. All the regiments had to join together and each man had to thrust his sword into the side of the elephant before it died. Well, Robinson Crusoe was gone many days and people wondered about him: "Perhaps he has been eaten by a lion," they said. "Robinson likes to be a solitary person and do foolish things. We won't ever go out into the bush by ourselves because we know it is dangerous." Well, one day, Robinson suddenly appeared in their midst and people could see that he had a great thing on his mind. They all gathered around him. He said: "I have killed an elephant for all the people." The people were surprised: "Robinson!" they said. "It is impossible! How did you do it? The very thought of an elephant approaching the village makes us shiver!" And Robinson said: "Ah, people, I saw a terrible sight! I was standing at the feet of the elephant. I was just a small ant. I could not see the world any more. Elephant was above me until his very head touched the sky and his ears spread out like great winds. He was angry but I only looked into one eye which was turning round and round in anger. What to do now? I thought it better to put that eye out. I raised my spear and threw it at the angry eye. People! It went right inside. Elephant said not a word and he fell to one side. Come, I will show you what I have done." They ran to fetch their containers as some wanted the meat of the elephant; some wanted the fat. The men made their knives sharp. They would make shoes and many things from the skin and bones. There was something for all the people in the great work Robinson Crusoe did.'

All this while, as he listened to the story, the boy's eyes had glowed softly. At the end of it, he drew in a long breath.

'Grandmother,' he whispered, adroitly stepping into the role of Robinson Crusoe, the great hunter. 'One day, I'm going to be like that. I'm going to be a hunter like Robinson Crusoe and bring meat to all the people.' He paused for breath and then added tensely: 'And what other great thing did Robinson Crusoe do?'

'Tsaa!' she said clicking her tongue in exhaustion. 'Am I then going away that I must tell *all* the stories at once?'

Although his image of Robinson Crusoe, the great hunter, was never to grow beyond his everyday boyish activities of pushing wire cars, hunting in the fields for wild rabbits, climbing trees to pull down old bird's nests and yelling out in alarm to find that a small snake now occupied the abandoned abode, or racing against the wind with the spoils of his latest theft, the stories awakened a great tenderness in him. If Robinson Crusoe was not churning up the dust in deadly hand-to-hand combat with an enemy, he was crossing swollen rivers and wild jungles as the great messenger and ambassador of the chief — all his activities were touchingly in aid of or in defence of the people. One day Friedman expressed this awakened compassion for life in a strange way. After a particularly violent storm, people found their huts invaded by many small mice and they were hard-pressed to rid themselves of these pests. Sejosenye ordered Friedman to kill the mice.

'But grandmother,' he protested. 'They have come to us for shelter. They lost all their homes in the storm. It's better that I put them in a box and carry them out into the fields again once the rains are over.'

She had laughed in surprise at this and spread the story around among her women friends, who smiled tenderly then said to their own offspring:

'Friedman isn't as bad as you.'

Life and its responsibilities began to weigh down heavily on Friedman as he approached his fourteenth year. Less time was spent in boyish activities. He grew more and more devoted to his grandmother and concerned to assist her in every way. He wanted a bicycle so that he might run up and down to the shops for her, deliver messages, or do any other chore she might have in mind. His mother, who worked in a town far away, sent him the money to purchase the bicycle. The gift brought the story of his life abruptly to a close.

Toward the beginning of the rainy season, he accompanied his grandmother to her lands, which were some twenty miles outside the village. They sowed seed together after the hired tractor had turned up the lands but the boy's main chore was to keep the household pot filled with meat. Sometimes they ate birds Friedman had trapped, sometimes they ate fried tortoise-meat or wild rabbit; but there was always something as the bush abounded with animal life. Sejosenye only had to take a bag of mealie meal, packets of sugar, tea, and powdered milk as provisions for their stay at the lands; meat was never a problem. Midway through the ploughing season, she began to run out of sugar, tea, and milk.

'Friedman,' she said that evening. 'I shall wake you early tomorrow morning. You will have to take the bicycle into the village and purchase some more sugar, tea, and milk.'

He was up at dawn with the birds, a solitary figure cycling on a pathway through the empty bush. By nine, he had reached the village and first made his way to Ga-Sefete-Molemo ward and the yard of a friend of his grandmother, who gave him a cup of tea and a plate of porridge. Then he put one foot on the bicycle and turned to smile at the woman with his beautiful gazelle eyes. His smile was to linger vividly before her for many days as a short while later, hard pounding feet came running into her yard to report that Friedman was dead.

He pushed the bicycle through the winding, sandy pathways of the village ward, reached the high embankment of the main road, pedalled vigorously up it and, out of the corner of his eye, saw a small green truck speeding towards him. In the devil-may-care fashion of all the small boys, he cycled right into its path, turned his head and smiled appealingly at the driver. The truck caught him on the front bumper, squashed the bicycle and dragged the boy along at a crazy speed for another hundred yards, dropped him and careered on another twenty yards before coming to a halt. The boy's pretty face was a smear all along the road and he only had a torso left.

People of Ga-Sefete-Molemo ward never forgot the last coherent word Sejosenye spoke to the police. A number of them climbed into the police truck and accompanied it to her lands. They saw her walk slowly and inquiringly towards the truck, they heard the matter-of-fact voice of the policeman announce the death, then they heard Sejosenye say piteously: 'Can't you return those words back?'

She turned away from them, either to collect her wits or the few possession she had brought with her. Her feet and buttocks quivered anxiously as she stumbled towards her hut. Then her feet tripped her up and she fell to the ground like a stunned log.

The people of Ga-Sefete-Molemo ward buried the boy Friedman but none of them would go near the hospital where Sejosenye lay. The stories brought to them by way of the nurses were too terrible for words. They said the old woman sang and laughed and talked to herself all the time. So they merely asked each other, 'Have you been to see Mma-Sejosenye?' 'I'm afraid I cannot. It would kill my heart.' Two weeks later, they buried her.

As was village habit, the incident was discussed thoroughly from all sides till it was understood. In this timeless, sleepy village, the goats stood and suckled their young ones on the main road or lay down and took their afternoon naps there. The motorists either stopped for them or gave way. But it appeared that the driver of the truck had neither brakes on his car nor a driving licence. He belonged to the new, rich civil-servant class whose salaries had become fantastically high since independence. They had to have cars in keeping with their new status; they had to have any car, as long it was a car; they were in such a hurry about everything that they couldn't be bothered to take driving lessons. And thus progress, development, and a preoccupation with status and living-standards first announced themselves to the village. It looked like being an ugly story with many decapitated bodies on the main road.

AHMED ESSOP

Gerty's Brother

I first saw Gerty in a shop in Vrededorp. Vrededorp, as everyone knows, is cleft in two by Delarey Street: on the one side it is colonised by us blacks and on the other side by whites. The whites come over to our side when they want to do their shopping, and return with a spurious bargain or two. I saw her in a shop in the garishly decorated Indian shopping lane called Fourteenth Street. I had gone there with my friend Hussein who wanted to see a shopkeeper friend of his. I think the shop was called Dior Fashions, but of that I am not quite sure because shop follows shop there and this one didn't strike me as being in any way fashionable. Anyway, that is where I saw her. My friend spoke to the shopkeeper — a fat dark man with a darker moustache — and I just looked around and smoked a cigarette.

I sat down on a chair and then I noticed two figures darken the doorway and enter the shop, a girl and a boy. The shopkeeper spoke to the girl and then suddenly laughed. She laughed too, I think. I wouldn't have taken any further notice of the group as I was seated at the back of the shop. But then the shopkeeper switched to Gujarati and spoke to my friend. I heard him say that she was easy and would not give much trouble in removing her undergarments to anyone, but one had to be careful as there was the usual risk involved. Hussein replied that he was keen and wouldn't like to waste much time about the matter. I think the shopkeeper introduced him to her at this stage. Then I heard him telling Hussein that he was going to organize a dance at his place on the following Saturday evening, that he was going to invite Gerty, and that if Hussein was interested he could take her away from his place. All this he said in Gujarati, rather coarsely I thought.

Later, when Hussein and I had climbed into his Volkswagen and were on our way to Fordsburg, he informed me that to soften her before the party on Saturday he had bought the girl a frock. He asked me how I liked her and I said she was all right as

far as I was concerned, though, of course, I had not been near
enough to see her properly and size her up. But I said she was all
right and he felt very satisfied at having bumped into a white
girl. He told me that she lived in Vrededorp, 'on the other side',
and that she seemed to be very easy. He said that when he had
done with her he would throw her over to me and I could have
her as well. I answered with a vague 'Let the time come'. He
then said something about 'pillar to post', and laughed as the car
tore its way through the traffic into Fordsburg.

Saturday night I was at my landlady's, stripped to the waist
because of the heat, reading an old issue of the *New Statesman*.
There was a knock on the door and somebody asked for me and
entered. It was Hussein all dressed up with bow tie and cuff-
links and gleaming shoes that were out of place in my spartan
room.

'Where to, my dandy friend?' I asked admiringly.

'To the dance party. I thought you would be ready. You
promised to come with me.'

I said I had forgotten, but that I would be ready in a minute. I
dressed quickly, but didn't care to put on a white shirt or a tie. I
wasn't very particular about what I wore and I think it pleased
my friend because my appearance was something of a foil to his,
and set off to advantage his carefully put-together looks.

We set off in his Volkswagen for Vrededorp and in a few
minutes the car braked sharply in Eleventh Street in front of the
house of Hussein's shopkeeper friend. We were quite early and
there were not many people present. Hussein's friend was
happy to see us and he introduced us to those who were there.
There were some lovely-looking girls in shimmering coral and
amber and amethyst-coloured saris and others in more sober
evening dress.

After a while Hussein asked to see the shopkeeper privately,
and I think they went out to the front verandah of the house.
When they returned I saw that Hussein was not too pleased
about something or other. Other girls arrived, all gaily dressed
and very chic and charming and I was beginning to look forward
to a swinging evening. The girls offered me tea and cake and
other tasty things to eat and I didn't refuse as my boarding-
house wasn't exactly a liberal establishment. All this time my
friend Hussein was walking in and out of the room, and was on

the look-out whenever someone knocked on the door and entered the house. The party got going and we danced, ate the refreshments provided and talked some euphonious nonsense.

I was just getting interested in a girl, when my friend interrupted me and said that he wanted to see me urgently. I followed him and we went to the verandah. Someone had switched off the lights and I saw two figures standing there, a girl and a small boy. He introduced her to me as Gerty. He then took me aside and asked me if I could drive the two of them to the Zoo Lake immediately and leave them in the park for a while, and if I could keep her brother company while he saw to Gerty's needs. As it was a risky business he didn't want the others in the party to know. He would like to get done with it before joining the party.

I said I didn't mind and the four of us got into the car. I drove to the Lake. It was a lovely night in December and we breathed in the luminous wind of the city streets as the car sped along. Hussein and Gerty sat in the back seat. They didn't say much to each other, but I guessed that they were holding hands and fondling. Gerty's brother sat beside me. He must have been seven or eight, but I didn't take much notice of him. He was eating some cakes and chocolates that Hussein had taken from the house. I dropped the pair in a park near the Lake. Hussein asked me to return in about an hour's time. The park was a darkness of trees and lawns and flowers, and it occurred to me that it made no difference if one slept with a white or black girl there.

Gerty told her brother that he mustn't worry and that she was all right and that he should go with me for a while. Before I drove off he asked me what they were going to do and I said they must be a bit tired and wanted to rest, but that did not sound convincing. Then I said they had something to discuss in private and the best place was in the park. He agreed with me and I started the car. I didn't feel like driving aimlessly about for an hour so I drove towards the lake. I asked the boy what his name was and he said Riekie.

I parked the car under some pine trees near a brightly-lit restaurant. There were people dining on the terrace amid blaring music, others were strolling on the lawns or resting on the benches. I asked Riekie if he would like an ice-cream and took him to the restaurant and bought him one. We went down to the

water's edge. The lake is small with a islet in the middle; a
fountain spouted water into shifting rays of variegated light.
Riekie was fascinated by it all and asked me several questions.

I asked him if he had ever sat in a boat. He said he hadn't. I
took him to the boat-house and hired one. The white attendant
looked at me for a moment and then at Riekie. I knew what he
was thinking about but I said nothing. He went towards the
landing-stage and pointed to a boat. I told Riekie to jump in, but
he hesitated. So I lifted him and put him into the boat. He was
light in weight and I felt the ribs under his arms. A sensation of
tenderness for the boy went through me. You must understand
that this was the first time I had ever picked up a white child.

I rowed out towards the middle of the lake, and went around
the fountain of kaleidoscopic lights. Riekie was gripped by
wonder. He trailed his hands in the cool water smelling of rotted
weeds, and tried to grab the overhanging branches of the wil-
lows along the banks.

It was time to pick up Hussein and Gerty. Riekie looked disappointed, but I said I would bring him there again. At this he
seemed satisfied and I rowed towards the landing-stage.

Hussein and Gerty were waiting for us. They got into the car
and we returned to the party in Eleventh Street.

The party was now in full swing. There were many girls and I
didn't waste much time. My friend stuck to Gerty, and if he was
not dancing with her he was talking to her. And by the time the
party ended at midnight Riekie had fallen asleep on a sofa and
had to be doused with water to wake him.

We dropped Gerty and her brother at a street corner on our
way to Fordsburg. Hussein had rooms of his own in Park Road,
situated in a small yard at the end of a passage. A tall iron gate
barred the entrance to the passage. There were only three rooms
in the yard. Hussein occupied two and the other was occupied
by a decrepit pensioner who lived in his room like some caged
animal, except that no one ever came to see him.

At first Hussein was afraid to tell Gerty where he lived. There
was the usual risk involved. But I think eventually he came to
the conclusion that in life certain risks had to be taken if one was
to live at all. And so Gerty and her brother came to his rooms
and she took on the role of mistress and domestic servant and
Riekie became the pageboy.

Gerty and Riekie were very fond of each other. The harsh realities of life - they were orphans and lived in poverty with an alcoholic elder brother — had entwined them. Hussein didn't mind Riekie's presence. In fact the boy attached himself to him. My friend was generous, and besides providing Gerty with frocks for summer, he bought the boy clothing and several pairs of shoes. Riekie was obedient and always ready to run to the shops for Hussein, to polish his shoes or wash the car. In time his cheeks began to take on colour and he began to look quite handsome. I noticed he wasn't interested in boys of his own age; his attachment to his sister seemed to satisfy him.

And then things took a different turn. Hussein came to understand that the police had an eye on him, that somehow they had come to know of Gerty and were waiting for an opportunity to arrest him in incriminating circumstances. Someone had seen a car parked for several nights near his rooms and noticed the movements of suspicious-looking persons. And he was convinced the police were after him when one night, returning home late, he saw a man examining the lock of the gate. As he was not in the mood for a spell of prison, he told her that she should keep away from him for some time, and that he would see her again as soon as things were clear. But I think both of them realised that there wasn't much chance of that.

There wasn't much that one could tell Riekie about the end of the affair. My friend left it to Gerty, and went to Durban to attend to his late father's affairs.

One Sunday morning I was on my way to post some letters and when I turned the corner in Park Road there was Riekie, standing beside the iron gate that led to my friend's rooms. He was clutching two bars with his hands, and shouting for Hussein. I stood and watched as he shouted. His voice was bewildered.

The ugly animal living in the yard lurched out of his room and croaked. 'Goh way boy, goh way white boy. No Hussein here. Goh way.'

Riekie shook the barred gate and called for Hussein over and over again, and his voice was smothered by the croaks of the old man.

I stood at the corner of the street, in my hand the two letters I intended to post, and I felt again the child's body as I lifted him

and put him into the boat many nights ago, a child's body in my
arms embraced by the beauty of the night on the lake, and I
returned to my landlady's with the hackles of revolt rising
within me.

DAMBUDZO MARECHERA

The Christmas Reunion

I had never killed a goat before. But it was Christmas. And father who had always done it was dead. He had been dead for seven years. My sister, Ruth, could not possibly be expected to kill the goat. It was supposed to be a man's job. And mother was dead too. There were the two of us in the house, Ruth and I. I was on sabbatical from the university and Christmas would, I had hoped, be a break from the book I was writing. But there had to be a goat to spoil everything. Actually it was Christmas Eve, and that was the time of killing and skinning the goat. Everybody in the township would be killing their own family goat. While I tried to find an excuse to get out of having to kill the goat myself, I reminded Ruth that a goat was a passionate creature beloved of Pan and how could I kill that beast in me? I was, I said, myself a hardy, lively, wanton, horned and bearded ruminant quadruped – if not in fact, at least in spirit. I had always been wicked. I was up there in the sky with Capricorn, I said. If all this isn't convincing, I said, what about that all-important Tropic of Capricorn which seemed to make those who lived close to it vicious, nasty, spoilt, bloody Boers, and in short to kill the goat would be to disrespect a substantial part of the human extremities and interiorities. Besides, I added, you know I can't eat what I have killed. Also I was mere goat's wool in the general fabric of this great fiction we call life and could not logically be capable of such a monstrosity as murdering a poor old goat. Imagine a large assembly of bloodthirsty Germans shouting GEISS at a terrified little Jewish boy. All this mass-extermination of perfectly harmless but god-created goats seemed to me to be nothing but a distortion of what Christmas was really about. Which was? Which was? Well, we're Africans anyway and all this nonsense about Christmas was merely a sordid distraction. After all, I said, aren't whites and blacks skinning each other now ready for the Christmas pot, lugging each other by the heels into the universal kitchen to dress each one up with chillies and mustard and black pepper and chips and afterwards everybody would pat their stomachs and belch gently and scratch their bellies in which the feeling of Freedom and Christmas was being slowly digested. The whole business of expressing Christian glee by cutting the throats of much-maligned goats was indeed sickening, not to mention the so-called domestication of goats in concentration-camp-style kraals when what could be more majestic and courageous and rugged than pure mountain goats? I could not for the life of me see anything but inhumanity in buying a goat for a few shillings and tethering it to an old barbed-wire fence and having babies watch its throat and guts being cut up. Besides, I was not a real killer at all. Perhaps sometimes I inadvertently stepped on a beetle that was not watching where it was going, and of course I did murder all those damned mosquitoes that were plaguing my rooms at the university, and that nasty fat fly which so maddened me that I took a swipe at it with a hardback *Complete Shakespeare*. I think I only grazed its compound eyes and chucked it into the waste-paper basket and then the crafty insect played so hard at being dead it actually died. I agree that snake which was skulking around in the apple tree when you were looking longingly at the red-ripest one probably did not deserve to be scared to death by my shotgun. And every self-respecting pimply boy had a rubber sling to stone birds to death. And fighting is not a different business: you raise your fist at somebody and at once you are a potential killer – there is nothing manly in that. This business about 'being a real man' is what is driving all of us crazy. I'll have none of it. There's nothing different between you and me except what's hanging between our legs. And if you want goat meat, kill it yourself. If I'm supposed to become a 'real man' in the twinkling of an eye by cutting the human throats of these human goats, then I don't see why you shouldn't suddenly become a 'real woman' by the same horrible atrocity. How can you ever possibly look any living thing in the eye after becoming a grown-up by cutting the throat of a living being? What I mean is, my mind is in such a mess because every step eats up the step before it and where will this grand staircase of everything eating everything else lead us to? Who wants to be the first step and who will be the last all-eating step? God? I know that goat has probably exterminated a lot of cowering grass, and the grass itself ate up

the salt and water in the earth, and the salt and the water
probably came from stinking corpses in the ground, and the
corpses probably ate up something else – I mean, what the hell!
At least we have got that within us which does not kill when all
the bloody world out there is killing. Look, you're my sister, so
don't rush me – at least give me a chance. This is not a guerrilla
band from which a man cannot desert alive. It isn't Smith's army
either. It's me. Me. And I'm just goat's wool that nobody can see.
The way the goat is staring at me is making me nervous. But
that's natural; how would you stare at people who were, in your
presence, openly discussing the subject of doing away with you,
skinning you and dressing you up so that you'd not be even a
corpse but something good to eat, which would an hour later
come out of their arses and be flushed away into a labyrinth of
sewers? I know we can't eat air or stone or fire, but we can at any
rate drink water. But why do we have to eat and drink at all?
Whoever created us had a nasty mind! How would you feel if
somebody skinned you and then hung out your skin to dry and
made a pair of shoes out of it? I mean, there's people out there
who'd boil your very bones to make fertilizer – and if your bones
are not good enough, they boil them again and make glue out of
them and give it to little schoolkids to paste up their paperdolls
and stick them on a time chart that's supposed to explain how
human civilisation worked out from the Neanderthal to the man
of today who is supposed to see things like a camera lens looks
at you just before the shutter falls. I refuse to see things that way!
They look at you like you want me to look at that goat. They
look at you like you were a potential meal, and they digest your
innards and fart you out and call it progress. It terrifies me the
way we are capable of imprisoning whole populations of pigs,
cattle, poultry, goats and sheep and fatten them up and then
herd them into gas-chambers and when they are dead strip them
of their flesh and bones and brains and gold teeth and marriage
rings and spectacles – strip them of everything and call it what,
intensive farming, modern progress. And we call it everything
else but exactly what it is. The world was not created to serve for
a meal for us. If it was, then god help the likes of me. God? It's
his Christmas and in 1915 and 1916 on the western front they
took a break from shooting each other up and pushed a football
about and then as soon as his holy birthday was over they began

blasting the tonsils out of each other again. One of the bloody Germans was a clown with a goldfish. I don't want to be a gold-fish in somebody's idea of a cosmic farce. The goat doesn't want to be either. And that poor archbishop in Uganda probably did not want to be a goldfish in Amin's head, either. And probably the goldfish would prefer it if I left its name out of this.

Heavens! it's so late already. What time is supper? What do you mean, I'll have to kill the goat if I want any supper? I want my supper. This is the first time I've been able to come home in seven years, and would you deny me a humble repast? The goat? Him? He is really the humble repast, is he? Then – god help me – I'll ... Let's give him to those starving Makonis. They probably haven't had anything again today. Hey – look out! It's broken its tether. See how it runs, like Pan himself, or like a scapegoat, or like me when I was younger. It's burst through that crowd! It's in the forest! Well good luck to you, Pan. Don't look so offended, Ruth, because we are eating out. I've reserved the table already. At that posh place, Brett's. My wife will be joining us there in – let's see – five minutes. You two have got a lot to talk about – it's been seven years, you know. I just hope I won't be booked for speeding.

XOLILE GUMA

African Trombone

It was a clear October morning, graced by the warmth of the sun, caressed by a capricious breeze typical of such a morning in sub-equatorial Africa. Towards the arena they came, in all shapes and sizes. Big ones, small ones, tall ones, short ones, fat ones, thin ones, a seething mass of people. Colourfully adorned in costumes of origin as varied as the people who wore them. Africans, independent Africans, proud of their independence and gathered now to celebrate the occasion, commemorating the day on which the colonial flag was brought down and theirs slowly and triumphantly raised to the heavens, there to flutter and sway, symbol of the African dream accomplished; Africans – and known as such, not the 'native hordes' of the old textbook descriptions, descending onto the plains to meet the long-haired gentlemen from across the sea.

Within the arena, festivities had begun. The army, resplendent in their new uniforms, stood in formation in the centre, flanked on the left by the youth league, on the right by the police, while in the background one saw 'Dad's army', veterans of the Second World War. How graphically that arena portrayed history, the old and the new, unable to merge but seemingly capable of peaceful co-existence. The neat, disciplined, modern, rectangular formation of the armed forces framed by the veterans: rugged, too old for discipline, outdated, standing in a rough semi-circle, a formation dating back to the Africa which was being rediscovered.

I sat in the covered area immediately to the left of the seats reserved for 'honourable members of the diplomatic corps'. Further to the left, people were streaming in through all possible gates, filling whatever space there was, losing themselves in the sea of people with amazing ease. To the right, beyond a stately row of red seats enclosed by a green rope threaded through a progression of stainless steel rings, the sea of faces flowed endlessly, reaching the furthest boundaries of the arena, finally merging into the people to my left, thus completing the circle, punctuated only by the red hiatus, reserved for foreign emissaries and 'honourable members of the diplomatic corps'.

Intent as I was on surveying the panorama bedecking that green arena, my attention was arrested by one piercing note. The semi-circle composed of the veterans was now alive with motion, swaying in a manner not unlike a giant millipede unsuccessfully attempting to do the twist: uncoordinated and ragged and yet, in some grotesque way, orderly. Nor did the matter end there, for from that undisciplined writhing mass came sounds, rich sounds of deep voices, tremulously raised in haphazard fashion, accompanied by the honking of an assortment of brassware; bugles, trumpets, French horns, all relics of the Second World War, manfully handled by the veterans. And then I saw him, resplendent in the uniform of a regimental sergeant-major, medals proudly displayed, complemented by a loin-cloth of cowhide, feet encased in brown boots which had long resigned themselves to the inevitability of decay, blowing a trombone. He emerged from the ranks, taking halting, measured steps, veins bulging from the neck upwards, testimony of the magnitude of his exertion, blowing his trombone. Bent double but refusing to be cowed, his face lined by years of insecurity and anguish, hands gnarled by the experience of war and the passage of time, he blew his trombone. His trombone became vehicle of his emotions, emotions aroused by his peers, who like himself had actively fought for the day when their country would be free. The notes emanating from that trombone were not amenable to chromatic definition: they emanated from his guts and seemed to be directed at my guts, like the sound of a cow being slaughtered, blood flowing in viscous rivulets of red, drawing my stomach along for companionship. 'What does all this mean?' he seemed to be saying. 'Is this what I fought for, all those many years ago?' I watched transfixed. I could imagine the scene as it must have been thirty years earlier, in this same arena, when the then young men answered the call to arms. How straight and tall they must have stood then. Fired by the zeal of youth, prepared to die for their country. Now they were bent double.

The British ambassador's daughter, seated in the red hiatus, lisped, 'Goth, ithn't that old man wif the trombone thweet?'

Intent on discovering the truth about that old man, I made my way through the crowds, pushing and heaving, cursing and pleading as the occasion demanded, until I too emerged through the iron gate leading out of the arena, feeling as I did so, as exalted as I would imagine the biblical camel feels when it manages to negotiate the proverbial eye of the needle. My task seemed almost hopeless. Where amongst that impossible mob, was I going to find an aged man, member of a royal regiment, in the uniform of a regimental sergeant-major, carrying a shiny trombone, whom the British ambassador's daughter had described as 'thweet'? On every side the people thronged, ululating and gesticulating in wild abandon, emerging from that arena as though it was a giant dam, pregnant with people, whose sluice gates had just been opened. I reluctantly decided to drown myself in that sea of people, to be carried along by it like some bottle tossed in desperation by a marooned sailor, he not knowing where it would land, but hopeful that it would.

I 'landed' in town, part of a band of travellers which had boarded a bus whose bonnet bore some resemblance to a pig's snout. Looking about me, I noticed that people were gravitating towards various centres of amusement: pubs and discotheques, with neon lights brazenly announcing their wares. The bus stop was opposite a church whose wares, not being amenable to advertisement by neon lights, were surreptitiously implicit in the mystical darkness which it exuded. I paused a while, reflecting on all that had passed. The green snout coughed as the bus, 'Maphala Special: Never Say Die', jerked into clumsy motion, panting blue smoke through its posterior; low and squat, straddling the road like an overfed pig, obviously intent on returning to the arena, there to swallow more people before returning once again to relieve itself before the church.

The sun setting in the western sky spread the last rays of day with the tenderness of a mother laying her first-born to sleep. In the east, the moon made its coy appearance. Depressed by my inability to locate the trombonist and yet soothed by the sky's version of the day's aftermath, I stood, pensive.

A woman came walking down the street towards me, with the strange, jerky gait peculiar to one who is two-in-one. I say a woman, in fact she was more of a girl than a woman, with narrow shoulders accentuating the bulge which was the source of

her discomfort. As she passed, she seemed to smile ever so
slightly, obviously amused by what must have been a look of
incredulity on my face. 'Men,' she seemed to be saying, 'can
never understand these things. Theirs is only to plant seed —
forgetting that, given a fertile environment, that seed must
prosper and grow.' She waddled on, pausing to examine the
flow of traffic before crossing to the church, eternal refuge of the
desperate. To this day, I still wonder which startled me more, the
sound of the piercing trombone, or the frenzied screech of tyres.
I jumped, startled, rudely jolted by the reality of life and death.
She lay in a pool of blood, which only seconds earlier had given
radiance to her coy smile; blood which only seconds earlier had
held the promise of life. He came prancing down the street,
rejuvenated by heaven-knows-what, trombone in hand. Absent
was any of the 'thweetness' which the British ambassador's
daughter might have seen. This was a man driven by frustration,
like a lion mortally wounded, maddened by pain and seeking
revenge. Cognizant of the fact that death was at hand, and yet
mindful of the sweetness of life, he pranced down the street,
coming towards us.

Meanwhile the crowds had converged on that pitiful spectacle; drawn and yet repelled by the horror of it. Like green flies
around a dump of manure they buzzed, none venturing to do
anything and none prepared to sacrifice his vantage point. 'Get
the police, somebody!' I howled, and immediately felt ashamed.
Why the hell wouldn't I go and fetch the police? The refrain was
picked up by others. 'Get the police, somebody!' – and still she
bled.

The cavernous door of the church opened and the priest
emerged. We all breathed a sigh of relief. The minister was come,
defender of the faith, anointer of God, healer supreme; for who,
but the minister, can heal what he cannot see? His appearance
was greeted by a frenzied run of notes from the trombonist. Like
an angel in mourning, white upon black the minister floated out
of the church.

'Do not touch the woman, old one,' he said, 'she needs medical attention which you are not capable of giving.'

Frightened by the tone of the 'angel', the old man who had
been cradling the injured woman, let go. Her head hit the
ground with a sickening thud; we all winced simultaneously.

'Fool,' the angel roared, 'now look what you've done.'

The old man picked up his trombone from the congealing blood, shook his head slowly from side to side, and began to walk away.

'Do you know who I am, young man?' he whispered, obviously hurt. I edged a little closer, hopefully.

'Be gone, old one,' the minister threatened, 'your filthy loin skin and unwashed hands have already done damage not only to this poor woman but to us all. We who have self-respect and acceptable standards of conduct.'

He left, trombone in hand, disappearing into the night. To this day I have not been able to find him, possessor of the history of this land, without whose efforts we would not today be where we are. What he said to me with that trombone was, 'What is this independence for which I fought, but which now passes me by? Children for whom I selected education and not bribery as a means of salvation now use that education as a means of bribery, and call me a fool. I must stand as a curio for children. But always remember that with my death, your greatest source of information also dies. You will become the curiosity of the international society, a people denying their history.'

If you ever meet an old man carrying a trombone, or as is more likely, blowing his trombone, stop and listen. That African trombone has a great deal to say, and not much time in which to say it.

ACHMAT DANGOR

The Homecoming

He did not receive a hero's welcome. No press photographers, no former headmasters came to welcome the return of the prodigal son. Only Jacobs was there, exuding a generous eagerness and haste. He had to be back at work. His lunchtime was over already.

'Things are changing,' Jacobs told him in the taxi, and after a hasty glance at his watch told the driver to go direct to Johannesburg station.

'I'm glad to see you've none of the airs the other fellows bring with them from abroad, Nick.'

'There's not all that much that is worth bringing back.'

'Yes, I know, but not even a degree, a diploma, or something to make your old people feel good? What did you do in Europe, Nick?'

'Travelled.'

'For eight years?'

'Nine.'

'Yes, well. They'll still be glad to see you.'

'How are they?'

'Fine. Old, but fine. Waited for their brilliant son all these years.'

Brilliant Coloured boys go to Europe and bring back degrees, professorships and an air of permanent exile. Except Nicholas Dassault. The rebuke in Jacobs's voice did not escape him. His parents must be extremely disappointed in him. A truck-driver and cinema-usher in London, a taxi-driver in Marseilles, labourer in Germany, a prisoner in Istanbul. Speaks five European languages, but not one degree. His clothes and the age of his face will tell them this. His parents and their friends.

'Here's the station, Nick. Just go up there and ask for a single to Newclare. And listen, this place is still full of good people, hear? Ask them if you get lost. Go on, meet the people, travel Third Class if you like. Sorry I've got to rush.'

After a muttered thanks, Nicholas walked out into the African sun, baking in his heavy suit.

Home, home and another Third Class journey.

'Took a train from Troy to Ithaca, died in his sleep on a wooden bench,' he hummed. Something he wrote or read, long ago. Third Class journeys are the same the world over. And their sojourners. Workmen in greasy protective clothes, scratching the dirt of their interminable labours from under their uncut fingernails. Heavy-hipped women burdened by the paraphernalia necessary for survival, stoically ignoring the insults of passengers they jostle with their unwieldy parcels.

He clung to the leather thong with an expertise unknown to a stranger, and yet they knew he was a stranger. Some stared at him, and at his suitcase, then yawned and returned to their preoccupation with the little world at their crowded feet. The Third Class insignia becomes recognisable before long.

The familiar little stations, with quaint English names (Grosvenor, Mayfair, Westbury) slid past. He alighted at Newclare, gently but firmly brushing aside a large woman who clung resolutely to the pillar in the doorway. Politeness was an instant sign of weakness in his Third Class environment, nor is it wise to accede to a request to stand aside. That woman would have lost her place in such a crowded train.

And here was his Ithaca.

He stood on the platform, feeling lost, despite his experience, despite the immunity he had acquired to physical change.

But the valley was gone. In place of the huge expanse of grass that had swept to the swamp verging on the mine-dump stood large complexes of duplex flats. Washing streamed from the sweep of iron railings on the never-ending balconies. And children. Hundreds of urchins, minions of the middle-class, well-fed and badly dressed, played in grassed playing terrains. Symbols of urban life, mass euthanasia.

A sense of familiarity returned to him. He shrugged and walked on. Here the broken road ran, and ended where this river ran. The road had become a black and gleaming ribbon, the river (beginning to shrink even when he left) was now a sluice for industrial waste, covered with concrete slabs. Daniel had died here, drowned. He recalled the inquest: Ratlogo, Daniel Ongopotso, death by drowning while attempting to escape arrest. No blameworthy party can be established. Death deemed accidental. And Aaron had lived. Because he hid in our tree.

The rain fell softly onto the window pane.

'Go away from the window. If they see you staring at the tree, they will know there's someone in it.'

'Where's Potso?'

'He went to the river to warn his father. Modimu!'

'Quiet. There's somebody coming.'

The policeman had courteously inquired whether any Marussians (Basotho) were on the premises. His mother shook her head. His throat was dry. 'Don't worry, we'll protect you,' the policeman had said.

Afterwards his father, driven by his son's begging, took the torch and went to search the river.

They found Daniel floating in the swamp early the next morning. His body was swollen, but he had a strange, elated expression on his face. They had found the body of Daniel's father floating a hundred yards away from his son. Nicholas could never forget the heavy, bloated face.

Now he walked down Griffith Avenue, where his parents lived – the lucky few, away from the 'Compounds' as he would hear them called. In that valley, beyond the broken road, the houses had always cascaded back-to-back, like a turbulent river, and washed up in gradual serenity to this hill where the well-to-do had always lived.

But the demarcation then was not one of race, but one of class, and class was decided by money. The African bus-owner lived alongside the Indian shopkeeper and the Coloured artisan who ran his own business.

Here on this hill, large terraces had jutted out into neat gardens and on many a summer night the fashionable music of the time flowed out into the darkness, competing with the beat of the Sangoma drums that boomed insistently from the edge of the broken road.

Silk saris and soutane gowns mingled with homespun African prints, swirled around in an oasis of gaiety to the sound of the tango. Shebeen queens away from their shebeens, priests far from their paltry parishes, doctors, lawyers, teachers and Fah-

Fee kings formed the inner society. Man was man, race did not matter, for money was the common denominator, no matter how ill-begotten.

His father still lived here. But the shebeen queen was gone, the bus-owner and the Indian shopkeeper too. Many of the terraces had disappeared, leaving the neighbourhood looking naked and seedy. His father, a retired furniture manufacturer, had retained his terrace, now overgrown with creepers.

'My goeie God. Dis Nicky. Pat Dassault se seun wat oorsee gegaan het.'

'Kyk hoe groot is hy. Haai! Hoe gaan dit?'

'Onthou jy ons nog? Sieker almal al ve'giet, nê?'

His father and mother were standing at the edge of their garden. His father's face, once hard, had gained an inscrutable softness. His mother's hair was an iron-grey. The lovely Lena, old and gnarled.

A crowd gathered around the gate while he embraced first his mother, then his father. A tear gathered in the old man's eye, and rolled into his bushy moustache, with a motion that seemed contrived.

Nicholas viciously repressed the feeling of revulsion that welled up in him as he watched the old man's tear-filled eyes and reddened face.

He shook hands with the neighbours he remembered, kissed their wives on the cheeks, and then the whole crowd flowed indoors, the newer neighbours watching questioningly from their porches.

Home, home. He had returned, he who had left to be a better slave than they.

They were people whose lives, reaching a point of ennui with age, found sustenance in nostalgia. The gathering grew spontaneously into a social occasion.

Almost forgetting their new arrival, they reminisced over cups of hastily-brewed coffee. Everybody recalled somebody who had left the neighbourhood, chance meetings with forgotten friends and neighbours, deaths, marriages. Many also took the opportunity of retelling, probably for the hundredth time, the fates and fortunes of their own children.

'Andrew and his wife are doing very well in Canada. They have two children now. Lovely things.'

'Bruim and Janie are in Cape Town. Beautiful house in Skotches Kloof they have.'

Old Mrs Samuels lamented the younger generation's apparent lack of gratitude and disregard for custom and convention. Her son, after qualifying as a doctor went to practise in the Transkei and married an African woman.

'Sy is lieflik. Maar tog … nie ons mense nie.'

Nicholas welcomed their disregard for his presence. It obviated the need for small talk, the need to tell them about Europe. It helped him to evade the question of why he did not complete his education.

During his first year at university in England, he met Simon Musi, a fellow expatriate student from Soweto. Simon prodded him into taking a month's holiday and travelling the continent with him.

Three months later they parted in Vienna, Simon abruptly announcing his return to South Africa.

Nicholas stayed, and travelled. He had grown to love this life of a carefree vagrant. His greatest joy was the train journeys. A comfortable passenger on a hard wooden bench, criss-crossing the continent, Eastern Europe and the Levant. He was the ideal passenger, sitting back and enjoying without complaint the rigour of journeys over somewhat archaic rail-systems. He made no conscious decisions about the direction of his journeys, buying tickets from destination to destination at random. After a year he became the perennial passenger, being taken from place to place without any act of will on his part.

Once he was stopped at the Czechoslovakian border because of his South African passport. He sat on the platform of the small Greek frontier station for days, basking in the warm Greek summer, drinking a strange, pungent liquor proffered by the only café there.

The Greek authorities served him with a deportation order, putting him on a train for Turkey, where he travelled extensively. His travels came to an end, temporarily, after two years when his father's cash grant ceased. News of his son's wanderings reached the ageing Dassault, who promptly stopped the grant and solicited the South African government through its various embassies to find Nicholas and send him home.

Nicholas returned to London, a city he hated, to settle what little affairs he had there. He found himself forced to work illegally, first as a truck-driver, then as a cinema-usher to earn his keep.

Within a year he returned to Paris, whence his journeys resumed. He travelled from city to city, in a more orderly fashion, however, due to his financial circumstances. He worked as a labourer, lived with workmen, farmers and pimps. After six years he ended up in a Turkish prison for entering the country illegally after the South African embassy in Athens had refused to renew his much-travelled passport for the fourth time.

He was flown home at the South African government's expense (repaid by his father) to this homely welcome, eight years after leaving the country of his birth.

After the evening meal, which his father presided over with the air of austerity that he had imposed when the home was filled with the garrulous noise of five restless sons, Nicholas and the old Dassault sat uneasily opposite each other at the edge of the terrace.

Nicholas's eye roved over the terrace and garden, glimpsing the darkened corners of his childhood where the Dassault sons sat, hot and stiff in their black serge suits, sipping the iced sherbet their Indian neighbour had taught their mother to make. All around them, with a dreamlike incandescence on their faces, the adult guests at their parents' anniversary party drifted about, glasses of prohibited whisky in their hands.

It was here that young ladies in frail white gowns and young men with slicked-down hair began, tremulously, to flaunt the conventions of the day by openly courting each other.

It was on such a night that the boom of the Sangoma drums rose with such surprising intensity, that it momentarily stilled the gaiety on the terrace. With a short nervous laugh, his father had turned the radiogram louder and waved the party-goers on to resume their dancing.

Nicholas had heard a whistle from the edge of the garden, and quietly slipped away when his father's attention was diverted. Aaron and Potso leaned against the wall, panting after the hard run up the hill from Dikies Diek.

'Come. The Sangomas are dancing tonight.'

'So?'

'It's a special dance. Chief Magubane is dead.'

'What!'

'They are going to smell out his killer.'

Without further demur, Nicholas took off his shoes and socks and climbed over the wall. Aaron, 'the one with the wild eye' Nicholas's mother had called him, led them down the cobbled street, running full out. When Nicholas and the other Dassault sons had first run on their shoe-softened bare feet, their soles had cracked and bled. But they healed and hardened, and soon they too pounded over the cobblestones with ease and comfort.

The 'smelling out' dance took place in an open patch surrounded by a cluster of tin shanties. The Sangomas, about five in number, danced in wild gyrations amongst the small crowd that had gathered there. They pounded their feet frantically on the ground, until a cloud of dust hung immobile in the still summer air. The dust cloud turned the colour of dead blood in the light of a bonfire burning in the centre of the clearing.

The Sangomas, the bones of their ankles and wrists clattering like broken glass, had by now reduced the crowd to a state of paralysis.

Nicholas and his two friends also felt this strange enthralment. Aaron clutched the railings on the wooden fence with whitened fingers, Potso sat pale and deathly still. Nicholas felt a lump in his throat; he suppressed the wild desire to flee.

The spell, and the quietude of fear it had inseminated, was broken when a stick-wielding young man dragged in a screaming and frantically gesticulating figure. The Sangomas howled, in uncanny unison, like the scavenger dogs that inhabited Dikies Diek. With a wave of his kierie, the young man silenced the witches, and spoke harshly in a fluent Sotho which was beyond Nicholas's grasp of the language.

'What is he saying?'

'It is the Chief's son. He says he does not need old women to tell him who his father's killer was, he knows the killer.'

A vociferous argument had ensued between the chief's son and the Sangomas, who were cackling like geese. The chief's son raised the still-struggling figure he had dragged in by the collar of a worn coat, and displaying his captive to the crowd, he fetched the man a stunning blow with his kierie.

From the other end of the cluster of shacks, a new intrusion occurred. With flashing torches two policemen, one black and one white, rushed in. They waved their revolvers in the air. The black policeman ordered the crowd to remain where they were while his white counterpart rushed to rescue the man who had been beaten, now lying inert on the ground.

Pandemonium erupted. Shots were fired. Soon the two policemen emerged from the confusion, bleeding profusely from numerous blows inflicted by kieries. Dragging the unconscious man they had rescued, they retreated, guns pointed at the crowd, which melted away rapidly into the darkness.

'Let's go,' Aaron whispered, but as the trio rose from their hiding place, strong hands grasped them by the wrist. Two huge Marussians accosted the frightened boys. Nicholas had an irrepressible urge to cry.

One of the men spoke to Potso, but Aaron answered in a pleading voice.

'Tsamay!' the men whispered, and disappeared into the shanties.

The boys ran, and did not stop until they reached the station.

'He wanted to kill us.'

'He said they would skin us alive, the way they skin cats.'

Nicholas had seen them in the veld, skinning cats with non-chalant ease. Fearfully he bade his companions goodnight.

'Nick,' Aaron said earnestly, 'they will, so keep your mouth shut. That man they killed was a policeman.'

Nicholas ran home, where he found that the party had ended. He looked downhill towards Dikies Diek, where the headlights of police cars wove through the narrow streets.

By the light of the moon he could discern the vague outline of blanketed Basoto men fleeing into the veld.

The next day was Sunday, and Nicholas performed the rituals of their Christian living with unusual zeal, praying fiercely in church for obviation of the threat he had received the previous night. His mind continuously conjured up the thought of himself whimpering as frantically as a cat in the grip of those strong black hands.

After the simple but joyous festivities of their Sunday lunch, Nicholas had almost forgotten the occurrences of the previous

night. As was customary on Sundays, the family would be joined
by various relatives and friends. The women would gather on
the terrace drinking coffee and talking while the men,
accompanied by their sons, would retire to a huge plot the Dassault family owned alongside Dikies Diek.

After each of the man had imbibed a glass of the pungent
home-brewed peach liquor that the plot's caretaker unfailingly
provided, they would assist the caretaker in penning the sheep
that roamed the property, and put up a cricket wicket at the end
of an improvised pitch.

Here, surrounded by tin shanties and to the accompaniment
of the bleat of sheep, the cream of Newclare's society — artisans,
teachers, shopkeepers and men from such sublime professions as
gambling, liquor peddling and Fah-Fee running — would
indulge in an afternoon's game of cricket. This exercise in
incongruous gentility usually attracted a sizeable group of
curious spectators who whiled away their afternoon's drinking
in unconcealed amusement at the strange, arm-waving, hoarse-
voiced antics of men who in normal times were cold, calculating
and 'respectable' businessmen.

But this day the spectators were strangely absent, and only a
few boys sat around. Aaron was there, nervous and withdrawn.
Clouds were gathering and the birds were gone from the trees.

'There's a storm coming,' Aaron said.

'It never rains on Sunday,' Nicholas answered, hoping that
nothing would upset this idyllic, if temporary, escape from the
terrible event of which he had a distinct foreboding.

On their way from church they had seen unusual activity at
the police station. His father had remarked that there was going
to be some raid or other, but Nicholas had immediately linked
this activity with last night's events.

'You did not tell anybody about last night, did you?'

'No,' Nicholas answered angrily. Being reminded of the
previous night's events angered him more than the obvious tone
of mistrust in Aaron's voice.

His father's thick hairy arms were entwined around the bat.
As the ball made its erratic passage across the uneven pitch, the
fielders crouched forward. In their multi-coloured shirts they
resembled a group of graceless praying mantises. Dassault hit
the cork ball skywards with a resounding thwack. And then it

began to rain without warning. The flight of the ball was abandoned and the players began feverishly to collect the jackets they had discarded, and run for the shelter of their cars.

Aaron was on his feet, staring at the railway line. Nicholas had seen them too, hordes of khaki-clad policemen, their batons gleaming as wet wood does.

Aaron began to run up the hill, and everywhere, with screams of panic, men, women and children began to run towards the veld. Nicholas stood staring at this awesome sight, hundreds of men waving their long batons, rushing down the railway embankment, their tunics flapping in the wind.

'I can't see their eyes,' he thought as his father bundled him into the car.

The downpour continued all afternoon, muting the screams, the sounds of shattering glass and the inevitable screech of tyres. As dusk fell, the rain stopped and an anguished mourning cry (eLele, eLele!) which Nicholas associated with funerals, was heard. Mothers and sons began to search for their husbands and fathers in alleyways, on roofs and in drainage-holes.

The Dassault children were forbidden to go outdoors, and Nicholas saw Aaron descend from the tree in their garden and run towards the river.

He returned a while later and stood in the darkness of the Dassault terrace, water and tears streaming down his face.

'Nick, Nick? It's Aaron.'

Nicholas opened the door despite his mother's angry remonstrations.

'Did you find him?'

'No. His father's not home either.'

Dassault drove Aaron to his home in Dikies Diek, angrily telling both boys that it was useless to go and search the river in the darkness. The river would be flooded by now.

But Nicholas begged his father, until Dassault relented with a weary sigh. It was nearing midnight when Dassault, accompanied by his male servant and two neighbours, left armed with torches.

They returned when the sun had risen over the drenched township, Dassault thanking his neighbours and calmly informing his wife that the bodies of both Potso and his father had been found, floating in the swamp. Dassault retired, wearily telling his son that nothing could be done for them.

Nicholas woke up, startled out of his reverie by his father's hand on his shoulder. 'I think you should go to bed. You must be tired, son.'

Nicholas rose, walked to the end of the terrace, and stood looking down at the cluster of duplex flats known as 'the Compounds'. They stood dark and brooding in the base of the valley.

'It's all gone, Nick. The hovels, the shebeens, the natives and their faction fights. Those people down there have homes, schools, churches. And the people they removed are all living better than they did in the hole that it was.'

Nicholas nodded but did not answer. The garden had a wet rank smell. Once, on a hot summer night like this, the smell of the moist earth would rise, warm and fragrant. The terrace too, showed signs of decay. The stone flooring was crumbling in places, and there were brown rusty patches on the roof. 'Things have changed,' Jacobs had said. He wondered whether Matt, also a childhood friend, would know what had happened to Aaron. The people that lived in 'the hole that it was'.

The early fifties had been a time of economic depression in Johannesburg. Even in the Dassault household there were certain austerities that had to be observed, but in Dikies Diek there was mass unemployment and even hunger. Nicholas used to sit on those smoky evenings in that small brick house, waiting for Aaron's father to return with a loaf of bread. Or the lack of bread reflected in the red of a drunken eye. Aaron would turn away with a shrug, an uncaring smile on his lips.

He had learnt other things from Aaron, apart from hiding his feelings when denied something he desperately wanted. He had learnt the freedom of uncombed hair, that poverty was freedom to a child for whom in manhood even liberty would be impoverished. That freedom grew in an empty belly, like a stunted flower, and took Third Class journeys to nowhere. And quietude, and the ability to be your own master, were found in a void, without decisions, without the application of will.

They had come one morning, when the winter had ended, white men in black suits. They came with saracens and empty trucks

and departed laden with the sparse furnishing of the households
of Dikies Diek, whose inhabitants sat on these trucks, resignation
on their faces. Their destination was Meadowlands, Soweto.

They waved to those whom they left behind. 'Chip-Chip' the
barber, Chong the butcher, Dassault, Khan, Lepere, people
whose names and skins kept them in Newclare.

Dassault did not wave back. He stood on his terrace, his face
hard and controlled. Nicholas scrambled down the hill, but was
kept back from the truck that carried Aaron and his family by a
uniformed policeman. Nicholas waved, tears streaming down
his face, as the truck pulled off, but there was no reaction from
Aaron, who merely smiled that uncaring smile.

Nicholas stayed behind in Dikies Diek, which was a ghost
town by the end of the day. He watched, with a strange feeling
of detachment, teams of workmen pulling down the corrugated
iron shanties, and laying them out in neat piles.

He watched as other trucks brought people from nearby
Sophiatown to live in the few brick houses in Dikies Diek. People
with children like him, who looked like him, had fathers like
him.

In one day Dikies Diek was gone.

That night, many years ago, he had acceded readily to a
request he had denied his father for months, and agreed to
attend a boarding school in Aliwal North.

He rose early, and breakfasted with his parents as he had done
as a scholar all those years ago. He had an appointment that
morning. His father had arranged with a friend to see Nicholas
about employment.

'It's a good opportunity. In South Africa no one becomes
labourers or ushers unless they're crippled,' Dassault said.

The train was full, and as it swayed, Nicholas felt the ebb of
an apprehension that had beset him the moment he alighted at
Newclare station the day before.

At Johannesburg station he locked himself in a toilet and
counted out the exact amount of money the ticket office said the
fare would be.

As inconspicuous as all the others in the queue, he shuffled
along until his turn came at the window.

'Third Class to Cape Town. Single please.'

NORMAN RUSH

Bruns

Poor Bruns. They hated him so much it was baroque. But then so is Keteng baroque, everything about it.

Probably the Boers were going to hate Bruns no matter what. Boers run Keteng. They've been up there for generations, since before the Protectorate. When independence came, it meant next to nothing to them. They ignored it. They're all citizens of Botswana, but they are Boers underneath forever, really unregenerate. Also, in Keteng you're very close to the border with South Africa. They still mostly use rands for money instead of pula. Boers slightly intrigue me. For a woman, I'm somewhat an elitist, and hierarchy always interests me. I admit these things. The Boers own everything in Keteng, including the chief. They wave him to the head of the queue for petrol, which he gets for free, naturally, just like the cane liquor they give him. They own the shops. Also they think they really know how to manage the Bakorwa, which actually they do. You have to realize that the Bakorwa have the reputation of being the most violent and petulant tribe in the country, which is about right. All the other tribes say so. And in fact the Boers do get along with them. In fact, the original whites in Keteng — that would be the Vissers, Du Toits, Pieterses ... seven families altogether — were all rescued by the Bakorwa when their oxwagons broke down in the desert when they were trekking somewhere. They started out as bankrupts and now they own the place. It's so feudal up there you cannot conceive. That is, it has been until now.

I know at lot about Keteng. I got interested in Keteng out of boredom with my project. Actually, my project collapsed. My thesis adviser at Stanford talked me into my topic anyway, so it wasn't all that unbearable when it flopped. At certain moments I can even get a certain vicious satisfaction out of it. Frankly, the problem is partly too many anthropologists in one small area. We are thick on the ground. And actually we hate each other. The problem is that people are contaminating one another's research, so hatred is structural and I don't need to apologize. At any rate, I was getting zero. I was supposed to be showing a relationship between diet and fertility among the Bakorwa up near Tswapong, in the hills. The theory was that fertility would show some seasonality because the diet in the deep bush was supposedly ninety per cent hunting–gathering, which would mean sharp seasonal changes in diet content. But the sad fact is you go into the middle of nowhere and people are eating Simba chips and cornflakes and drinking Castle Lager. The problem is Americans, partly. Take the hartebeest domestication project, where they give away so much food and scraps and things that you have a kind of permanent beggar settlement outside the gate. And just to mention the other research people you have encumbering the ground – you have me, you have the anthropologists from the stupid Migration Study and the census, and you have people from some land-grant college someplace following baboons around. By the way, there were several baboon attacks on Bakorwa gathering firewood around Keteng, which they blame on the Americans for pestering the baboons. Or Imiricans, as the Boers would say. America gets the blame.

The other thing is that Keteng is remote. It's five hours from the rail line, over unspeakable roads, through broiling-hot empty thornveld. In one place there's no road and you just creep over red granite swells for a kilometer, following a little line of rocks. So the Boers got used to doing what they wanted, black government or not. They still pay their farm labor in sugar and salt and permission to crawl underneath their cows and suck fresh milk. It is baroque. So I got interested in Keteng and started weekending. At my project site, camping was getting uncomfortable, I should mention, with strange figures hanging around my perimeter. Nobody did anything, but it makes you nervous. In Keteng I can always get a room from the sisters at the mission hospital and a bath instead of washing my armpits under my shirt because you never know who's watching.

The place I stay when I descend into Keteng is interesting and is one reason I keep going back. I can see everything from the room the sisters give me. The hospital is up on the side of a hill, and the sisters' hostel is higher than that, on the very top. My room is right under the roof, the second story, where there's a water tank and therefore a perpetual sound of water gurgling down through pipes, a sound you get famished for in a place so arid. Also in tubs on the roof they have vines growing that drape down over the face of the building, so you have this green-curtain effect over your window. The sisters have a little tiny enclosed locked-up courtyard where they hang their under-things to dry, which is supposed to be secret and sacrosanct, which you can see into from my room. You can also see where Bruns stayed – a pathetic bare little shack near the hospital with gravel around the stoop and a camp stool so he could sit in the sun and watch his carrots wither. At the foot of the hill the one street in Keteng begins at the hospital gate and runs straight to the chief's court at the other end of town. Downtown amounts to a dozen one-story buildings – shops with big houses behind them. You can see the Bakorwa wards spreading away from the center of Keteng – log kraals, mud rondavels with thatch, mostly, although cement block square houses with sheet-metal roofs held down by cobbles are infiltrating the scene. Sometimes I think anthropology should be considered a form of voyeurism rather than a science, with all the probing into reproductive life and so forth we do. I'm voyeuristic. I like to pull my bed up to the window and lie there naked, studying Keteng. Not that the street life is so exotic. Mostly it's goats and cattle. I did once see a guy frying a piece of meat on a stove. The nuns have really hard beds, which I happen to prefer.

Poor Bruns. The first thing I ever heard about him was that there was somebody new in Keteng who was making people as ner-vous as poultry, as they put it. That's an Afrikaans idiom. They meant Bruns. He was a volunteer from some Netherlands religious outfit and a conscientious objector like practically all the Dutch and German volunteers are. He was assigned to be the fleet mechanic at the mission hospital. He was a demon mechanic, it turned out, who could fix anything. Including the X-ray machine, for example, which was an old British Army World War 1 field unit, an antique everybody had given up on. Of course, what do the Boers care, because when they get even just a little cut it's into the Cessna and over the border into the Republic or Potgietersrust or even Pretoria. But other people were ecstatic. Bruns was truly amazing. People found out. A few of the Bakorwa farmers have tractors or old trucks, and Bruns, being hyper-Christian, of course started fixing them up for free in his spare time. On Saturdays you'd see Bakorwa pushing these old wrecks, hordes of them pushing these three or four old wrecks toward Keteng for Bruns. So, number one, right away that made Bruns less than popular around Du Toit's garage. Du Toit didn't like it. It even got a little mean, with some of Bruns's tools disappearing from his workroom at the hospital until he started really locking things up.

The other thing that fed into making people nervous right away was Bruns physically. He was very beautiful. I don't know how else to put it. He was very Aryan, with those pale-blue eyes that are apparently so de rigueur for male movie stars these days. He had a wonderful physique. At some point possibly he had been a physical culturist, or maybe it was just the effect of constant manual work and lifting. Also I can't resist mentioning a funny thing about Boer men. Or, rather, let me back into it: there is a thing with black African men called the African Physiological Stance, which means essentially that men, when they stand around, don't bother to hold their bellies in. It might seem like a funny cultural trait to borrow, but Boer men picked it up. It doesn't look so bad with blacks because the men stay pretty skinny, usually. But in whites, especially in Boers, who run to fat anyway, it isn't so enthralling. They wear their belts underneath their paunches, somewhat on the order of a sling. Now consider Bruns strictly as a specimen walking around with his nice flat belly, a real waist, and, face it, a very compact nice little behind, and also keep in mind that he's Dutch, so in a remote way he's the same stock as the Boer men there, and the contrast was not going to be lost on the women, who are another story. The women have nothing to do. Help is thick on the ground. They get up at noon. They consume bales of true-romance magazines from Britain and the Republic, so incredibly crude. They do makeup. And they can get very flirtatious in an incredibly heavy-handed way after a couple of brandies. Bruns was the opposite of flirtatious. I wonder what the women thought it meant. He was very scrupulous when he was talking to you, unlike everybody else. He kept his eyes on your face. As a person with large breasts I'm sensitized to this. Boer men are not normal. They think they're a godsend to any white woman who turns up in this wilderness. Their sex ideas are derived from their animals. I've heard they just unbanned *Love Without Fear* in South Africa this year, which says something. The book was published in 1941.

On top of that, the Dutch–Boer interface is so freakish and tense anyway. The Dutch call Afrikaans 'baby Dutch'. Boers are a humiliation to the Dutch, like they are their ids set free in the world or something similar. The Dutch Parliament keeps almost voting to get an oil boycott going against South Africa.

So it wasn't helpful that Bruns was some kind of absolute vegetarian, which he combined with fasting. He was whatever is beyond lactovegetarian in strictness. You have never seen people consume meat on the scale of the Boers. As a friend of mine says, Boers and meat go together like piss and porcelain. Biltong, sausages, any kind of meat product, pieces of pure solid fat — they love meat. So there was another rub.

Bruns was so naïve. He apparently had no idea he was coming to live in a shame culture. Among the Bakorwa, if you do something wrong and somebody catches you, they take you to the customary court and give you a certain number of strokes with a switch in public. They wet it first so it hurts more. This is far from being something whites thought up and imposed. It's the way it is. The nearest regular magistrate is — where? Bobonong? Who knows? Bakorwa justice is based on beatings and fear of beatings and shame, full stop. It's premodern. But here comes Bruns wearing his crucifix and wondering what is going on. The problem was he had an unfortunate introduction to the culture. You could call wife-beating among the Bakorwa pretty routine. I think he saw an admission to the hospital related to that. Also he himself was an ex-battered child, somebody said. I'm thinking of setting up a course for people who get sent there. I can give you an example of the kind of thing people should know about and not think twice about. The manager of the butchery in one of the towns caught two women shoplifting and he made them stand against the wall while he whipped them with an extension cord instead of calling the police. This shamed them and was probably effective and they didn't lose time from work or their families. You need anthropologists to prepare people for the culture here. Bruns needed help. He needed information.

Bruns belonged to some sect. It was something like the people in England who jump out and disrupt fox hunts. Or there was a similar group, also in England, of people who were interposing themselves between prizefighters, to stop prizefighting. Bruns was from some milieu like that. I think he felt like he'd wandered into something by Hieronymus Bosch which he was supposed to do something about.

The fact is that the amount of fighting and beating there is in Bakorwa culture is fairly staggering to a person at first. Kids get beaten at school and at home, really hard sometimes. Wives naturally get beaten. Animals. Pets. Donkeys. And of course the whole traditional court process, the *kgotla*, is based on it. I think he was amazed. Every Wednesday at the *kgotla* the chief hears charges and your shirt comes off and you get two to twenty strokes, depending. Then there's the universal recreational punching and shoving that goes on when the locals start drinking. So it's not something you can afford to be sensitive about if you're going to work here for any length of time.

Bruns decided to do something. The first thing he tried was absurd and made everything worse.

He started showing up at the *kgotla* when they were giving judgment and just stood there watching them give strokes. He was male, so he could get right up in the front row. I understand he never said anything, the idea being just to be a sorrowful witness. I guess he thought it would have some effect. But the Bakorwa didn't get it and didn't care. He was welcome.

Maybe I'm just a relativist on corporal punishment. Our own wonderful culture is falling apart with crime, more than Keteng is, and you could take the position that substituting imprisonment for the various kinds of rough justice there used to be had only made things worse. Who knows if there was less crime when people just formed mobs in a cooperative spirit and rode people out of town on a rail or horsewhipped them, when that was the risk you were running rather than plea bargaining and courses in basket weaving or some other fatuous find of so-called rehabilitation? I don't.

Bruns convinced himself that the seven families were to blame for all the violence — spiritually to blame at least. He was going to ask them to do something about it, take some kind of stand, and he was going to the center of power, Deon Du Toit.

There's some disagreement as to whether Bruns went once to

Du Toit's house or twice. Everybody agrees Du Toit wasn't home and that Bruns went in and stayed, however many times he went, stayed talking with Marika, Du Toit's slutty wife. The one time everybody agrees on was at night. Bruns started to turn away when the maid told him Du Toit wasn't there. But then somehow Bruns was invited in. That's established. Then subsequently there was one long afternoon encounter, supposedly.

Bruns was going to blame the families for everything — for making money off liquor, which leads to violence, for doing nothing about violence to women and not even appearing in *kgotla* for women who worked for them when they were brutalized by their husbands or boyfriends, for corrupting the chief, who was an incompetent anyway, for doing nothing about conditions at the jail. I can generate this list out of my own knowledge of Bruns's mind: everything on it is true. Finally there was something new he was incensed about. The drought had been bad and Du Toit had just started selling water for three pula a drum. You know a drought is bad when cattle come into town and bite the brass taps off cisterns. A wildebeest charged an old woman carrying melons and knocked her down so it could get the moisture in the melons.

We know what Du Toit did when he came back and found out Bruns had been there. First he punched the housemaid, Myriad Gofetile (her twin sister also works for Du Toit), for letting Bruns in or for not telling him about it, one or the other. And Marika wasn't seen outside the house for a while, although the Boers usually try not to mark their women where it shows when they beat them.

Those are two people I would love to see fighting. Deon and Marika Du Toit, tooth and nail. It would be gorgeous. Both of them are types. He's fairly gigantic. Marika has skin like a store dummy's. She's proud of it. She's one of those people who are between twenty-five and forty but you can't tell where. She has high cheekbones you can't help envying, and these long eyes, rather Eurasian-looking. She wears her hair like a fool, though — lacquered, like a scoop around her head. Her hair is yellowish. She hardly says anything. But she doesn't need to because she's so brilliant with her cigarette, smoking and posing.

Deon was away hunting during the time or times Bruns visited. The inevitable thing happened, besides beating up on his

household, when Deon found out. This was the day he got back,
midmorning. He sent a yard boy to the hospital with a message
to the effect that Bruns is ordered to drop whatever he's doing
and come immediately to see Deon at the house.

Bruns is cool. He sends back the message that he's engaged on
work for the hospital and regrets he isn't free to visit.

So that message went back, and the yard boy comes back with
a new command that Bruns should come to Du Toit's at tea,
which would be at about eleven. Bruns sends the message back
that he doesn't break for tea, which was true.

Suddenly you have Deon himself materializing in the hospital
garage, enraged, still covered with gore from hauling game out
of his pickup. He had shot some eland.

'You can't come by my wife when I am away!' He ended up
screaming this at Bruns, who just carried on fixing some vehicle.

He now orders Bruns to come to his house at lunch, calling
him a worm and so on, which was apropos Bruns being a
pacifist.

Bruns took the position that he had authority over who was
present in the garage and ordered Du Toit to leave.

Then there was a stupid exchange to the effect that Bruns
would come only if Du Toit was in actual fact inviting him to a
meal at noon.

Throughout all this Bruns is projecting a more and more sorrowful calmness. Also, everything Bruns says is an aside, since
he keeps steadily working. Deon gets frantic. The sun is pounding down. You have this silent chorus of Africans standing
around. There is no question that they are loving every moment.

It ends with Deon telling Bruns he had better be at his house
at noon if he expects to live to have sons.

Of course, after the fact everybody wanted to know why somebody didn't intervene.

Bruns did go at lunchtime to Deon's.

The whole front of Deon's place is a screened veranda he uses
for making biltong. From the street it looks like red laundry.
There are eight or nine clotheslines perpetually hung with rags
of red meat turning purple, air-drying. This is where they met.
Out in the road you had an audience of Bakorwa pretending to
be going somewhere, slowly.

Meat means flies. Here is where the absurd takes a hand. Deon comes onto the porch from the house. Bruns goes onto the porch from the yard. The confrontation is about to begin. Deon is just filling his lungs to launch out at Bruns when the absurd thing happens: he inhales a fly. Suddenly you have a farce going. The fly apparently got rather far up his nostril. Deon goes into a fit, stamping and snorting. He's in a state of terror. You inhale a fly and the body takes over. Also you have to remember that there are certain flies that fly up the nostrils of wildebeests and lay eggs that turn into maggots that eat the brains of the animals, which makes them gallop in circles until they die of exhaustion. Deon has seen this, of course.

The scene is over before it begins. Deon crashes back into his living room screaming for help. It is total public humiliation. The Bakorwa see Bruns walk away nonchalantly and hear Du Toit thrashing and yelling.

Marika got the fly out with tweezers, I heard. By then Bruns was back at work.

Here is my theory of the last act. Deon's next move was inevitable – to arrange for a proxy to catch Bruns that same night and give him a beating. For symbolic and other reasons, it had to be one of the Bakorwa. At this point both Bruns and Deon are deep in the grip of the process of the Duel, capital D. Pragmatically, there would be no problem for Deon in getting one of the Bakorwa to do the job and probably even take the blame for it in the unlikely event he got caught. This is not to say there was no risk to Deon, because there was, some. But if you dare a Boer to do something, which is undoubtedly the way Deon perceived it, he is lost. An example is a man who dared to kiss a rabid ox on the lips, at the abattoir in Cape Town. It was in the *Rand Daily Mail*. By the way, the point of kissing the ox on the lips is that it gives rabies its best chance of getting directly to your brain. So he did it. Not only that, he defaulted on the course of rabies injections the health department was frantically trying to get him to take. Here is your typical Boer folk hero. Add to that the Duel psychology, which is like a spell that spreads out and paralyzes people who might otherwise be expected to step in and put a stop to something so weird. Still, when someone you know personally like Bruns is found dead, it shocks you. I had cut this man's hair.

I'm positive two things happened the last night, although the official version is that only one did.

The first is that Deon sent somebody, a local, to beat Bruns up. When night falls in Keteng it's like being under a rock. There's no street lighting. The stores are closed. The whites pull their curtains. Very few Bakorwa can afford candles or paraffin lamps. It can seem unreal, because the Bakorwa are used to getting out and about in the dark and you can hear conversations and deals going down and so on, all in complete blackness. They even have parties in the dark where you can hear bojalwa being poured and people singing and playing those one-string tin-can violins. There was no moon that night and it was cloudy.

Bruns would often go out after dinner and sit on one of the big rocks up on the hill and do his own private vespers. He'd go out at sunset and sit there into the night thinking pure thoughts. He had a little missal he took with him, but what he could do with it in the dark except fondle it I have no idea.

So I think Bruns went out, got waylaid and beaten up as a lesson, and went back to his hut. I think the point of it was mainly just to humiliate him and mark him up. Of course, because of his beliefs, he would feel compelled just to endure the beating. He might try to shield his head or kidneys, but he couldn't fight back. He would not be in the slightest doubt that it was Bakorwa doing it and that they had been commissioned by Du Toit. So he comes back messed up, and what is he supposed to do?

Even very nice people find it hard to resist paradox. For example, whenever somebody who knows anything about it tells the story of poor Bruns, they always begin with the end of the story, which is that he drowned, their little irony being that of course everybody knows Botswana is a desert and Keteng is a desert. So poor Bruns, his whole story and what he did is reduced to getting this cheap initial sensation out of other people.

As I reconstruct the second thing that happened, it went like this: Bruns wandered back from his beating and possibly went into his place with the idea of cleaning himself up. His state of mind would have to be fairly terrible at this point. He has been abused by the very people he is trying to champion. At the same time, he knows Du Toit is responsible and that he can never prove it. And also he is in the grip of the need to retaliate. And he is a pacifist. He gets an idea and slips out again in to the dark.

They found Bruns the next morning, all beaten up, drowned, his head and shoulders submerged in the watering trough in Du Toit's side yard. The police found Deon still in bed, in his clothes, hung over and incoherent. Marika was also still in bed, also under the weather, and she also was marked up and made a bad exhibit. They say Deon was struck dumb when they took him outside to show him the body.

Here's what I see. Bruns goes to Deon's, goes to the trough and plunges his head underwater and fills his lungs. I believe he could do it. It would be like he was beaten and pushed under. He was capable of this. He would see himself striking at the centre of the web and convicting Du Toit for a thousand unrecorded crimes. It's self-immolation. It's non-violent.

Deon protested that he was innocent, but he made some serious mistakes. He got panicky. He tried to contend he was with one of the other families that night, but that story collapsed when somebody else got panicky. Also it led to some perjury charges against the Vissers. Then Deon changed his story, saying how he remembered hearing some noises during the night, going out to see what they were, seeing nothing, and going back in and to bed. This could be the truth, but by the time he said it nobody believed him.

The ruin is absolute. It is a real Götterdämmerung. Deon is in jail, charged, and the least he can get is five years. He will have to eat out of a bucket. The chief is disgraced and they are discussing a regency. Bruns was under his protection, formally, and all the volunteer agencies are upset. In order to defend himself the chief is telling everything he can about how helpless he is in fact in Keteng, because the real power is with the seven families. He's pouring out details, so there are going to be charges against the families on other grounds, mostly about bribery and taxes. Also, an election is coming, so the local Member of Parliament has a chance to be zealous about white citizens acting like they're outside the law. Business licenses are getting suspended. Theunis Pieters is selling out. There's a new police compound going up and more police coming in. They're posting a magistrate.

There is ruin. It's perfect.

The Music of the Violin

Vukani was doing homework in his bedroom when voices in the living-room slowly filtered into his mind. He lifted his head to look up, as if to focus his ears. No. He could not recognise the voices. Now and again the hum of conversation was punctuated with laughter. Then he grew apprehensive, the continuing conversation suddenly filling him with dread. He tried to concentrate on his work. 'Answer the following questions: How did the coming of the whites lead to the establishment of prosperity and peace among the various Bantu tribes? ...' But the peace had gone from his mind. The questions had become a meaningless task. Instinctively he turned round to look at his music stand at the foot of his bed. Yesterday he had practised some Mozart. Then he saw the violin leaning against the wall next to the stand. Would they come to interrupt him? He felt certain they would. He stood up, thinking of a way to escape.

There was another peal of laughter from the living-room, and Vukani wondered again who the visitors were. As he opened the door slowly he was met by another thunderous roar. Escape would be impossible. He had to go through the living-room and would certainly be called by his mother to be introduced to the visitors, and then the usual agony would follow. A delicate clink of cups and saucers told Vukani the visitors had been served tea. Perhaps it was coffee. Most probably tea. Visitors generally preferred tea. Another roar. His father and the male visitor were laughing. He knew now that the visitors were a man and a woman, but he did not know them. Curious now, he opened the door another inch or so, and saw the woman visitor, who sat close to where the passage to the bedrooms began. Vukani's mother, in her white nursing uniform, sat close to the woman in another heavily cushioned chair. They were separated by the coffee table.

'I couldn't make it at all to the meeting last Saturday,' said Vukani's mother.

'Which meeting, dearie?' asked the woman.

The men laughed again during their own conversation.

'Don't you laugh so loudly,' Vukani's mother shouted.

'You see,' Vukani's father was saying. 'I had caught the fellow by surprise, as I usually do.'

'That's the only way to ensure that the work gets done,' said the other man.

'So I said: "Show me the students' garden plots." I saw a twitch of anguish cross his face. But he was a clever fellow, you see. He quickly recovered and said: "Of course sir, of course, come along." So we went. There was a wilderness around the school. These bush schools! I wouldn't have been surprised if a python had stopped us in our tracks. So, after about two hundred yards of walking and all the wilderness around us, I began to wonder. So I say to this teacher: "Mr Mabaso" – that was the fellow's name – "these plots, they are quite far, aren't they?" "We're just about there, sir," he said.'

'Man alive!' exclaimed the other man. 'This story is getting hot. Let me sip one more time.' There was some silence while the man sipped his tea. Vukani's mother also lifted her cup to her lips. The women were now listening too.

'So,' continued Vukani's father, 'we walked another two hundred yards and I turned to look at the man. "We're just about there, sir." I only needed to look at him and he would say: "We're just about there, sir." '

Everybody laughed. 'You see, the fellow was now sweating like a horse.'

'So?' asked the woman visitor, laughing. She was wiping her eyes with Kleenex.

'Then this fellow, Mabaso, shows me a hill about a mile away and says: "We're going there to that hill, sir, the plots are behind it. You see, sir, I figured that since the wind normally hits the hill on the side we are looking at now, I should have the plots on the leeward side to protect the plants." What bosh!'

There was more laughter and the male visitor said, in the middle of laughter: 'Beatrice, give me some Kleenex, please.' His wife stood up and disappeared from Vukani's view. She returned soon. Vukani heard a nose being blown.

'Please don't laugh, fellow Africans,' said Vukani's father. 'The man is a genius. What's this poem by the English poet, "The man blushes unseen in the wilderness." He knew I would not go any further. So I really have no proof that there were no garden plots.'

'Of course there weren't any,' asserted Vukani's mother.

'Of course there weren't,' everybody agreed.

'You school inspectors,' said the male visitor, 'have real problems with these bush schools.'

'You don't know, you!' agreed Vukani's father. 'We just can't get it into these teachers' heads that we have to uplift the Black nation. And we cannot do that through cheating and laziness. We will not develop self-reliance that way. The fellow was just not teaching the students gardening, and that is dead against government policy.' Vukani shut the door. In spite of himself he had been amused by the story. He went back to the desk and tried to continue with the homework. He could not. What about going out through the window? No. That would be taking things too far. He wondered where Teboho, his sister, was. Probably in her bedroom. Teboho and their mother were having too many heated exchanges these days. Their mother tended to make too many demands on them. Vukani wished he could go and talk to Teboho. They had grown very close. Then he suddenly became frantic again and went back to the door. He had to escape. When he opened the door, as slightly as before, it was the woman visitor who was talking.

'You just don't know what you missed, you,' she was saying. The men laughed again.

'Please, you men!' appealed Vukani's mother. But they laughed once again.

'Do you want us to leave you and go to the bedroom?' threatened Vukani's mother. 'And you know if we go in there we won't come out.'

'Peace! Peace!' said Vukani's father. 'Peace, women of Africa!' Then he lowered his voice as he continued to talk to the other man.

'Now, come on, what have I missed?' asked Vukani's mother eagerly.

'Well, you just don't know what you missed,' said Mrs Beatrice, pulling the bait away from the fish.

'Please don't play with my anxiety.'

'I want to do just that,' said Mrs Beatrice, clapping her hands

once and sitting forward in her chair, her legs thrust underneath.
She kept on pulling down her tight-fitting skirt over her big
knees. But after each effort the skirt slipped back, revealing the
knees again.

'You women are on again about the Housewives' League?'
remarked Vukani's father, interrupting the women.

'Day in and day out,' said the other man, supporting Vukani's
father.

'Of course yes!' said Mrs Beatrice with emphatic pride.

'Forget about these men,' pleaded Vukani's mother, 'and give
me a pinch of the story.'

'Mother-of-Teboho, you really missed,' Mrs Beatrice started.
'A white woman came all the way from Emmarentia – high-class
exclusive suburb, mind you – to address the meeting on Jewish
recipes. Came all the way to Soweto for that. It was wonderful.'

'Was it not Mrs Kaplinsky?'

'As if you know!'

'Ha, woman! Please, give me! Give me!' begged Vukani's
mother with great excitement, clapping her hands repeatedly.
'I'm fetching my pen, I'm fetching my pen. Give me those
recipes.' But she did not leave to go and fetch her pen.

'I'm selling them, dearie. Business first, friendship after.' They
laughed.

'Ei! Women and food ...' exclaimed the other man.

'What! We cook for you men,' retorted his wife.

'Exactly,' concurred Vukani's mother. 'More tea?'

'No thanks, dearie.'

'Hey you men, more tea?' But the men were already back to
their conversation, and burst out laughing. Vukani's father answered while laughing, suddenly coming into Vukani's view as
he brought his empty cup to the coffee table between the
women. 'No thanks,' he was saying. 'No thanks ... he he he
heheheee ... that was a good one ... no thanks ... what a good
one.' Then he took out a handkerchief from the pocket of his
trousers, wiped his eyes, wiped his whole face, and then wiped
his lips. 'A jolly good evening tonight,' he remarked. Then he
went back to his chair, disappearing from Vukani's view.

'Thanks for the tea,' said the other man, blowing his nose.

'Teboho!' called Vukani's mother. 'Please come and clear up
here!' Teboho appeared carrying a tray. She had on denim jeans

and a loose blouse.

'That was a nice cup of tea, Teboho,' said the other man. Teboho smiled shyly.

'When are you going back to 'varsity?' he asked.

'We have six more weeks,' replied Teboho.

'You are lucky to have children who are educating themselves, dearie,' said Mrs Beatrice.

'Oh, well,' said Vukani's mother, shrugging her shoulders as Teboho disappeared into the kitchen. There was some silence.

'Sometimes these South African Jews sicken me,' said the other man reflectively.

'Why?' the two women asked.

'Well, they're hypocrites! I mean look, they say they were killed left and right by the Germans, but here they are, here, helping the Boers to sit on us.'

'How can you say such a thing?' asked his wife. 'People like Mrs Kaplinsky are very good friends of ours. Some of her best friends are Africans.'

'Because she gives you recipes.'

'Food, my dear husband, belongs to mankind, not just to one race.'

'Yes, exactly,' agreed Vukani's mother. 'Like art, literature and things. Completely universal.'

'Well! …' said the man, but he did not pursue the matter further.

'In fact this reminds me,' said Vukani's mother with sudden enthusiasm, her eyes glittering. 'Instead of sitting here talking politics, we should be listening to some music. Have you heard my son play? He plays the violin. A most wonderful instrument.'

'Yes,' said Vukani's father, 'you know … '

Vukani swiftly shut the door, shutting out the living-room conversation with an abruptness that brought him sharply to himself as he moved to the centre of the room. He began to feel very lonely and noticed he was trembling. It was coming now. He looked at the history homework on the desk; then looked at the reading lamp with its circular light which seemed to be baking the open pages of the books on the desk with its intensity, so that the books looked as if they were waiting for that delicate moment when they would burst into flame.

Then he thought of Doksi, his friend. He wondered where he

was and what he was doing at that moment. Friday evening? Probably watching his father cutting the late evening customers' hair and trimming it carefully while he murmured a song, as always. Doksi had said to Vukani one day that when he was a grown-up he would like to be a barber like his father. Doksi seemed to love hair. Vukani remembered his favourite game: a weekly ritual of hair burning. Every Saturday afternoon Doksi would make a fire out in the yard and when it was burning steadily, toss knots of hair into it. The hair would catch fire with a crackling brilliance that always sent him into raptures of delight. He never seemed to mind the smell of the burning hair. One Saturday after his bonfire Doksi had said, while making the sign of the cross over the smoking fire: 'When God had finished burning hair he thought that it was good.' Vukani had playfully accused him of sacrilege. But Doksi, suddenly looking serious, had said: 'Dead things catch fire.'

Now, Vukani was suddenly fascinated by a desire to see the books on the desk aflame. Perhaps he should lower the lamp: bring it closer to the books. It was a silly idea, yet he lowered the lamp all the same. But the papers shone defiantly with a sheen. It was futile. Then he saw his violin again, and felt the sensation of fear deep in his breast.

He looked at the violin with dread, as something that could bring both pain and pleasure at once. It was like the red dress which Miss Yende, their class teacher in Standard Four, occasionally wore. She had once said to the class: 'When I wear this red dress, children, know that I will not stomach any nonsense that day. Know that I will expect sharp minds; I will expect quick responses to my questions; and I will expect absolute seriousness. And I shall use the stick with the vengeance of the God of the Old Testament.' That dress! It was a deep, rich, velvety red that gave the impression that the dress had a flowery fragrance. Yet, because it signalled the possibility of pain, it also had a dreadful repulsiveness.

Vukani tried to brace himself for the coming of the visitors. It was always like that. Every visitor was brought to his room, where he was required to be doing his school work or practising on the violin. Then he had to entertain these visitors with violin music. It was always an agonising nuisance to be an unwilling entertainer. What would happen if he should refuse to play that night? He knew what his mother would say. It was the same thing every time. His eyes swept round the room. He was well provided for. There was the beautiful desk on which he did his work; bookshelves full of books, including a set of *Encyclopaedia Britannica*; a reading lamp on the desk; two comfortable easy chairs; a wardrobe full of clothes; his own portable transistor radio; a violin and a music stand; a chest full of games: Monopoly, chess and many others. His mother never tired of telling him how lucky he was. 'There is not a single boy in the whole of Soweto – including here in Dube – who has a room like yours. Can you count them for me? Never! This room is as good as any white boy's. Isn't it exactly like Ronnie Simpson's? You yourself, you ungrateful boy, have seen that room when we visited the Simpsons in Parktown North. Kaffir children! That's what. Always ungrateful!'

What did all this really mean to him when it brought so much pain? Vukani remembered what teacher Maseko had said at assembly one morning: 'Children, I would rather be a hungry dog that runs freely in the streets, than a fat, chained dog burdened with itself and the weight of the chain. Whenever the white man tells you he has made you much better off than Africans elsewhere on this continent, tell him he is lying before God!' There were cheers that morning at assembly, and the children had sung the hymn with a feeling of energetic release:

> *I will make you fishers of men*
> *Fishers of men*
> *Fishers of men*
> *I will make you fishers of men*
> *If you follow me.*

Three weeks later teacher Maseko was fired. The Principal made the announcement at morning assembly. He spoke in Afrikaans, always. Concluding the announcement he said: 'Children, a wandering dog that upsets garbage bins and ejects its dung all over the place, is a very dangerous animal. It is a carrier of disease and pestilence, and when you see it, pelt it with stones. What should you do to it?'

'Pelt it with stones!' was the sombre response of the assembled children that morning. Vukani wondered whether teacher Maseko was that dog. But how could anybody pelt teacher Maseko with stones?

Vukani heard another roar of laughter from the living-room. But why did his mother have to show off at his expense in this manner? That Friday, as on all Mondays, Wednesdays and Fridays, he had carried his violin to school. The other children at school just never got used to it. It was a constant source of wonder and ridicule. 'Here's a fellow with a strange guitar!' some would say. Others would ask him to play the current township hits. It was so every day. Then one day his violin had disappeared from class while he had gone out to the toilet. He was met with stony faces when after school he pleaded for its return. Everybody simply went home and there was no sign of the violin. What would he say to his music teacher in town? What would he say to his mother? When he went out of the classroom he found Doksi waiting for him. They always went home together, except on the days when Vukani had to go to town for music lessons after school.

'Doksi,' he said, 'I can't find my violin. Somebody took it.'

'These boys of shit!' Doksi cursed sympathetically. He had not waited for details. He knew his friend's problem. 'Do you suspect anybody?'

'I can't say,' replied Vukani. 'The whole class seems to have ganged up on me. There are some things that will always bring them together.'

'Even Gwendoline?' asked Doksi with a mischievous smirk on his face.

Gwendoline was the frail, brilliant, beautiful girl who vied with Vukani for first position in class. Vukani had always told Doksi that he would like to marry her one day. And Doksi would always say: 'With you it's talk, talk all the time. Why don't you just go to this girl and tell her you love her? Just look at how she looks at you. She is suffering, man!'

'Look,' said Vukani, 'this is no time for jokes. My violin is lost.'

'The trouble with you, Vukani, is that you are too soft. I would never stand this nonsense. I'd just face the whole class and say: "Whoever took my violin is a coward. Why doesn't he come out and fight?" I'm sure it was taken by one of those big boys whom everybody fears. Big bodies without minds! They ought to be working in town. Just at school to avoid paying tax.

But me, they know me. They know what my brothers would do. My whole family would come here looking for the bastards.'

'Let's go tell the principal,' suggested Vukani. The principal was one of those Vukani had entertained one day in his bedroom. 'But maybe we shouldn't,' said Vukani changing his mind.

'Let's go and find out from the girls sweeping your classroom,' suggested Doksi. They went back.

Most of the children had gone now. Only those whose turn it was to clean the classrooms remained. The girls were singing loudly and the room was full of dust.

'Leave it to me,' said Doksi.

There were four girls in the classroom. Gwendoline and Manana were as old as Doksi and Vukani. The other two girls, Topsana and Sarah, were much older.

'Hey, you girls,' shouted Doksi, squaring his shoulders and looking like a cowboy about to draw. 'Where is the bloody violin?' The bigger girls simply laughed.

'And who are you, toughie?' said Sarah pushing a desk out of the way for Topsana to sweep.

'Hey you, Vukani,' called Topsana, 'I want to soothe your heart. I've long been waiting for this moment. Come and kiss me.' The smaller girls giggled and Vukani regretted that they had come back. 'I mean it,' said Topsana. 'I know who took your violin. It's safe. You'll find it at home. I made them promise to take it there. There now, I want my kiss. I want to kiss the inspector's son.'

Meanwhile, Doksi turned to the younger girls: 'Hey you, what is the joke? What's there to laugh at?'

'Hha!' protested Manana, sweeping rather purposefully. 'Laughing is laughing.'

'I can show you a thing or two,' Doksi said. 'Punch you up or something.'

'Doksi,' appealed Vukani. 'Please let's go.' Doksi clearly felt the need for retreat, but it had to be done with dignity. He addressed all the girls with a sweep of his hands. 'You are all useless. One of these days I'll get you. Come on, Vukani, let's go.'

The walk home for Vukani had been a long one. Better not to tell the parents. If Topsana had been telling the truth, then he should wait. Nobody asked about the violin that night. But he would never forget the morning following that day, when his mother stormed into his bedroom, black with anger. She simply came in and pulled the blankets off him. Then she glared at him, holding the violin in one of her hands. Vukani had felt so exposed, as if his mother would hit him with the violin. It was very early in the morning. His mother was already dressed up in her uniform, ready to go to work. If she was on day duty, she had to leave very early for the hospital.

'Vukani!' she shouted. 'What desecration is this? What ultimate act of ungratefulness is this? Is this to spite me? Is this an insult? Tell me before I finish you off.'

'What's happening, Dorcas?' Vukani saw his father entering the bedroom.

'Can you believe this? I found this violin on the doorstep outside as I was leaving for work. Can you believe this?'

'Vukani,' said his father. 'What on earth should have made you do such a thing?'

'I didn't put it there, *Baba*,' Vukani replied.

'Nonsense,' shouted his mother. 'You don't have to lie. Ungrateful boy, you have the nerve to tell your parents a lie.'

'Wait a minute, dear, maybe we should hear what he has to say.' Vukani had nothing to say. The deep feeling of having been wronged could only find expression in tears. He heard the violin land next to him and he recoiled from its coldness. He also heard his mother leave, saying that he was crying because of his sins. She never knew what had happened and seemed not to care.

But that was last year. Today he had been humiliated again in public, and there were people in that living-room who wanted to humiliate him again. Right inside his home. It was all because of this violin. The homework had made him forget the latest ordeal for a while. The homework was like a jigsaw puzzle; you simply looked for pieces which fitted. All the answers were there in the chapter. You just moved your finger up and down the page until you spotted the correct answer. There was no thinking involved. But now it was all gone. It was not South African History, the story of the coming of the white man, he was looking at; he was now faced with the reality of the violin.

There was that gang of boys who always stood under the shop veranda at Maponya's shopping complex. They shouted:

'Hey, music man!' whenever he went past their 'headquarters'
on his way home to Dube. That very Friday they had done more
than shout at him from a distance. They had stopped him and
humiliated him before all those workers who were returning
from work in town.

'Hey, music man!' the one who seemed to be their leader had
called. Vukani, as a rule, never answered them. He just walked
on as if he had not heard anything. But that afternoon as he was
coming up from Phefeni station and was turning round the
corner to go down towards the AME Church, it was as if the
gang had been waiting for him.

'Hey, music man!' This time it was a chorus. A rowdy chorus.
Out of the corner of his eye Vukani saw two boys detach themselves from the gang. He dare not turn to look. He had to act
unconcerned. He tried to quicken his step as imperceptibly as
possible.

'Music man! Don't you know your name?' They were behind
him now. Crossing the street had been no problem for them.
They simply walked into the street and cars came to a screeching
halt. They were the kings of the township. They just parted the
traffic as Moses must have parted the waves of the sea. Vukani
wanted to run, but he was not going to give himself away. If he
ran and they caught up with him they could do a lot of harm to
him. He had had that feeling once – of wanting to take
advantage of something weaker than him – when he'd found a
stray dog trying to topple a garbage bin. If the dog had stood its
ground and growled, he would have been afraid. But the dog
had taken to its heels, tail tucked between legs, and Vukani had
been filled with the urge to run after the dog, catch it, and beat it
to death. As fleeing impala must excite the worst destructive
urge in a lion. Vukani had once seen a film in which a lion
charged at a frightened impala. There had been a confidence in
the purposeful strides of the lion, as if it felt this was just a game
that would surely end with the bringing down of the prey.

A hand grabbed Vukani's collar from behind and jerked him
violently to a halt. The leader of the gang came round and faced
him. He held Vukani by the knot of his tie. He was short but
heavily built. He had puffed-up cheeks with scars on them. His
bloodshot eyes suggested the violence in him. He must have
been four or five years older than Vukani.

'Spy!' the leader cursed, glaring at Vukani. 'So you are special! So we had to cross the street and risk death in order to talk to you. You don't know your name, music man? Every day we greet you nice-nice and you don't answer. Because you think you are being greeted by shit. By scum, hey? Why, spy? Are we shit?'

'Ja! Just answer that,' said the fellow behind. 'Are we shit?' Vukani tried to free his neck.

'Shit!' screamed the leader. 'We just wanted to talk to you nice-nice. That's all. We just wanted to dance to your music a little. Dance to your guitar a little. But no. You don't even look at us. Do we smell, music man? Do we smell?' There was a crowd of workers now who were watching the spectacle quietly.

'Shake him up, Bhuka!' was the chorus from the rest of the gang about thirty yards away at the shop.

'What are you rogues doing to this poor boy?' asked an old lady who had a bundle of washing on her head.

'Shut up!' said Bhuka. 'Go and do your white man's washing, he'll want it tomorrow.' Some in the crowd laughed at this.

'Dogs of the street! Don't talk like that to your mother. Whose child are you?'

'I'm your child,' said Bhuka with a certain flourish. This time more of the crowd laughed.

'He's the child of his mother!' said the boy behind Vukani. None laughed at that one. He was in the shadow of his leader.

'You are laughing,' said the woman, bravely addressing the crowd. 'You are laughing at this boy being harassed, and you are laughing at me being insulted by these street urchins. I could be your mother, and this could be your son. *Sies!* You rogues, just let decent people be.' The woman then left, taking Vukani's hopes with her. But she had not left Bhuka unsettled. He had to move his prey to safer ground. Too many lesser animals could be a disturbance. He tightened his grip around Vukani's tie pulling him across the street towards the 'headquarters'. Vukani looked at the fist below his chin, and saw that it had a little sixth finger. There were two shining copper bangles round the wrist.

Part of the crowd left, but another part wanted to see the game to its end. They followed the trio to the shop. The gang then had Vukani completely encircled.

'Do you have a sister?' Bhuka snapped. Vukani had trouble

breathing now. Bhuka realised this and loosened the grip.
Vukani thought of Teboho at home. If she came here she would
fight for him. 'I asked you a question. Do you have a sister?'
Vukani nodded. 'Hey man, talk! Is your voice precious? His
master's voice!'

'Yes,' answered Vukani in a whisper.

'I want to fuck her. Do you hear? I want to eat her up
thoroughly. Do you hear? Tell her that.' Bhuka paused and
jerked Vukani to and fro so that Vukani's head bobbed. He then
stopped and glowered at Vukani. 'And what song will you play
when I am on top of her?' There was a festive laugh from the
crowd. Bhuka looked round with acknowledgement. 'Tell me
now, can you play *Thoka Ujola Nobani?*' It was a current hit.

Vukani felt tears in his eyes. He winked many times to keep
them in. Why couldn't they just leave him alone? That day
would be final, he would simply tell his parents that he did not
want to play the violin again. If they still insisted he would run
away from home.

'Please leave me alone,' he heard himself say.

'I asked you. Can you play *Thoko Ujola Nobani?*'

Vukani shook his head.

'Why, music man?

'I'd have to learn how to play it first. I can't just play it like
that.'

'Next time you pass here you must be knowing that song.
And come with your sister.' Then he gave Vukani a shove at the
chest, and Vukani reeled backwards and fell on his back. But he
still held on to the violin.

'Next time we greet you nice-nice, you must greet nice-nice.'
Vukani got up timidly and hurried away, glancing back
occasionally. Somehow he felt relieved. It could have been
worse. The stories he had heard about the violence of this gang
were simply unbelievable. He felt deep inside him the laughter
that followed him as he slunk away. Just after passing the AME
church he saw the rubbish heap people had created at the corner
and wished he were brave enough to throw the violin there.

'My son,' his mother had said one day when Vukani com-
plained about the harassment he suffered as a result of the
violin, 'you should never yield to ignorance.'

'But maybe you should buy me a piano,' Vukani had said. 'I

can't carry that in the street.'

'If Yehudi Menuhin had listened to fools he wouldn't be the greatest living violinist. A violin you have and a violin you will play.' That's how it had ended. But his agony continued, three times a week.

Then the door opened. 'Here he is!' said Vukani's mother as she led the visitors in. His father took the rear. Vukani looked blankly at the homework. Question three: Who introduced the European type of education among the Bantu? ... But Vukani felt only the solid presence of four people behind him.

'Vuka,' said his mother. 'I did not hear you practise today.' It was not clear from her voice whether she was finding fault with her son or was just trying to have something to say by way of introduction. Vukani turned round and smiled sheepishly. They all looked at him as if they expected him to defend himself, their eyes occasionally going to the table as if to see what he was doing.

'Are you doing your homework, son?' asked the male visitor.

'E!'

'Good, hard-working boy!' he said patting Vukani on the shoulders. Vukani felt in that hand the heaviness of condescension.

'He's a very serious-minded boy,' added his mother with obvious pride.

'You are very happy, dearie, to have a child who loves school,' observed Mrs Beatrice.

'And here is my Mozart's violin,' said Vukani's father, pointing at the violin against the wall. He took the case, opened it and took out the violin.

'Vuka!'

'Ma!'

'These visitors are the mother and father of Lauretta. Do you know her?'

'No, I don't think I do,' said Vukani shaking his head.

'But you are at the same school together. Surely you know Lauretta, the daughter of Doctor Zwane. Stand up to greet them.'

Now Vukani remembered the girl who was well known at school for her brilliance. She was two classes ahead of Vukani. But Vukani wondered if she could beat Gwendoline. Vukani greeted the visitors and went back to his seat.

'Vuka, you will play the visitors something, won't you? What will you play us?' asked his mother. Vukani looked at the violin in his father's hands. He was explaining to Dr Zwane the various kinds of violins.

'This type,' he was saying, 'is very rare. You do not find it easily these days. Not at all.'

'It must have been very expensive,' observed Dr Zwane appreciatively. 'One can judge from its looks.'

'Five hundred and fifty rands down,' butted in Vukani's mother.

'Made to specifications. You just tell them how you want it and they make it. This is special.'

'One has to pay to produce a Mozart,' said Vukani's father with finality.

'We had Lauretta started on ballet recently,' said Mrs Zwane, as if suggesting that they were also doing their duty. 'I'm happy to note that she seems to be doing well. All these things have to be taught at our schools. You school inspectors have a duty to ensure that it happens.'

'Indeed,' agreed Vukani's father. 'But do you think the Boers would agree? Never. Remember they say Western Civilisation is spoiling us, and so we have to cultivate the indigenous way of life.' The conversation was stopped by Vukani's mother.

'Okay now,' she clapped her hands, 'what will you play us?'

Vukani's father brought the violin to Vukani who took it with his visibly shaking hands. He saw the red, glowering eyes of Bhuka that afternoon. He heard the laughter of people in the streets. He remembered being violently shaken awake by his angry mother one morning. He remembered one of his dreams which came very frequently. He was naked in the streets and people were laughing. He did not know how he became naked. It always occurred that way. He would be naked in the streets and people would be laughing. Suddenly he would reach home and his mother would scold him for bringing shame to the family. But the dream would always end with his leaving home and flying out into the sky with his hands as wings.

Vukani found he had instinctively put the violin on his left shoulder. And when he realised that, he felt its irksome weight on him. What did people want of him? He did not want to play.

He did not want to play. And for the second time that day, he felt tears coming to his eyes, and again he winked repeatedly to keep them from flowing. This was the time.

'Mama!'

'Yes son.' But Vukani did not go on. His mother continued. 'Why don't you play some selections from Brahms? You know some excerpts from his *only* violin concerto. What about Liszt? Where are your music books? There is something on the music stand; what is it? Ahh! It's the glorious, beautiful Dvorak! Tum tee tum! Tum tee tum!' She shook her head, conducting an imaginary orchestra. 'Come and play some of this Dvorak.'

Vukani wanted to shout but his throat felt completely dry. He wanted to sink into the ground. He tried to swallow. It was only dryness he swallowed, and it hurt against the throat. Standing up would be agonising. His strength and resistance were all gathered up in his sitting position. All that strength would be dissipated if he stood up. And he would feel exposed, lonely and vulnerable. The visitors and his parents soon noticed there was something amiss.

'What is it, Vuka?' asked his mother. 'Is there something wrong?'

'Nothing wrong, Ma,' said Vukani, shaking his head. He had missed his opportunity. Why was he afraid? Why did he not act decisively for his own good? Then he felt anger building up in him, but he was not sure whether he was angry with himself, or with his parents, together with the visitors whose visit was now forcing him to come to terms with his hitherto unexpressed determination to stop doing what brought him suffering.

At that moment there was a dull explosion seemingly coming from the kitchen, of something massive suddenly disintegrating into pieces. There was a moment's silence, then Vukani's mother muttered: 'The bloody street girl has done it again,' and she stormed out of the bedroom. Her voice could be heard clearly in the kitchen: 'Awu, Lord of the heavens! my ... my expensive ... my precious ... my expensive ... this girl has done it again. Teboho! Has the devil got into you again? Do you have to be breaking something every day?'

'It slipped out of my hand,' said Teboho in a subdued voice.

'What kind of hands do you have?' said her mother shrieking

with anger.

'It was a mistake,' replied Teboho, her voice now a pitch higher.

'What a costly mistake! Oh, my God. What a costly one! I gave Mrs Willard three hundred rands to bring me this set from Hong Kong when she went there on holiday. And I've pleaded with you countless times to be extra careful with the china!'

'Ma, I didn't just dash the pot to the floor ... '

'And such care doesn't cost much. How many households in the whole of Johannesburg, white and black, can boast of owning such a set ... a genuine set? Will you not appreciate that? Don't just stand there ...'

'Mama, can you please stop that.' Teboho's voice sounded urgently restrained.

'Is that how you are talking to me?'

'You don't want to listen to anybody. You just came in here shouting.' Teboho's voice was loud with a note of defiance. It seemed to have lost all restraint.

'Is that how they teach you to talk to your parents at the University?'

'Mama, that is not the point.'

'Are you arguing with me?'

'I'm not ... '

'Then what are you saying?'

'You're always telling us not to break dishes, not to scratch the furniture, not to break your house plants, there are so many things one cannot do in this house ... Haven't you been showing more interest in your dishes than in your children?'

'What?'

'I'm not going to say anything more.'

'What decent girl, but a slut, can talk like that to her mother, and there are visitors in the house?'

'Mama, will you stop!' There was a sound of a slap. Another explosion. Lighter this time; perhaps a glass.

'You've slapped me!' screamed Teboho. 'I'm leaving this house; you can stay with it. If you want to be a slave to things, then do it alone.' There was the sound of a little scuffle, followed by hurrying footsteps. Then the door to Teboho's bedroom banged shut, rattling some cutlery.

Vukani's father was about to leave for the kitchen when he

met his wife at the door. She brushed past him into Vukani's bedroom, grinning at the visitors.

'I'm sorry for that unfortunate diversion,' she said. 'Children can be destructive. Since Teboho went to that university in the north she has some very strange ideas. Opposes everything. Defiant. Can you have your own child calling you a white black woman, a slave of things?'

And then she mimicked Teboho's voice: ' "That's how it's planned. That we be given a little of everything, and so prize the little we have that we forget about freedom." Fancy. Forgive me; but I had to remind this show-off girl that I was her parent.'

There was a moment's silence of embarrassment. The adults all exchanged glances. A wave of sadness crossed Vukani's mother's face. But it did not last.

'One can never know with children, dearie,' observed Mrs Zwane, breaking the silence.

'Indeed!' said her husband. There was another silence.

'Well Vuka,' said Vukani's father at last. 'Can you heal our broken spirits?'

'Yes!' agreed his mother. 'We have been waiting for too long.'

Vukani thought of his sister. He wanted to go to her. They were very lonely. Their parents disapproved of many of their friends. Even Doksi. His mother had said he should have friends of his own station in life. What would a barber's son bring him? All this had brought Vukani and Teboho very close. He decided then that he would not let his sister down. But what could he do? He thought of dashing the violin against the wall, and then rushing out of the house. But where would he go? Who did he know nearby? The relatives he knew lived very far away. He did not know them all that well, anyhow. He remembered how envious he would be whenever he heard other children saying they were going to spend their holidays with their relatives. Perhaps a grandmother or an uncle. He remembered once asking his mother when were they ever going to visit his uncle. His mother had not answered him. But then there was that conversation between his parents.

'By the way,' Vukani's mother had started it, 'when did you say your sister would be coming?'

'Next month.' There had been a brief silence before his father continued. 'Why do you ask? I have been telling you practically every day.'

'I was just asking for interest's sake.'

'Well,' his father had said, putting down the *Daily Mail* and picking up the *Star*, 'I just feel there is more to the question than meets the eye.'

'You think so?'

'Yes, I think so.' There had been silence.

'Relatives,' his mother had come out eventually 'can be a real nuisance. Once you have opened the door, they come trooping in like ants. We cannot afford it these days. Not with the cost of living. These are different times. Whites saw this problem a long time ago. That is why they have very little time for relatives. Nuclear family! That's what matters. I believe in it. I've always maintained that. If relatives want to visit, they must help with the groceries. There I'm clear, my dear. Very clear.' Vukani's father had said something about 'Whites are whites; Africans are Africans.' But Vukani's aunt never came. Nobody ever said anything about her. Yet, Doksi liked to say: 'It's nice to have many relatives. Then when you are in trouble at home, you can always hide with one of them. And your father will go from relative to relative looking for you. When he finds you, he will be all smiles trying to please the relatives.'

'Vukani!' called his mother. 'We are still waiting. Will you start playing now?'

Vukani stood up slowly, feeling every movement of his body, and walked round to the music stand. Then he faced his mother, and something yielded in him.

'Ma, I don't want to play the violin any more.' There was a stunned silence. Vukani's mother looked at her husband, a puzzled expression on her face. But she quickly recovered.

'What?' she shouted.

'I don't want to play the violin any more.' Vukani was surprised at his steadiness.

'This is enough!' screamed his mother. 'Right now ... right now. You are going to play that violin right now.'

'Now you just play that instrument. What's going on in this house?' His father's voice put some fear into him.

'Wait, dearie,' pleaded Mrs Zwane. 'Maybe the boy is not well.'

'Beatrice,' answered Vukani's mother, 'there is nothing like that. We are not going to be humiliated by such a little flea. Play, cheeky brute!'

'Today those boys stopped me again ... ' Vukani attempted to justify his stand.

'Who?' shrieked his mother. 'Those dogs of the street? Those low things?'

'What's bothering him?' asked Dr Zwane. Vukani's mother explained briefly. Then turning toward her husband she said, 'As I told you the other day, he keeps complaining that people laugh at him because he plays the violin.'

'Jealousy!' shouted Mrs Zwane. 'Plain jealousy. Jealousy number one. Nothing else. Township people do not want to see other Africans advance.'

'Dear,' answered Vukani's mother, 'you are showing them some respect they do not deserve. If you say they are jealous you make them people with feelings. No. They do not have that. They are not people. They are animals. Absolutely raw. They have no respect for what is better than they. Not these. They just trample over everything. Hey, you, play that instrument and stop telling us about savages.'

Vukani trembled. He felt his head going round now. He did not know what to do to escape from this ordeal. The tears came back, but this time he did not stop them. He felt them going down his cheeks, and he gave in to the fury in him. 'I do not want to play ... I do not want to play ... not any more! ... ' Then he choked and could not say anything more. But what he had said had carried everything he felt deep inside him. He felt free. There was a vast expanse of open space deep inside him. He was free. He could fly into the sky.

Then he heard Dr Zwane say: 'How difficult it is to bring up a child properly in Soweto! To give him culture. African people just turn away from advancement.'

Those words seemed to build a fire in Vukani's mother. They sounded like a reflection on her. She let go at Vukani with the back of her hand. Vukani reeled back and fell on the bed letting the violin drop to the floor. It made no noise on the thick carpet. Then she lifted him from the bed, and was about to strike him again when Teboho rushed into the bedroom and pulled her mother away from her brother.

'Ma! What are you doing? What are you doing?' she

screamed.

'Are you fighting me? 'shrieked her mother. 'You laid a hand on your mother. Am I bewitched?'

'You never think of anybody else. Just yourself.'

'Teboho,' called her father. 'Don't say that to your mother.'

'Please, dearie, please,' appealed Mrs Zwane. 'There is no need for all this. How can you do this to your children?'

'*Sies*! What disgraceful children! I am a nursing sister, your father is an inspector of schools. What are you going to be, listening to savages. You cannot please everybody. Either you please the street, in which case you are going to be a heap of rubbish, something to be swept away, or you please your home, which is going to give you something to be proud of for the rest of your useless life!'

'Dorcas! That's enough now,' said Vukani's father with calm, but firm finality. Vukani's mother looked at her husband with disbelief, a wave of shock crossing her face. She looked at the visitors who stared at her. Then she turned for the door and went to her bedroom, banging the door violently. Soon there was bitter sobbing in the main bedroom. Then it turned into the wail of the bereaved.

MIA COUTO

The Barber's Most Famous Customer

Firipe Beruberu's barber's shop was situated under the great tree in the market at Maquinino. Its ceiling was the shade of the crab apple. Walls, there were none: which is why it blew all the cooler round the chair where Firipe sat his customers. A sign on the tree trunk displayed his prices. On it was written: '7$50 per head'. But with the rising cost of living, Firipe had amended the inscription to: '20$00 per headful'.

On the ageing timbers there hung a mirror, and next to it, a yellowing photo of Elvis Presley. On a crate, by the bench where the customers sat waiting, a radio shook to the rhythm of the *chimandjemandje*.

Firipe would weed heads while talking all the while. Barber's talk about this and that. But he didn't like his chitchat to tire his customers. When someone fell asleep in the chair, Beruberu would slap a tax on the final bill. Underneath the prices listed on his sign, he had even added: 'Headful plus sleep – extra 5 escudos'.

But in the generous shade of the crab apple tree there was no room for anger. The barber distributed affabilities, handshakes. Whoever let his ears wander in that direction heard only genial talk. When it came to advertising his services, Firipe never held back:

'I'm telling you: me, I'm the best barber there is. You can walk anywhere round here, look into every neighbourhood: they'll all tell you Firipe Beruberu is the greatest.'

Some customers just sat there patiently. But others provoked him, pretending to contradict him:

'That's fine salestalk, Master Firipe.'

'Salestalk? It's the truth! I've even cut top quality white man's hair.'

'What? Don't tell me you've ever had a white man in this bar-ber's shop … '

'I didn't say a white had been here. I said I'd cut his hair. And

I did, you take my word for it.'

'Explain yourself, Firipe, come on. If the white didn't come here, how did you cut him?'

'I was called to his house, that's what happened. I cut his, and his children's too. Because they were ashamed to sit down here in this seat. That's all.'

'I'm sorry, Master Firipe. But it can't have been a rich white. It must have been a *chikaka*.'

Firipe made his scissors sing while, with his left hand, he pulled out his wallet.

'Ahh! You folk? You're always doubting and disbelieving. I'm going to prove it to you. Wait there, now where is the ... ? Ah! Here it is.'

With a thousand cares he unwrapped a coloured postcard of Sidney Poitier.

'Look at this photo. Can you see this fellow? See how nice his hair is: it was cut here, with these very hands of mine. I scissored him without knowing what his importance was. I just saw that he spoke English.'

The customers cultivated their disbelief. Firipe replied:

'I'm telling you: this fellow brought his head all the way from over there in America to this barber's shop of mine ... '

While he talked, he kept looking up into the tree. He was keeping a watchful eye in case he had to dodge falling fruit.

'These bloody crab apples! They make a mess of my barber's shop. And then there are always kids round here, trying to get at them. If I catch one, I'll kick him to pieces.'

'What's this, Master Firipe? Don't you like children?'

'Like children? Why, only the other day a kid brought a sling and aimed it at the filthy tree, hoping to shoot down an apple. The stone hit the leaves and, mbaaa! it fell on top of a customer's head. Result: instead of that customer having a haircut here, he had to have a head shave at the first aid post.'

Customers changed, the conversation remained the same. From out of Master Firipe's pocket, the old postcard of the American actor would appear in order to lend truth to his glories. But the most difficult to convince was Baba Afonso, a fat man with an impeccably groomed heart, who dragged his haunches along at a slow pace. Afonso had his doubts:

'That man was here? I'm sorry, Master Firipe. I don't believe a bit of it.'

The indignant barber stood there, arms akimbo:

'You don't believe it? But he sat right there in that chair where you're sitting.'

'But a rich man like that, and a foreigner to boot, would have gone to a white man's saloon. He wouldn't have sat down here, Master Firipe. Never.'

The barber feigned offence. He could not have his word doubted. Then he resorted to a desperate measure:

'You don't believe me? Then I'll bring you a witness. You'll see, wait there.'

And off he went, leaving his customers to wait with bated breath. Afonso was calmed down by the others.

'Baba Afonso, don't be angry. This argument, it's only a game, nothing more.'

'I don't like people who tell lies.'

'But this one isn't even a lie. It's propaganda. Let's pretend we believe it and have done with it.'

'As far as I am concerned, it's a lie,' fat old Afonso kept saying.

'Okay, Baba. But it's a lie that doesn't harm anyone.'

The barber hadn't gone far. He had walked no more than a few steps to talk to an old man who was selling tobacco leaf. Then the two of them returned together, Firipe and the old man.

'This is old Jaimco.'

And turning to the tobacco seller, Firipe ordered:

'You tell them, Jaimco.'

The old man coughed up all his hoarseness before attesting.

'Yes. In truthfully I saw the man of the photo. It was cut the hair of him here. I am witness.'

And the customers showered him with questions.

'But did you get to listen to this foreigner? What language did he speak?'

'Shingrish.'

'And what money did he pay with?'

'With copper coin.'

'But which type, escudos?'

'No, it was money from outside.'

The barber gloated, self-satisfied, his chest puffed out. From time to time the old man breached the limit of their agreement and risked using his own initiative.

'Then, that man went in the market for to buy things.'

'What things?'

'Onion, orange, soap. He bought baccy leaf too.'

Baba Afonso leapt from his chair, pointing a chubby finger at him:

'Now I've caught you: a man like that wouldn't buy baccy leaf. You've made that up. That category of fellow would smoke filter cigarettes. Jaimco, you're just telling lies, nothing more.'

Jaimco was taken aback by this sudden attack. Fearful, he looked at the barber and tried one last line of argument:

'Ahh! It's not a lie, I remember even: it was a Saturday.'

Then there was laughter. For it wasn't a serious fight, their scruples were little more than playfulness.

Firipe pretended to be upset and advised the doubters to find another barber.

'Okay, there's no need to get angry, we believe you. We accept your witness.'

And even Baba Afonso gave in, prolonging the game:

'I expect that singer, Elvis Presley, was also here in Maquinino, having his hair cut ... '

But Firipe Beruberu did not work alone. Gaspar Vivito, a young cripple, helped him with the clearing up. He swept the sand with care, so as not to spread dust. He shook out the cloth covers far away.

Firipe Beruberu always told him to take care with the hair clippings.

'Bury them deep, Vivito. I don't want the *n'uantché-cuta* to play any tricks.'

He was referring to a little bird that steals people's hair to make its nest. Legend has it that once the owner's head has been raided, not a single whisker will ever grow on it again. Firipe blamed any decrease in the clientèle on Gaspar Vivito's carelessness.

Yet he could not expect much from his assistant. For he was completely crippled: his rubbery legs danced a never-ending *marrabenta*. His tiny head tottered lamely on his shoulders. He slobbered over his words, slavered his vowels, and smeared his consonants with spittle. And he tripped and stumbled as he tried to shoo away the children who were collecting crab apples.

At the end of the afternoon, when there was only one customer left, Firipe told Vivito to tidy up. This was the hour when complaints were received. If Vivito could find no way of being like other folk, Firipe paid more attention to jokes than to barbering skills.

'Excuse me, Master Firipe. My cousin Salomco told me to come and complain at the way his hair was cut.'

'How was it cut?'

'There's not a hair left, he's been completely plucked. His head is bald, it even shines like a mirror.'

'And wasn't it he who asked for it like that?'

'No. Now he's ashamed to go out. That's why he sent me to complain.'

The barber took the complaint in good humour. He made his scissors click loudly as he spoke:

'Listen, my friend: tell him to leave it as it is. A bald man saves on combs. And if I cut off too much, I won't charge.'

He circled the chair this way and that, then stood back to admire his talent.

'There you go, get off the chair, I've finished. But you'd better take a good look in the mirror, otherwise you might send your cousin to complain later.'

The barber shook the towel, scattering hairs. Then the customer joined his protests to those of the plaintiff.

'But Master Firipe, you've cut off almost everything in front. Have you seen where my forehead reaches to?'

'Ahh! I haven't touched your forehead. Talk to your father, or your mother, if you want to complain about the shape of your head. It's not my fault.'

The malcontents joined forces, bemoaning their double baldness. It was an opportunity for the barber to philosophise on capillary misfortunes:

'Do you know what makes a person go bald? It's using another man's hat. That's what makes a man lose his hair. I, for instance, won't even wear a shirt if I'm not sure where it's come from. Much less trousers. Just think, my brother-in-law bought a pair of underpants second-hand ...'

'But Master Firipe, I can't pay for this haircut.'

'You don't have to pay. And you, tell your cousin Salomco to pass this way tomorrow: I'll give him back his money. Money, money ... '

And that's how it was: a dissatisfied customer earned the right not to pay. Beruberu only charged for satisfaction. Standing from morning to nightfall, weariness began to burden his legs.

'Hell, what a dog's life! Ever since morning: snip-snip-snip. I've had enough! Living's hard, Gaspar Vivito.'

And the two of them would sit down. The barber in his chair, his assistant on the ground. It was Master Firipe's sundown, a time to meditate on his sadness.

'Vivito, I'm worried that you may not be burying the hair properly. It looks as if the *n'uantché-cuta* is losing me customers.'

The boy replied with choked sounds, he spoke a language that was his alone.

'Shut up, Vivito. Go see if we made much money.'

Vivito shook the wooden box. From inside there was the jingle of some coins. Their faces lit up with a smile.

'How well they sing! This shop of mine is going to grow, mark my words. In fact I'm even thinking of putting in a telephone here. Maybe later I'll close it to the public. What do you think, Vivito? If we only take bookings. Are you listening, Vivito?'

The assistant was watching his boss, who had got up. Firipe walked round his chair, talking all the while, enjoying imagined futures. Then, the barber looked at the cripple and it was as if his dream had had its wings shattered and had plummeted into the dark sand.

'Vivito, you should be asking: but how will you close this place if it hasn't got a wall? That's what you should be saying, Gaspar Vivito.' But it wasn't an accusation. His voice lay prostrated on the ground. Then he went over to Vivito and let his hand ripple over the boy's dangling head.

'I can see that hair of yours needs cutting. But your head won't stand still, always moving this way and that, fiddle-de-dee, fiddle-de-dee.'

With difficulty, Gaspar climbed up into the chair and put the cloth round his neck. Agitated, the boy pointed to the darkness round about.

'There's still some time for a scissorful or two. Now see if you can sit still, so that we can hurry.'

And so the two preened themselves under the great tree. All the shadows had died by that hour. Bats scratched the surface of the sky with their screeches. Yet it was at this very hour that Rosinha, the market girl, passed by, on her way home. She appeared out of the gloom and the barber stood hesitant, totally enveloped in an anxious look.

'Did you see that woman, Vivito? Pretty, too pretty even. She usually goes by here at this hour. I sometimes wonder whether I don't linger here on purpose: dragging time until the moment she passes.'

Only then did Master Firipe admit his sadness to himself, and another Firipe emerged. But he didn't confide in anyone: as for the mute Vivito, could it be that he understood the barber's sorrow?

'It's true, Vivito, I'm tired of living alone. It's a long time since my wife left me. The bitch ran off with another. But it's this barber's profession too. A fellow's tied here, can't even go and take a look at what's happening at home, control the situation. And that's what happens.' By this time he was masking his rage. He diverted the human grief from himself and imposed it upon the creatures of the earth. He threw a stone up into the branches, trying to hit bats.

'Filthy animals! Can't they see this is my barber's shop? This place has got an owner; it's the property of master Firipe Beruberu.'

And the two of them chased imaginary enemies. In the end they stumbled into each other, without a heart to be angry. Then, exhausted, they let out a chuckle, as if forgiving the world its insult.

It happened one day. The barber's shop continued its sleepy service, and on that morning, just as on all the others, gentle banter flowed from one topic to another. Firipe was explaining the sign and its warning about the tax on sleeping.

'Only those who fall asleep in the chair have to pay. It often happens with that fat one. I start putting the towel round him and he starts snoozing straightaway. Now me, I don't like that. I'm not anybody's wife to have to put heads to sleep. This is a proper barber's shop.'

At that point two strangers appeared. Only one of them

entered the shade. He was a mulatto, nearly white in colour. Conversation died under the weight of fear. The mulatto went up to the barber and ordered him to show his papers.

'Why my papers? Am I, Firipe Beruberu, disbelieved?'

One of the customers came over to Firipe and whispered to him:

'Firipe, you'd better do as he says. This man's from the PIDE.'

The barber bent over the wooden crate and took out his papers:

'Here are all my bits of plastic.'

The man examined his identity card. Then, he screwed it up and threw it on the ground.

'Hey, barber, there's something missing in this card.'

'Something missing, what do you mean? I've given you all my papers.'

'Where's the photograph of the foreigner?'

'The foreigner?'

'Yes, the foreigner who sheltered here in your barber's shop.'

Firipe was puzzled at first, then he smiled. He had realised what the fuss was about and prepared to explain:

'But officer, this business of the foreigner is a story I made up, a joke … '

The mulatto pushed him, silencing him suddenly.

'A joke, let's see about that. We know only too well there are subversives here from Tanzania, Zambia, wherever. Terrorists! It's probably one of those you put up here.'

'But put up, how? I don't put anyone up, I don't get mixed up in politics.'

The policeman inspected the place, unhearing. He stopped in front of the sign and read it clumsily under his breath. 'You don't put anyone up? Then explain what this here means: "Headful plus sleep – extra 5 escudos". Explain what this sleep means … '

'That's just because of some customers who fall asleep in the chair.'

The policeman was already growing in his anger.

'Give me the photo.'

The barber took the postcard from his pocket. The policeman interrupted his movement, snatching the photo with such force that he tore it.

'Did this one fall asleep in the chair too, did he?'

'But he was never here, I swear. Christ's honour. That's a photo of a film star. Haven't you ever seen him in films, the ones the Americans make?'

'Americans, did you say? Okay, that's it. He's probably a friend of the other one, the one called Mondlane who came from America. So this one came from there too, did he?'

'But this one didn't come from anywhere. It's all a lie, propaganda.'

'Propaganda? Then you must be the one in charge of propaganda in the organisation ...'

The policeman seized the barber by his overall and shook him until the buttons fell to the ground. Vivito tried to pick them up, but the mulatto gave him a kick.

'Get back, you son-of-a-bitch. We'll arrest the lot of you before we finish here.'

The mulatto called the other policeman and whispered something in his ear. The other one walked down the path and returned some minutes later, bringing with him old Jaimco.

'We've already interrogated this old man. He's confirmed that you received the American in the photograph here.'

Firipe, smiling feebly, almost had no strength left to explain.

'There, you see, officer? More confusion. It was me who paid Jaimco to testify to my lie. Jaimco is mixed up in it with me.'

'That he is, to be sure.'

'Hey, Jaimco, admit it, wasn't it a trick we agreed on?'

The old wretch turned this way and that inside his tattered coat, baffled.

'Yes. In truthfully I saw the man of which. In that chair he was.'

The policeman pushed the old man and handcuffed him to the barber. He looked round with eyes of a hungry vulture. He faced the small crowd which was silently witnessing the incident. He gave the chair a kick, smashed the mirror, tore up the poster. It was then that Vivito became involved and began shouting. The cripple clutched the mulatto's arm but soon lost his balance, and fell to his knees.

'And who's this? What language does he speak? Is he a foreigner too?'

'The boy's my assistant.'

'Assistant, is he? Then he'd better come along too. Okay, let's go! You, the old man and this dancing monkey, get moving. Walk in front of me.'

'But Vivito … '

'Shut up, mister barber, the time for talking's finished. You'll see, in prison, you'll have a special barber to cut your and your little friend's hair.'

And before the helpless gaze of the whole market, Firipe Beruberu, wearing his immaculate overall, scissors and comb in the left-hand pocket, trod the sandy path of Maquinino for the last time. Behind him, with ancient dignity, came old Jaimco. Following him lurched Vivito with a drunkard's step. Bringing up the rear of this cortège were the two policemen, proud of their catch. Then, the humdrum haggling over prices ceased, and the market sank into the deepest gloom.

The following week, two guards arrived. They tore out the barber's sign. But as they looked around, they were struck by surprise: nobody had touched anything. Instruments, towels, the radio and even the cash box were just as they had been left, waiting for the return of Firipe Beruberu, master of all the barbers in Maquinino.

Translated by David Bradshaw

GCINA MHLOPHE

The Toilet

Sometimes I wanted to give up and be a good girl who listened to her elders. Maybe I should have done something like teaching or nursing as my mother wished. People thought these professions were respectable, but I knew I wanted to do something different, though I was not sure what. I thought a lot about acting ... My mother said that it had been a waste of good money educating me because I did not know what to do with the knowledge I had acquired. I'd come to Johannesburg for the December holidays after writing my matric exams, and then stayed on, hoping to find something to do.

My elder sister worked in Orange Grove as a domestic worker, and I stayed with her in her back room. I didn't know anybody in Jo'burg except my sister's friends whom we went to church with. The Methodist church up Fourteenth Avenue was about the only outing we had together. I was very bored and lonely.

On weekdays, I was locked in my sister's room so that the Madam wouldn't see me. She was at home most of the time, painting her nails, having tea with her friends, or lying in the sun by the swimming pool. The swimming pool was very close to the room, which is why I had to keep very quiet. My sister felt bad about locking me in there, but she had no alternative. I couldn't even play the radio, so she brought me books, old magazines, and newspapers from the white people. I just read every single thing I came across: *Fair Lady*, *Woman's Weekly*, anything. But then my sister thought I was reading too much.

'What kind of wife will you make if you can't even make baby clothes, or knit yourself a jersey? I suppose you will marry an educated man like yourself, who won't mind going to bed with a book and an empty stomach.'

We would play cards at night when she knocked off, and listen to the radio, singing along softly with the songs we liked.

Then I got this temporary job in a clothing factory in town. I looked forward to meeting new people, and liked the idea of being out of that room for a change. The factory made clothes for ladies' boutiques.

The whole place was full of machines of all kinds. Some people were sewing, others were ironing with big heavy irons that pressed with a lot of steam. I had to cut all the loose threads that hang after a dress or a jacket is finished. As soon as a number of dresses in a certain style were finished, they would be sent to me and I had to count them, write the number down, and then start with the cutting of the threads. I was fascinated to discover that one person made only sleeves, another the collars, and so on until the last lady put all the pieces together, sewed on buttons, or whatever was necessary to finish.

Most people at the factory spoke Sotho, but they were nice to me – they tried to speak to me in Zulu or Xhosa, and they gave me all kinds of advice on things I didn't know. There was this girl, Gwendolene – she thought I was very stupid – she called me a 'bari' because I always sat inside the changing-room with something to read when it was time to eat my lunch, instead of going outside to meet guys. She told me it was cheaper to get myself a 'lunch boy' – somebody to buy me lunch. She told me it was wise not to sleep with him, because then I could dump him anytime I wanted to. I was very nervous about such things. I thought it was better to be a 'bari' than to be stabbed by a city boy for his money.

The factory knocked off at four-thirty, and then I went to a park near where my sister worked. I waited there till half past six, when I could sneak into the house again without the white people seeing me. I had to leave the house before half past five in the mornings as well. That meant I had to find something to do with the time I had before I could catch the seven-thirty bus to work – about two hours. I would go to the public toilet in the park. For some reason it was never locked, so I would go in and sit on the toilet seat to read some magazine or other until the right time to catch the bus.

The first time I went into this toilet, I was on my way to the bus stop. Usually I went straight to the bus stop outside the OK Bazaars where it was well lit, and I could see. I would wait there, reading, or just looking at the growing number of cars and buses on their way to town. On this day it was raining quite hard, so I thought I would shelter in the toilet until the rain had passed. I knocked first to see if there was anyone inside. As there was no reply, I pushed the door open and went in. It smelled a little – a dryish kind of smell, as if the toilet was not used all that often, but it was quite clean compared to many 'Non-European' toilets I knew. The floor was painted red and the walls were cream white. It did not look like it had been painted for a few years. I stood looking around, with the rain coming very hard on the zinc roof. The noise was comforting – to know I had escaped the wet – only a few of the heavy drops had got me. The plastic bag in which I carried my book and purse and neatly folded pink handkerchief was a little damp, but that was because I had used it to cover my head when I ran to the toilet. I pulled my dress down a little so that it would not get creased when I sat down. The closed lid of the toilet was going to be my seat for many mornings after that.

I was really lucky to have found that toilet because the winter was very cold. Not that it was any warmer in there, but once I'd closed the door it used to be a little less windy. Also the toilet was very small – the walls were wonderfully close to me – it felt like it was made to fit me alone. I enjoyed that kind of privacy. I did a lot of thinking while I sat on the toilet seat. I did a lot of daydreaming too – many times imagining myself in some big hall doing a really popular play with other young actors. At school, we took set books like *Buzani KuBawo* or *A Man for All Seasons* and made school plays which we toured to the other schools on weekends. I loved it very much. When I was even younger I had done little sketches taken from the Bible and on big days like Good Friday, we acted and sang happily.

I would sit there dreaming …

I was getting bored with the books I was reading – the love stories all sounded the same, and besides that I just lost interest. I started asking myself why I had not written anything since I left school. At least at school I had written some poems, or stories for the school magazine, school competitions and other magazines like *Bona* or *Inkqubela*. Our English teacher was always so encouraging; I remembered the day I showed him my first poem – I was so excited I couldn't concentrate in class for the whole day. I didn't know anything about publishing then, and I didn't ask myself if my stories were good enough. I just enjoyed writing things down when I had the time. So one Friday, after I'd started being that toilet's best customer, I bought myself a notebook in which I was hoping to write something. I didn't use it for quite a while, until one evening.

My sister had taken her usual Thursday afternoon off, and she had delayed somewhere. I came back from work, then waited in the park for the right time to go back into the yard. The white people always had their supper at six-thirty and that was the time I used to steal my way in without disturbing them or being seen. My comings and goings had to be secret because they still didn't know I stayed there.

Then I realised that she hadn't come back, and I was scared to go out again, in case something went wrong this time. I decided to sit down in front of my sister's room, where I thought I wouldn't be noticed. I was reading a copy of *Drum Magazine* and hoping that she would come back soon – before the dogs sniffed me out. For the first time I realised how stupid it was of me not to have cut myself a spare key long ago. I kept on hearing noises that sounded like the gate opening. A few times I was sure I had heard her footsteps on the concrete steps leading to the servant's quarters, but it turned out to be something or someone else.

I was trying hard to concentrate on my reading again, when I heard the two dogs playing, chasing each other nearer and nearer to where I was sitting. And then, there they were in front of me, looking as surprised as I was. For a brief moment we stared at each other, then they started to bark at me. I was sure they would tear me to pieces if I moved just one finger, so I sat very still, trying not to look at them, while my heart pounded and my mouth went dry as paper.

They barked even louder when the dogs next door joined in, glared at me through the openings in the hedge. Then the Madam's high-pitched voice rang out above the dogs' barking.

'Ireeeeeeeene!' That's my sister's English name, which we never use. I couldn't move or answer the call – the dogs were standing right in front of me, their teeth so threateningly long. When there was no reply, she came to see what was going on.

'Oh, it's you? Hello.' She was smiling at me, chewing that gum which never left her mouth, instead of calling the dogs away from me. They had stopped barking, but they hadn't moved – they were still growling at me, waiting for her to tell them what to do.

'Please Madam, the dogs will bite me,' I pleaded, not moving my eyes from them.

'No, they won't bite you.' Then she spoke to them nicely, 'Get away now – go on,' and they went off. She was like a doll, her hair almost orange in colour, all curls round her made-up face. Her eyelashes fluttered like a doll's. Her thin lips were bright red like her long nails, and she wore very high-heeled shoes. She was still smiling; I wondered if it didn't hurt after a while. When her friends came for a swim, I could always hear her forever laughing at something or other.

She scared me – I couldn't understand how she could smile like that but not want me to stay in her house.

'When did you come in? We didn't see you.'

'I've been here for some time now – my sister isn't here. I'm waiting to talk to her.'

'Oh – she's not here?' She was laughing, for no reason that I could see. 'I can give her a message – you go on home – I'll tell her that you want to see her.'

Once I was outside the gate, I didn't know what to do or where to go. I walked slowly, kicking my heels. The street lights were so very bright! Like big eyes staring at me. I wondered what the people who saw me thought I was doing, walking around at that time of night. But then I didn't really care, because there wasn't much I could do about the situation right then. I was just thinking how things had to go wrong on that day particularly, because my sister and I were not on such good terms. Early that morning, when the alarm had gone for me to wake up, I did not jump to turn it off, so my sister got really angry with me. She had gone on about me always leaving it to ring for too long, as if it was set for her, and not for me. And when I went out to wash, I had left the door open a second too long, and that was enough to earn me another scolding.

Every morning I had to wake up straight away, roll my bedding and put it all under the bed where my sister was sleeping. I was not supposed to put on the light although it was still dark. I'd light a candle, and tiptoe my way out with a soap dish and a toothbrush. My clothes were on a hanger on a nail at the back of the door. I'd take the hanger and close the door as quietly as I could. Everything had to be ready set the night before. A washing basin full of cold water was also ready outside the door, put there because the sound of running water and the loud screech the taps made in the morning could wake the white people, and they would wonder what my sister was doing up so early. I'd do my everything and be off the premises by five-thirty with my shoes in my bag – I only put them on once I was safely out of the gate. And that gate made such a noise too. Many times I wished I could jump over it and save myself all that sickening careful-careful business!

Thinking about all these things took my mind away from the biting cold of the night and my wet nose, until I saw my sister walking towards me.

'Mholo, what are you doing outside in the street?' she greeted me. I quickly briefed her on what had happened.

'Oh Yehovah! You can be so dumb sometimes! What were you doing inside in the first place? You know you should have waited for me so we could walk in together. Then I could say you were visiting or something. Now, you tell me, what am I supposed to say to them if they see you come in again? Hayi!'

She walked angrily towards the gate, with me hesitantly following her. When she opened the gate, she turned to me with an impatient whisper.

'And now why don't you come in, stupid?'

I mumbled my apologies, and followed her in. By some miracle no one seemed to have noticed us, and we quickly munched a snack of cold chicken and boiled potatoes and drank our tea, hardly on speaking terms. I just wanted to howl like a dog. I wished somebody would come and be my friend, and tell me that I was not useless, and that my sister did not hate me, and tell me that one day I would have a nice place to live … anything. It would have been really great to have someone my own age to talk to.

But also I knew that my sister was worried for me, she was scared of her employers. If they were to find out that I lived with her, they would fire her, and then we would both be walking up and down the streets. My eleven rand wages wasn't going to help us at all. I don't know how long I lay like that, unable to fall asleep, just wishing and wishing with tears running into my ears.

The next morning I woke up long before the alarm went off,

but I just lay there feeling tired and depressed. If there was a way out, I would not have gone to work, but there was this other strong feeling or longing inside me. It was some kind of pain that pushed me to do everything at double speed and run to my toilet. I call it my toilet because that is exactly how I felt about it. It was very rare that I ever saw anybody else go in there in the mornings. It was like they all knew I was using it, and they had to lay off or something. When I went there, I didn't really expect to find it occupied.

I felt my spirits really lifting as I put on my shoes outside the gate. I made sure that my notebook was in my bag. In my haste I even forgot my lunchbox, but it didn't matter. I was walking faster and my feet were feeling lighter all the time. Then I noticed that the door had been painted, and that a new window pane had replaced the old broken one. I smiled to myself as I reached the door. Before long I was sitting on that toilet seat, writing a poem.

Many mornings saw me sitting there writing. Sometimes it did not need to be a poem; I wrote anything that came into my head – in the same way I would have done if I'd had a friend to talk to. I remember some days when I felt like I was hiding something from my sister. She did not know about my toilet in the park, and she was not in the least interested in my notebook.

Then one morning I wanted to write a story about what had happened at work the day before; the supervisor screaming at me for not calling her when I'd seen the people who stole two dresses at lunch time. I had found it really funny. I had to write about it and I just hoped there were enough pages left in my notebook. It all came back to me, and I was smiling when I reached for the door, but it wouldn't open – it was locked!

I think for the first time I accepted that the toilet was not mine after all … Slowly I walked over to a bench nearby, watched the early spring sun come up, and wrote my story anyway.

Ash On My Sleeve

Desmond is a man who relies on the communicative powers of the handshake. Which renders my hand, a cluster of crushed bones, inert as he takes a step back and nods approvingly while still applying the pressure. He attempts what proves impossible in spite of my decision to cooperate. This is to stand back even further in order to inspect me more thoroughly without releasing my hand. The distance between us cannot be lengthened and I am about to point out this unalterable fact when his smile relaxes into speech.

'Well what a surprise!'

'Yes, what a surprise,' I contribute.

It is of course no longer a surprise. I arranged the meeting two months ago when I wrote to Moira after years of silence between us, and yesterday I telephoned to confirm the visit. And I had met Desmond before, in fact at the same party at which Moira had been struck by the eloquence of his handshake. Then we discussed the role of the Student Representative Council, his voice remaining even as he bent down to tie a shoe-lace. And while I floundered, lost in subordinate clauses, he excused himself with a hurried, 'Back in a moment.' We have not spoken since.

'You're looking wonderful, so youthful. Turning into something of a swan in your middle age hey!'

I had thought it prudent to arrange a one-night stay which would leave me the option of another if things went well. I am a guest in their house; I must not be rude. So I content myself with staring at his jaw where my eyes fortuitously alight on the telltale red of an incipient pimple. He releases my hand. He rubs index finger and thumb together, testing an imagined protuberance, and as he gestures me to sit down the left hand briefly brushes the jaw.

It always feels worse than it looks, he will comfort himself, feeling its enormity; say to himself that the tactual never corresponds with the appearance of such a blemish, and dismiss it. I

shall allow my eyes at strategic moments to explore his face, then
settle on the offending spot.

Somewhere at the back of the house Moira's voice has been
rising and falling, flashing familiar stills from the past. Will she
be as nervous as I am? A door clicks and a voice starts up again,
closer, already addressing me, so that the figure develops slowly,
fuzzily assumes form before she appears: '... to deal with these
people and I just had to be rude and say my friend's here, all the
way from England, she's waiting ...'

Standing in the doorway, she shakes her head. 'My God
Frieda Shenton, you plaasjapie, is it really you?'

I grin. Will we embrace? Shake hands? My arm hangs
foolishly. Then she puts her hands on my shoulders and says,
'It's all my fault. I'm hopeless at writing letters and we moved
around so much and what with my hands full with children I
lost touch with everyone. But I've thought of you, many a day
I've thought of you.'

'Oh nonsense,' I say awkwardly. 'I'm no good at writing letters either. We've both been very bad.'

Her laughter deals swiftly with the layer of dust on that old
intimacy but our speech, like the short letters we exchanged, is
awkward. We cannot tumble into the present while a decade
gapes between us.

Sitting before her I realise what had bothered me yesterday on
the telephone when she said, 'Good heavens man I can't believe
it ... Yes of course I've remembered ... OK, let me pick you up at
the station.'

Unease at what I now know to be the voice made me decline.
'No,' I said. 'I'd like to walk, get to see the place. I can't get
enough of Cape Town,' I gushed. For her voice is deeper, slowed
down eerily like the distortion of a faulty record player. Some
would say the voice of a woman who speaks evenly, avoiding
inflection.

'I bet,' she says, 'you regretted having to walk all that way.'

She is right. The even-numbered houses on the left side of this
interminable street are L-shaped with grey asbestos roofs. Their
stoeps alternate green, red and black, making spurious claims to
individuality. The macadamised street is very black and sticky
under the soles, its concrete edge of raised pavement a virgin
grey that invites you to scribble something rude, or just anything

at all. For all its neat edges, the garden sand spills on to the pavement as if the earth were wriggling in discomfort. It is the pale porous sand of the Cape Flats pushed out over centuries by the Atlantic Ocean. It does not bode well for the cultivation of prizewinning dahlias.

I was so sure that it was Moira's house. There it was, a black stoep inevitably after the green, the house inadequately fenced off so that the garden sand had been swept along the pavement in delicately waved watermark by the previous afternoon's wind.

A child's bucket and spade had been left in the garden and on a mound of sand a jaunty strip of astroturf testified to the untameable. I knocked without checking the number again and felt foolish as the occupier with hands on her hips directed me to the fourth house along.

Moira's is a house like all the others except for the determined effort in the garden. Young trees in bonsai uniformity, promising a dense hedge all around for those who are prepared to wait. The fence is efficient. The sand does not escape; it is held by the roots of a brave lawn visibly knitting beneath its coarse blades of grass. Number 288 is swathed in lace curtains. Even the glass-panelled front door has generously ruched lengths of lace between the wooden strips. Dense, so that you would not begin to guess at the outline approaching the door. It was Desmond.

'Goodness me, ten, no twelve years haven't done much to damage you,' Moira says generously.

'Think so, Moi,' Desmond adds. 'I think Frieda has a contract with time. Look, she's even developed a waistline,' and his hands hover as if to describe the chimerical curve. There is the possibility that I may be doing him an injustice.

'I suppose it's marriage that's done it for us. Very ageing, and of course the children don't help,' he says.

'It's not a week since I sewed up this cushion. What do the children do with them?' Moira tugs at the loose threads then picks up another cushion to check the stitching.

'See,' Desmond persists, 'a good figure in your youth is no guarantee against childbearing. There are veins and sagging breasts and of course some women get horribly fat; that is if they don't grow thin and haggard.' He looks sympathetically at

Moira. Why does she not spit in his eye? I fix my eye on his jaw so that he says, 'Count yourself lucky that you've missed the boat.'

Silence. And then we laugh. Under Desmond's stern eye we lean back in simultaneous laughter that cleaves through the years to where we sat on our twin beds recounting the events of our nights out. Stomach-clutching laughter as we whispered our adventures and decoded for each other the words grunted by boys through the smoke of the braaivleis. Or the tears, the stifled sobs of bruised love, quietly, in order not to disturb her parents. She slept lightly, Moira's mother, who said that a girl cannot keep the loss of her virginity a secret, that her very gait proclaims it to the world and especially to men, who will expect favours from her.

When our laughter subsides Desmond gets a bottle of whisky from the cabinet of the same oppressively carved dark wood as the rest of the sitting-room suite.

'Tell Susie to make some tea,' he says.

'It's her afternoon off. Eh ...' Moira's silence asserts itself as her own so that we wait and wait until she explains, 'We have a servant. People don't have servants in England, do they? Not ordinary people, I mean.'

'It's a matter of nomenclature, I think. The middle classes have cleaning ladies, a Mrs Thing, usually quite a character, whom we pretend to be in awe of. She does for those of us who are too sensitive or too important or intelligent to clean up our own mess. We pay a decent wage, that is for a cleaner, of course, and not to be compared with our own salaries.'

Moira bends closely over a cushion, then looks up at me and I recall a photograph of her in an op-art mini-skirt dangling very large black-and-white earrings from delicate lobes. The face is lifted quizzically at the photographer, almost in disbelief, and her cupped hand is caught in movement perhaps on the way to check the jaunty flickups. I cannot remember who took the photograph but at the bottom of the picture I recognise the intrusion of my right foot, a thick ankle growing out of an absurdly delicate high-heeled shoe.

I wish I could fill the ensuing silence with something conciliatory, no, something that will erase what I have said, but my trapped thoughts blunder insect-like against a glazed window. I

who in this strange house in a new Coloured suburb have just
accused and criticised my hostess. She will have seen through
the deception of the first-person usage; she will shrink from the
self-righteousness of my words and lift her face quizzically at
my contempt. I feel the dampness crawl along my hairline. But
Moira looks at me serenely while Desmond frowns. Then she
moves as if to rise.

'Don't bother with tea on my account,' I say with my eye
longingly on the whisky, and carry on in the same breath, 'Are
you still in touch with Martin? I wouldn't mind seeing him after
all these years.'

*Moira's admirers were plentiful and she generously shared the benefits
of her beauty with me. At parties young men straightened their jackets
and stepped over to ask me to dance. Their cool hands fell on my
shoulders, bare and damp with sweat. I glided past the rows of girls
waiting to be chosen. So they tested their charm – 'Can I get you a
lemonade? Shall we dance again?' – on me, the intermediary. In the
airless room my limbs obeyed the inexorable sweep of the ballroom
dances. But with the wilder Twist or Shake my broad shoulders buckled
under a young man's gaze and my feet grew leaden as I waited for the
casual enquiry after Moira. Then we would sit out a dance chatting
about Moira while the gardenia on my bosom meshed in maddening
fragrance our common interest. My hand squeezed in gratitude with a
quick goodnight, for there was no question about it: my friendship had
to be secured in order to be considered by Moira. Then in the early
hours, sitting cross-legged on her bed, we sifted his words and Moira
unpinned the gardenia, crushed by his fervour when his cool hand on
my shoulder drew me closer, closer in that first held dance.*

*Young men in Sunday ties and borrowed cars agreed to take me
with them on scenic drives along the foot of Table Mountain, or Chapman's Peak where we looked down dizzily at the sea. And I tactfully
wandered off licking at a jumbo ice-cream while they practised their
kissing. Moira's virginity unassailable. Below, the adult baboons
scrambled over the sand dunes and smacked the bald bottoms of their
young and the sunlicked waves beckoned at the mermaids on the rocks.*

Desmond replies, 'Martin's fallen in love with an AZAPO
woman, married her and stopped coming round. Shall we say
that he finally lost interest in Moi?'

The whisky in the glass lurches amber as he rolls the stem between his fingers.

'Would you like a Coke?' he asks.

I decline but I long to violate the alcohol taboo for women. 'A girl who drinks is nothing other than a prostitute,' Father said. And there's no such thing as just a little tot because girls get drunk instantly. Then they hitch up their skirts like the servant girls on their days off, caps scrunched into shopping bags, waving their Vaaljapie bottles defiantly. A nice girl's reputation would shatter with a single mouthful of liquor.

'The children are back from their party,' Moira says. There is shuffling outside and then they burst in blowing penny whistles and rattling their plastic spoils. Simultaneously they reel off the events of the party and correct each other's versions while the youngest scrambles on to his mother's lap. Moira listens, amused. She interrupts them, 'Look who's here. Say hallo to the auntie. Aunty Frieda's come all the way from England to see you.' They compose their stained faces and shake hands solemnly. Then the youngest bursts into tears and the other two discuss in undertones the legitimacy of his grievance.

'He's tired,' Desmond offers from the depth of his whisky reverie, 'probably eaten too much as well.'

This statement has a history, for Moira throws her head back and laughs and the little boy charges at his father and butts him in the stomach.

'Freddie, we've got a visitor, behave yourself hey,' the eldest admonishes.

I smile at her and get up to answer the persistent knock at the back door which the family seem not to hear. A man in overalls waiting on the doorstep looks at me bewildered but then says soberly, 'For the Missus,' and hands over a bunch of arum lilies which I stick in a pot by the sink. When I turn around Moira stands in the doorway watching me. She interrupts as I start explaining about the man.

'Yes, I'll put it in the children's room.'

I want to say that the pot is not tall enough for the lilies but she takes them off hurriedly, the erect spadices dusting yellow on to the funnelled white leaves. Soon they will droop; I did not have a chance to put water in the pot.

I wait awkwardly in the kitchen and watch a woman walk

past the window. No doubt there is a servant's room at the far end of the garden. The man must be the gardener but from the window it is clear that there are no flowers in the garden except for a rampant morning glory that covers the fence. When Moira comes back she prepares grenadilla juice and soda with which we settle around the table. I think of alcohol and say, 'It's a nice kitchen.' It is true that sunlight sifted through the lace curtains softens the electric blue of the melamine worksurfaces. But after the formality of the sitting-room the clutter of the kitchen comes as a surprise. The sink is grimy and filled with dirty dishes of surely the previous day. The grooved steel band around the table top holds a neat line of grease and dust compound.

'Yes,' she says, 'I like it. The living-room is Desmond's. He has no interest in the kitchen.'

And all the while she chops at the parsley, slowly chops it to a pulp. Then beneath the peelings and the spilled contents of brown paperbags she ferrets about until she drags out a comb.

'Where the hell are the bay leaves?' she laughs, and throws the comb across the worksurface. I rise to inspect a curious object on the windowsill from which the light bounces frantically. It is a baby's shoe dipped into a molten alloy, an instant sculpture of brassy brown that records the first wayward steps of a new biped. I tease it in the sunlight, turning it this way and that.

'Strange object,' I say, 'whose is it?'

'Ridiculous hey,' and we laugh in agreement. 'Desmond's idea,' she explains, 'but funnily enough I'm quite attached to that shoe now. It's Carol's, the eldest; you feel so proud of the things your child does. Obvious things, you know, like walking and talking you await anxiously as if they were the first steps on the moon and you're so absurdly pleased at the child's achievement. And so we ought to be, not proud I suppose, but grateful. I'm back at work, mornings only, at Manenberg, and you should see the township children. Things haven't changed much, don't you believe that.'

She picks up the shoe.

'Carol's right foot always leaned too far to the right and Desmond felt that that was the shoe to preserve. More character, he said. Ja,' she sighs, 'things were better in those early days. And anyway I didn't mind his kak so much then. But I'd better get on otherwise dinner'll be late.'

I lift the lace curtain and spread out the gathers to reveal a pattern of scallops with their sprays of stylised leaves. The flower man is walking in the shadow of the fence carrying a carrierbag full of books. He does not look at me holding up the nylon lace. I turn to Moira bent over a cheese grater, and with the sepia light of the evening streaming in, her face lifts its sadness to me, the nutbrown skin, as if under magnifying glass, singed translucent and taut across the high cheekbones.

'Moira,' I say, but at that moment she beats the tin grater against the bowl.

So I tug at things, peep, rummage through her kitchen, pick at this and that as if they were buttons to trigger off the mechanism of software that will gush out a neatly printed account of her life. I drop the curtain still held in my limp hand.

'What happened to Michael?' she asks.

'Dunno. There was no point in keeping in touch, not after all that. And there is in any case no such thing as friendship with men.' I surprise myself by adding, 'Mind you, I think quite neutrally about him, even positively at times. The horror of Michael must've been absorbed by the subsequent horror of others. But I don't, thank God, remember their names.'

Moira laughs. 'You must be kinder to men. We have to get on with them.'

'Yes,' I retort, 'but surely not behind their backs.'

'Heavens,' she says 'we were so blarry stupid and dishonest really. Obsessed with virginity, we imagined we weren't messing about with sex. Suppose that's what we thought sex was all about, breaking a membrane. I expect Michael was as stupid as you. Catholic, wasn't he?'

I do not want to talk about Michael. I am much more curious about Desmond. How did he slip through the net? Desmond scorned the methods of her other suitors and refused to ingratiate himself with me. On her first date Moira came back with a headache, bristling with secrecy no doubt sworn beneath his parted lips. We did not laugh at the way he pontificated, his hands held gravely together as if in prayer to prevent interruptions. Desmond left Cape Town at the end of that year and I had in the meantime met Michael.

There was the night on the bench under the loquat tree when we ate the

*tasteless little fruits and spat glossy pips over the fence. Moira's fingers
drummed the folder on her lap.*

*'Here,' she said in a strange voice, 'are the letters. You should just
read this, today's.'*

*I tugged at the branch just above my head so that it rustled in the
dark and overripe loquats fell plop on the ground.*

*'No, not his letters, that wouldn't be right,' I said. And my memory
skimmed the pages of Michael's letters. Love, holy love that made the
remembered words dance on that lined foolscap infused with his smell. I
could not, would not, share any of it.*

'Is he getting on OK in Durban?' I asked.

*'Yes, I expect he still has many friends there. I'm going up just after
finals and then perhaps he'll come back to Cape Town. Let's see if we
can spit two pips together and hit the fence at the same time.'*

*So we sat in the dark, between swotting sessions, under the tree with
yellow loquats lustrous in the black leaves. Perhaps she mimicked his
Durban voice, waiting for me to take up the routine of friendly mock-
ery.*

I try in vain to summon it all. I cannot separate the tangled
strands of conversation or remembered letters. Was it then, in
my Durban accent, that I replied with Michael's views about the
permanence and sanctity of marriage?

'Ja-ja-ja,' Moira sighs, pulling out a chair. And turning again
to check the pot on the stove, her neck is unbecomingly twisted,
the sinews thrown into relief. How old we have grown since that
night under the loquat tree and I know that there is no point in
enquiring after Desmond.

'Do you like living here?' I ask instead.

'It's OK, as good as anything.'

'I was thinking of your parents' home, the house where I
stayed. How lovely it was. Everything's so new here. Don't you
find it strange?'

'Ag Frieda, but we're so new, don't we belong in estates like
this? Coloureds haven't been around for that long, perhaps
that's why we stray. Just think, in our teens we wanted to be
white, now we want to be full-blooded Africans. We've never
wanted to be ourselves and that's why we stray … across the
continent, across the oceans and even here, right into the
Tricameral Parliament, playing into their hands. Actually,' and

she looks me straight in the eye, 'it suits me very well to live here.'

Chastened by her reply I drum my fingertips on the table so that she says gently, 'I don't mean to accuse you. At the time I would have done exactly the same. There was little else to do. Still, it's really nice to see you. I hope you'll be able to stay tomorrow.' Her hand burns for a moment on my shoulder.

It is time for dinner. Moira makes a perfunctory attempt at clearing the table, then, defeated by the chaos, she throws a cloth at me.

'Oh God, I'll never be ready by seven.'

I am drawn into the revolving circle of panic: washing down, screwing lids back on to jars, shutting doors on food that will rot long before discovery. Moira has always been hopeless in a kitchen so that there is really no point in my holding up the bag of potatoes enquiringly.

'Oh stick it in there,' and with her foot she deftly kicks open a dank cupboard where moisture tries in vain to escape from foul-smelling cloths. In here the potatoes will grow eyes and long pale etiolated limbs that will push open the creaking door next spring.

Her slow voice does not speed up with the frantic move-ments; instead, like a tape mangled in a machine, it trips and buzzes, dislocated from the darting sinewy body.

The children watch television. They do not want to eat, except for the youngest who rubs his distended tummy against the table. We stand in silence and listen to the child, 'I'm hungry, really hungry. I could eat and eat.' His black eyes glint with the success of subterfuge and in his pride he tugs at Moira's skirt. 'Can I sit on your knee?' and offers as reward, 'I'll be hungry on your knee, I really will.'

Something explodes in my mouth when Desmond produces a bottle of wine, and I resolve not to look at his chin, not even once.

'I've got something for you girls to celebrate with; you are staying in tonight, aren't you? Frieda, I promise you this is the first Wednesday night in years that Moira's been in. Nothing, not riots nor disease will keep her away from her Wednesday meetings. Now that women's lib's crept over the equator it would be most unbecoming of me to suspect my wife's commitment to her black-culture group. A worthy affair, affiliated to the UDF you know.' The wine which I drink too fast tingles in my toes and fingertips.

'So how is feminism received here?' I ask.

'Oh,' he smiles, 'you have to adapt in order to survive. No point in resisting for the sake of it, you have to move with the times ... but there are some worrying half-baked ideas about ... muddled women's talk.'

'Actually,' Moira interjects, 'our group has far more pressing matters to deal with.'

'Like?' he barks.

'Like community issues, consciousness raising,' but Desmond snorts and she changes direction. 'Anyway, I doubt whether women's oppression arises as an issue among whites. One of the functions of having servants is to obscure it.'

'Hm,' I say, and narrow my eyes thoughtfully, a stalling trick I've used with varying success. Then I look directly at Desmond so that he refills my glass and takes the opportunity to propose a toast to our reunion. This is hardly less embarrassing than the topic of servants. The wine on my tongue turns musty and mingles with the smell of incense, of weddings and christenings that his empty words resurrect.

Desmond is in a cooperative mood, intent on evoking the halcyon days of the sixties when students sat on the cafeteria steps soaking up the sun. Days of calm and stability, he sighs. He reels off the names of contemporaries. Faces struggle in formation through the fog of the past, rise and recede. Rita Jantjes detained under the Terrorism act.'The Jantjes of Lansdowne?' I ask.

'It's ridiculous of them to keep Rita. She knows nothing; she's far too emotional, an obvious security risk,' Moira interjects.

'No,' Desmond explains, 'not the Lansdowne Jantjes but the Port Elizabeth branch of the family. The eldest, Sammy, graduated in Science the year before me.'

I am unable to contribute anything else, but he is the perfect host. There are no silent moments. He explains his plans for the garden and defers to my knowledge of succulents. There will be an enormous rockery in the front with the widest possible variety of cacti. A pity, he says, that Moira has planted those horrible trees but he would take over responsibility for the garden, give her a bit more free time, perhaps I didn't know that she has started working again?

Moira makes no effort to contribute to the conversation so diligently made. She murmurs to the little one on her knee whose fat fingers she prevents from exploring her nostrils. They giggle and shh-ssht each other, marking out their orbit of intimacy. Which makes it easier for me to conduct this conversation. Only once does he falter and rub his chin but I avert my eyes and he embarks smoothly on the topic of red wine. I am the perfect guest, a deferential listener. I do not have the faintest interest in the production of wine.

When we finish dinner Desmond gets up briskly. He returns to the living-room and the children protest loudly as he switches off the television and puts on music. Something classical and rousing, as if he too is in need of revival.

'Moi,' he shouts above the trombones, 'Moi, the children are tired, they must go to bed. Remember, it's school tomorrow.'

'OK,' she shouts back. Then quietly, 'Thursdays are always schooldays. But then Desmond isn't always as sober as I'd like him to be.'

She lifts the sleeping child from her lap on to the bench. We rest our elbows on the table amongst the dirty dishes.

'He gets his drink too cheaply; has shares in an hotel.' Moira explains how the liquor business goes on expanding, how many professional people give up their jobs to become liquor moguls.

'Why are the booze shops called hotels? Who stays in them? Surely there's no call for hotels in a Coloured area?'

'Search me, as we used to say. Nobody stays in them, I'm sure. I imagine they need euphemisms when they know that they grow rich out of other people's misery. Cheap wine means everyone can drown his sorrows at the weekends, and people say that men go into teaching so that they have the afternoons to drink in as well. I swear the only sober man to be found on a Saturday afternoon is the liquor boss. The rest are dronkies, whether they loaf about on street corners in hanggat trousers or whether they slouch in upholstered chairs in front of television sets. And we all know a man of position is not a man unless he can guzzle a bottle or two of spirits. It's not surprising that the Soweto kids of '76 stormed the liquor stores and the shebeens. Not that I'd like to compare the shebeen queen making a miserable cent with the Coloured "elite" as they call themselves who build big houses and drive Mercedes and send their daughters to Europe to find husbands. And those who allow themselves be bought by the government to sit in Parliament ...'

She holds her head. 'Jesus, I don't know. Sometimes I'm optimistic and then it's worth fighting, but other times, here in this house, everything seems pointless. Actually that wine's given me a headache.'

I stare into the dirty plate so hard that surely my eyes will drop out and stare back at me. Like two fried eggs, sunny-side-up. Then I take her hand.

'Listen, I know a trick that takes headaches away instantly.' And I squeeze with my thumb and index finger deep into the webbed V formed by the thumb of her outstretched hand. 'See? Give me the other hand. See how it lifts?' Like a child she stares in wonderment at the hand still resting in mine.

The back door bursts open and Tillie rushes in balancing on her palm a curious object, a priapic confection.

'Look,' she shouts, 'look, isn't it lovely? It's the stale loaf I put out for the birds and they've pecked it really pretty.'

The perfectly shaped phallus with the crust as pedestal has been sculpted by a bird's beak. Delicately pecked so that the surface is as smooth as white bread cut with a finely serrated knife. We stare wanly at the child and her find, then we laugh. Tears run down Moira's face as she laughs. When she recovers her voice is stern. 'What are you doing outside at this hour? Don't you know it's ten o'clock? Where's Carol?'

Carol bursts in shouting. 'Do you know what? There are two African men in the playhouse, in our playhouse, and they've got our sleeping-bags. Two grown-ups can't sleep in there. And I went to tell Susie but she won't open the door. She spoke to me through the window and she said it's time to go to bed. But there's other people in her room. I heard them. And Susie shouldn't give people my sleeping-bag.'

Moira waves her arm at Carol throughout this excited account, her finger across her lips in an attempt to quieten the child.

'Ssht, ssht, for God's sake, ssht,' she hisses. 'Now you are not to prowl around outside at night and you are not to interfere in Susie's affairs. You know people have problems with passes and it's silly to talk about such things. Daddy'll be very cross if he knew that you're still up and messing about outside. I suggest you say nothing to him, nothing at all, and creep to bed as quietly as you can.'

She takes the children by the hands and leads them out of the room. Moments later she returns to carry off the little one sleeping on the bench. I start to clear the table and when she joins me she smiles.

'Aren't children dreadful? They can't be trusted an inch. I clean forgot about them, and they'll do anything not to go to bed. When adults long to get to bed at a reasonable hour which is always earlier than we can manage ... Of course sleep really becomes a precious commodity when you have children. Broken nights and all that. No,' she laughs, looking me straight in the eye, 'I can't see you ever coping with children.'

The dishes are done. There is a semblance of order which clearly pleases Moira. She looks around the kitchen appreciatively then yawns. 'We must go to bed. Go ahead, use the bathroom first. I'll get the windows and doors shut. Sleep well.'

I have one of the children's bedrooms. For a while I sit on the floor, the little painted chair will not accommodate me, grotesque in the Lilliputian world of the child. Gingerly I lay my clothes across the chair. It is not especially hot, but I open the window. For a while, I lie in my nightdress on the chaste little bed and try to read. The words dance and my eyes sting under heavy lids. But I wait. I stretch my eyes wide open and follow a mad moth circling the rabbit-shaped lamp by the side of the bed. I start to the mesmerising scent of crushed gardenia when the book slips and slips from under my fingers. In this diminutive world it does not fall with a thud. But I am awake once more. I wait.

DON MATTERA

Die Bushie is Dood ...

Johnny Jacobs lay bleeding in the road, his chestnut-brown eyes widened in disbelief. He covered his face with his hands and shook his head. Life was ebbing out of him and he knew it.

'Why me? Why me, comrade Mandla? Why did they have to attack me of all people? Am I not also in the struggle?'

The words frothed from his mouth and he gripped on to the denim jacket of his best friend. The friend who had introduced him to student politics. It was 4.30 pm. The sun shone without real warmth for the June 16 rallyists who poured into the streets.

Johnny gave a rasping cough and spat out a mouthful of blood. The knives had sagged into him five times – in the back and on the chest. It happened without warning and Johnny's friends had scattered in all directions.

'Take me home, I want to die in my mother's house. Take me home, comrade,' he said and began to cry. Mandla, who was equally baffled and angry at the attack on his friend, also cried. He put his hand on the injured boy's forehead.

'It's okay, Johnny. You are not going to die. It's okay my brother, I'm taking you home.'

How Mandla wished he could believe his own words. God, why did I bring him to Soweto? What will his family say? Remorse and anger burned inside him and brought more tears to his eyes. He lifted Johnny's head on to his lap. He looked up at the crowd whose numbers were increasing.

'Someone please call an ambulance! My friend is dying ...' The words slipped out unintentionally. Mandla had fetched his comrade from Eldorado Park for the annual June 16 commemoration rally at Regina Mundi. He recollected Johnny's fiery speech and his fervent call for greater unity and political and social interaction between the Coloureds, Indians and the African masses. Shouts of 'Viva! Viva!' had greeted his plea particularly at a time when many blacks were beginning to doubt the patriotism and loyalty of Coloureds and Indians to the broad, democratic struggle for liberation.

And now Johnny was dying.

When the comrade from Eldorado Park gasped for air, blood ran from the sides of his mouth and from the chest wounds. His yellow-and-red June 16 T-shirt with the historic Hector Pietersen emblem of sacrifice silkscreened on the front was drenched. The stain had begun to harden at the waist. An elderly man bent and loosened the belt, and remarked that the blood had wet Johnny's private parts. An irritated Mandla pushed the man's hands away.

'Who stabbed this Bushie?' enquired a deep baritone voice from the back of the crowd. Some people stared at the speaker wryly. 'It was the comrades from Dlamini,' volunteered a short, well-built girl dressed in a black skirt and yellow blouse – colours of the national student body which she supported. 'Three of them attacked the group that accompanied the Coloured chap. They stabbed him several times,' she said in a conscious attempt to set the racial record straight. One only used the term 'maboesman' when Coloureds were at a safe distance. Discretion at times like these was vital, thought the girl, even though there were many Indians and Coloureds who spoke in a derogatory way about Blacks.

'I heard the poor guy scream,' said an apple-and-peanut vendor, pointing to the victim. 'He shouted: "Please don't kill me, I'm also a comrade." But they said: "Jy's 'n Bushie. You fokken Bushies don't want to strike and boycott when we strike and boycott." They were drunk. One of them returned and stabbed him one more time, and called him a sellout,' said the vendor. There was a loud murmur. Rumours abounded of imminent confrontation with the Coloureds and Indians over their apparent reluctance to join the strikes, stayaways and boycotts organised by the national movements. Comrade Mandla rose to his feet.

'Bushie or no Bushie, Johnny is one of us. He's black just like us and he's no bloody sellout. No sellout dammit!' Pain and anger were visible in his face.

Johnny recognised his voice. 'Take me home, please,' he pleaded feebly. A woman dressed in the garb of a religious sect pushed through the crowd.

'Give him air,' she shouted. 'Give the boy air.' She removed a small blanket from around her waist, placed it under Johnny's head and stroked his curly brown hair. She did it gently, full of sympathy and concern. He could have been my own child, she thought.

'Give the poor boy air; move back,' she ordered again. She got up and pushed her way out.

The baritone voice came again: 'And what is he doing here, especially on a day like June 16? This is Soweto ...' The jibe was cold and it clearly affected the bystanders. Many shook their heads while others nodded.

Soweto ... Soweto ... The word echoed in the injured boy's mind and trailed off into a soft but jagged sound: So ... we ... to ... The argument that morning in the yard: His mother's anger and her words 'I hope they kill you in that Soweto of yours ...' drummed in his ears. Why did she have to curse me?

'Where the hell are you going to, Johnny? Why didn't you get up for college today?'

'It's June 16, Ma, no teachers' college for me. I'm going to Soweto to attend a rally.'

'You're not going anywhere near that place. I'm sick of your bleddy politics. Those bantus are going to hurt you someday. If not the police then those people are going to give it to you; just wait and see. The last time you were picked up. Before that you were sjambokked at college; next time you will die, my boy.'

'Ma, don't wish me bad luck and don't call them bantus. They are black people just like us.'

'Black, bantu, same bloody thing.' The speaker was Joe, Johnny's eldest brother. 'Stay in your own area, among your own people and forget those darkies. They gonna necklace you for sure!'

Johnny shook his head. It was not the first time that his family had had it out with him. Members of the coloured community and its teaching fraternity had also attacked him for his political views. He swallowed the hastily made sandwich and bent in front of the watertap. The cold winter water pushed the bread down his gullet. He belched, wiped his mouth and took his newly bought June 16 T-shirt from a chair.

'Don't talk shit, Joe. Blacks don't just go around necklacing everybody. In fact it has stopped altogether. Besides it was used on police informers and sellouts.'

'Not just on sellouts, boetie. Those comrade friends of yours still use it to kill one another. The papers are full of such stories.'

Joe jumped up from the chair, grabbed the T-shirt and flung it into the dustbin.

'There. That's where that thing belongs – in the dirtbox.'

Johnny's fist slammed into his brother's face. Joe fell on his back. His mouth bled. He tried to rise but slumped backwards. Their mother screamed and flung a saucepan lid at her younger son as he retrieved the T-shirt. Johnny headed towards the gate where comrade Mandla and three friends waited in a green Dodge Colt.

'Don't come back here! I hope they kill you in that Soweto of yours. Bleddy politics. Will it never end?'

'I don't care!' responded her son as he entered the Dodge.

'What's wrong, Com? Is your old lady going crazy to curse you like that?'

'Naa, it's that stupid brother of mine. He threw this T-shirt in the dirtbox and I hit him hard.'

'Good. He's bloody mad. Your brother must be dagga drunk; that skipper is sacred to us blacks. Maybe not to Coloureds but to us it is a symbol of great sacrifice.'

'Don't generalise, Com. Not all the Coloureds are the same. And there are blacks among you who don't respect the significance of this Hector Pietersen T-Shirt. Behind your backs they sleep in the city and go to work on June 16. Not just the Coloureds.'

'You are right. Put on your skipper, Soweto is calling us.'

'Soweto knows me. I've been attending June 16 rallies for the last seven years. When other kids in Eldorado go to college or school, I come to Soweto.'

'That's because you're a true comrade; one of us. What's more, you've been detained, shot at and assaulted. You're one of the people, Com.'

'One of us, one of the people …' As Johnny whispered the words he gave a loud cough.

'What's he saying?' asked a tall bespectacled man, craning his head towards the victim.

'Something about people. I think the Bushie wants to be taken to his own people. I wonder what the hell he was doing here in the first place?' It was the deep baritone voice and what it said really irked Mandla.

'Shut up, you fool; can't you see he's dying, dammit. Call the ambulance and stop talking shit. He's no bloody Bushie; he's black and he's my friend,' said Mandla and bit into his lip. Why, why did I bring him here?

Johnny lifted his head. 'Comrade, take me home. I want to go to my mother's house.'

Mandla comforted him and put his head back on to the blanket. 'Rest comrade, rest …'

The ambulance arrived in the fading dusk. Its lights flickered dimly before Johnny's eyes.

'Stand back! Stand back!' shouted one of the attendants and pushed Mandla's hand from his friend's forehead. 'Come on,' came the authoritative command. 'Move away.'

'I'm with him. He's my friend. He's my brother,' said Mandla. Johnny smiled blankly. He coughed and jerked and kicked violently. The bleeding stopped. In fact there was no more blood in his body. One final cough. One final kick. One final question.

'Why me, Com?'

The words were faint but Mandla heard them and cried uncontrollably. Johnny's eyes closed and his body released a great burst of air and then he lay still.

'He's gone,' said the deep baritone voice. 'Die Bushie is dood …'

NADINE GORDIMER

The Ultimate Safari

'THE AFRICAN ADVENTURE LIVES ON ... YOU CAN DO IT! THE
ULTIMATE SAFARI OR EXPEDITION WITH LEADERS WHO KNOW
AFRICA.'

Travel advertisement, Observer, 27 November 1988

That night our mother went to the shop and she didn't come
back. Ever. What happened? I don't know. My father also had
gone away one day and never come back; but he was fighting in
the war. We were in the war, too, but we were children, we were
like our grandmother and grandfather, we didn't have guns. The
people my father was fighting – the bandits, they are called by
our government – ran all over the place and we ran away from
them like chickens chased by dogs. We didn't know where to go.
Our mother went to the shop because someone said you could
get some oil for cooking. We were happy because we hadn't
tasted oil for a long time; perhaps she got the oil and someone
knocked her down in the dark and took that oil from her. Perhaps she met the bandits. If you meet them, they will kill you.
Twice they came to our village and we ran and hid in the bush
and when they'd gone we came back and found they had taken
everything; but the third time they came back there was nothing
to take, no oil, no food, so they burned the thatch and the roofs
of our houses fell in. My mother found some pieces of tin and we
put those up over part of the house. We were waiting there for
her that night she never came back.

We were frightened to go out, even to do our business,
because the bandits did come. Not into our house – without a
roof it must have looked as if there was no one in it, everything
gone – but all through the village. We heard people screaming
and running. We were afraid even to run, without our mother to
tell us where. I am the middle one, the girl, and my little brother
clung against my stomach with his arms round my neck and his
legs around my waist like a baby monkey to its mother. All night
my first-born brother kept in his hand a broken piece of wood

from one of our burnt house-poles. It was to save himself if the bandits found him.

We stayed there all day. Waiting for her. I don't know what day it was; there was no school, no church any more in our village, so you didn't know whether it was a Sunday or a Monday.

When the sun was going down, our grandmother and grandfather came. Someone from our village had told them we children were alone, our mother had not come back. I say 'grandmother' before 'grandfather' because it's like that: our grandmother is big and strong, not yet old, and our grandfather is small, you don't know where he is, in his loose trousers, he smiles but he hasn't heard what you're saying, and his hair looks as if he's left it full of soap suds. Our grandmother took us – me, the baby, my first-born brother, our grandfather – back to her house and we were all afraid (except the baby, asleep on our grandmother's back) of meeting the bandits on the way. We waited a long time at our grandmother's place. Perhaps it was a month. We were hungry. Our mother never came. While we were waiting for her to fetch us, our grandmother had no food for us, no food for our grandfather and herself. A woman with milk in her breasts gave us some for my little brother, although at our house he used to eat porridge, same as we did. Our grandmother took us to look for wild spinach but everyone else in the village did the same and there wasn't a leaf left.

Our grandfather, walking a little behind some young men, went to look for our mother but didn't find her. Our grandmother cried with other women and I sang hymns with them. They brought a little food – some beans – but after two days there was nothing again. Our grandfather used to have three sheep and a cow and a vegetable garden but the bandits had long ago taken the sheep and the cow, because they were hungry, too; and when planting time came our grandfather had no seed to plant.

So they decided – our grandmother did; our grandfather made little noises and rocked from side to side, but she took no notice – we would go away. We children were pleased. We wanted to go away from where our mother wasn't and where we were hungry. We wanted to go where there were no bandits and there was food. We were glad to think there must be such a place; away.

Our grandmother gave her church clothes to someone in exchange for some dried mealies and she boiled them and tied them in a rag. We took them with us when we went and she thought we would get water from the rivers but we didn't come to any river and we got so thirsty we had to turn back. Not all the way to our grandparents' place but to a village where there was a pump. She opened the basket where she carried some clothes and the mealies and she sold her shoes to buy a big plastic container for water. I said, *Gogo*, how will you go to church now even without shoes, but she said we had a long journey and too much to carry. At that village we met other people who were also going away. We joined them because they seemed to know where that was better than we did.

To get there we had to go through the Kruger Park. We knew about the Kruger Park. A kind of whole country of animals – elephants, lions, jackals, hyenas, hippos, crocodiles, all kinds of animals. We had some of them in our own country, before the war (our grandfather remembers; we children weren't born yet) but the bandits kill the elephants and sell their tusks, and the bandits and our soldiers have eaten all the buck. There was a man in our village without legs – a crocodile took them off, in our river; but all the same our country is a country of people, not animals. We knew about the Kruger Park because some of our men used to leave home to work there in the places where white people came to stay and look at the animals.

So we started to go away again. There were women and other children like me who had to carry the small ones on their backs when the women got tired. A man led us into the Kruger Park: are we there yet, are we there yet, I kept asking our grandmother. Not yet, the man said, when she asked him for me. He told us we had to take a long way to get round the fence, which he explained would kill you, roast off your skin the moment you touched it, like the wires high up on poles that give electric light in our towns. I've seen that sign of a head without ears or skin or hair on an iron box at the mission hospital we used to have before it was blown up.

When I asked the next time, they said we'd been walking in the Kruger Park for an hour. But it looked just like the bush we'd been walking through all day, and we hadn't seen any animals except the monkeys and birds which live around us at home, and a tortoise that, of course, couldn't get away from us. My first-born brother and other boys brought it to the man so it could be killed and we could cook and eat it. He let it go because he told us we could not make a fire; all the time we were in the Park we must not make a fire because the smoke would show we were there. Police, wardens would come and send us back where we came from. He said we must move like animals among the animals, away from the roads, away from the white people's camps. And at that moment I heard – I'm sure I was the first to hear – cracking branches and the sound of something parting grasses and I almost squealed because I thought it was the police, wardens – the people he was telling us to look out for – who had found us already. And it was an elephant, and another elephant, and more elephants, big blots of dark moved wherever you looked between the trees. They were curling their trunks round the red leaves of the mopane trees and stuffing them into their mouths. The babies leaned against their mothers. The almost grown-up ones wrestled like my first-born brother with his friends – only they used trunks instead of arms. I was so interested I forgot to be afraid. The man said we should just stand still and be quiet while the elephants passed. They passed very slowly because elephants are too big to need to run from anyone.

The buck ran from us. They jumped so high they seemed to fly. The wart-hogs stopped dead, when they heard us, and swerved off the way a boy in our village used to zigzag on the bicycle his father had brought back from the mines. We followed the animals to where they drank. When they had gone, we went to their waterholes. We were never thirsty without finding water, but the animals ate, ate all the time. Whenever you saw them they were eating, grass, trees, roots. And there was nothing for us. The mealies were finished. The only food we could eat was what the baboons ate, dry little figs full of ants, that grow along the branches of the trees at the rivers. It was hard to be like the animals.

When it was very hot during the day we would find lions lying asleep. They were the colour of the grass and we didn't see them at first but the man did, and he led us back and a long way round where they slept. I wanted to lie down like the lions. My little brother was getting thin but he was very heavy. When our grandmother looked for me, to put him on my back, I tried not to see. My first-born brother stopped talking; and when we rested he had to be shaken to get up again. I saw flies crawling on our grandmother's face and she didn't brush them off; I was frightened. I picked up a palm leaf and chased them.

We walked at night as well as by day. We could see the fires where the white people were cooking in the camps and we could smell the smoke and the meat. We watched the hyenas with their backs that slope as if they're ashamed, slipping through the bush after the smell. If one turned its head, you saw it had big brown shining eyes like our own, when we looked at each other in the dark. The wind brought voices in our own language from the compounds where the people who work in the camps live. A woman among us wanted to go to them at night and ask them to help us. They can give us the food from the dustbins, she said, she started wailing and our grandmother had to grab her and put a hand over her mouth. The men who led us had told us that we must keep out of the way of our people who worked at the Kruger Park, if they helped us they would lose their work. If they saw us, all they could do was pretend we were not there; they had seen only animals.

Sometimes we stopped to sleep for a little while at night. We slept close together. I don't know which night it was – because we were walking, walking, any time, all the time – we heard the lions very near. Not groaning loudly the way they did far off. Panting, like we do when we run, but it's a different kind of panting: you can hear they're not running, they're waiting, somewhere near. We all rolled closer together, on top of each other, the ones on the edge fighting to get into the middle. I was squashed against a woman who smelled bad because she was afraid but I was glad to hold tight on her. I shut my eyes not to see the tree from which a lion might jump right into the middle of us, where I was. The man who led us jumped up instead, and beat on the tree with a dead branch. He had taught us never to make a sound but he shouted. He shouted at the lions like a drunk man shouting at nobody in our village. The lions went away. We heard them groaning, shouting back at him from far off.

We were tired, so tired. My first-born brother and the man had to lift our grandfather from stone to stone where we found places to cross the rivers. Our grandmother is strong but her feet were bleeding. We could not carry the bucket on our heads any longer, we couldn't carry anything except my little brother. We left our things under a bush. As long as our bodies get there, our grandmother said. Then we ate some wild fruit we didn't know from home and our stomachs ran. We were in the grass called elephant grass because it is nearly as tall as an elephant, that day we had those pains, and our grandfather couldn't just get down in front of people like my little brother, he went off into the grass to be on his own. We had to keep up, the man who led us always kept telling us, we must catch up, but we asked him to wait for our grandfather.

So everyone waited for our grandfather to catch up. But he didn't. It was the middle of the day; insects were singing in our ears and we couldn't hear him moving through the grass. We couldn't see him because the grass was so high and he was so small. But he must have been somewhere there inside his loose trousers and his shirt that was torn and our grandmother couldn't sew because she had no cotton. We knew he couldn't have gone far because he was weak and slow. We all went to look for him, but in groups, so we too wouldn't be hidden from each other in that grass. It got into our eyes and noses; we called him softly but the noise of the insects must have filled the little space left for hearing in his ears. We looked and looked but we couldn't find him. We stayed in that long grass all night. In my sleep I found him curled round in a place he had tramped down for himself, like the places we'd seen where the buck hid their babies.

When I woke up he still wasn't anywhere. So we looked again, and by now there were paths we'd made by going through the grass many times, it would be easy for him to find us if we couldn't find him. All that day we just sat and waited. Everything is very quiet when the sun is on your head, inside your head, even if you lie, like the animals, under the trees. I lay on my back and saw those ugly birds with hooked beaks and plucked necks flying round and round above us. We had passed them often where they were feeding on the bones of dead animals, nothing was ever left there for us to eat. Round and

round, high up and then lower down and then high again. I saw
their necks poking this side and that. Flying round and round. I
saw our grandmother, who sat up all the time with my little
brother on her lap, was seeing them, too.

In the afternoon the man who led us came to our grandmother and told her the other people must move on. He said, if
their children don't eat soon they will die.

Our grandmother said nothing.

I'll bring you water before we go, he told her.

Our grandmother looked at us, me, my first-born brother, and
my little brother on her lap. We watched the other people getting
up to leave. I didn't believe the grass would be empty, all
around us, where they had been. That we would be alone in this
place, the Kruger Park, the police or the animals would find us.
Tears came out of my eyes and nose on to my hands but our
grandmother took no notice. She got up, with her feet apart the
way she puts them when she is going to lift firewood, at home in
our village, she swung my little brother on to her back, tied him
in her cloth – the top of her dress was torn and her big breasts
were showing but there was nothing in them for him. She said,
Come.

So we left the place with the long grass. Left behind. We went
with the others and the man who led us. We started to go away,
again.

There's a very big tent, bigger than a church or a school, tied
down to the ground. I didn't understand that was what it would
be, when we got there, away. I saw a thing like that the time our
mother took us to the town because she heard our soldiers were
there and she wanted to ask them if they knew where our father
was. In that tent, people were praying and singing. This one is
blue and white like that one but it's not for praying and singing,
we live in it with other people who've come from our country.
Sister from the clinic says we're 200 without counting the babies,
and we have new babies, some were born on the way through
the Kruger Park.

Inside, even when the sun is bright it's dark and there's a kind
of whole village in there. Instead of houses each family has a
little place closed off with sacks or cardboard from boxes –
whatever we can find – to show the other families it's yours and

they shouldn't come in even though there's no door and no windows and no thatch, so that if you're standing up and you're not a small child you can see into everybody's house. Some people have even made paint from ground rocks and drawn designs on the sacks.

Of course, there really is a roof – the tent is the roof, far, high up. It's like a sky. It's like a mountain and we're inside it; through the cracks paths of dust lead down, so thick you think you could climb them. The tent keeps off the rain overhead but the water comes in at the sides and in the little streets between our places – you can only move along them one person at a time – the small kids like my little brother play in the mud. You have to step over them. My little brother doesn't play. Our grandmother takes him to the clinic when the doctor comes on Mondays. Sister says there's something wrong with his head, she thinks it's because we didn't have enough food at home. Because of the war. Because our father wasn't there. And then because he was so hungry in the Kruger Park. He likes just to lie about on our grandmother all day, on her lap or against her somewhere and he looks at us and looks at us. He wants to ask something but you can see he can't. If I tickle him he may just smile. The clinic gives us special powder to make into porridge for him and perhaps one day he'll be all right.

When we arrived we were like him – my first-born brother and I. I can hardly remember. The people who lived in the village near the tent took us to the clinic, it's where you have to sign that you've come – away, through the Kruger Park. We sat on the grass and everything was muddled. One Sister was pretty with her hair straightened and beautiful high-heeled shoes and she brought us the special powder. She said we must mix it with water and drink it slowly. We tore the packets open with our teeth and licked it all up, it stuck round my mouth and I sucked it from my lips and fingers. Some other children who had walked with us vomited. But I only felt everything in my belly moving, the stuff going down and around like a snake, and hiccups hurt me. Another Sister called us to stand in line on the veranda of the clinic but we couldn't. We sat all over the place there, falling against each other: the Sisters helped each of us up by the arm and then stuck a needle in it. Other needles drew our blood into tiny bottles. This was against sickness, but I didn't understand, every time my eyes dropped closed I thought I was walking, the grass was long. I saw the elephants. I didn't know we were away.

But our grandmother was still strong, she could still stand up, she knows how to write and she signed for us. Our grandmother got us this place in the tent against one of the sides, it's the best kind of place there because although the rain comes in, we can lift the flap when the weather is good and then the sun shines on us, the smells in the tent go out. Our grandmother knows a woman here who showed her where there is good grass for sleeping mats, and our grandmother made some for us. Once every month the food truck comes to the clinic. Our grandmother takes along one of the cards she signed and when it has been punched we get a sack of mealie meal. There are wheelbarrows to take it back to the tent: my first-born brother does this for her and then he and the other boys have races, steering the empty wheelbarrows back to the clinic. Sometimes he's lucky and a man who's bought beer in the village gives him money to deliver it – though that's not allowed, you're supposed to take that wheelbarrow straight back to the Sisters. He buys a cold drink and shares it with me if I catch him. On another day, every month, the church leaves a pile of old clothes in the clinic yard. Our grandmother has another card to get punched, and then we can choose something: I have two dresses, two pants and a jersey, so I can go to school.

The people in the village have let us join their school. I was surprised to find they speak our language; our grandmother told me. That's why they allow us to stay on their land. Long ago, in the time of our fathers, there was no fence that kills you, there was no Kruger Park between them and us, we were the same people under our own king, right from our village we left to this place we've come to.

Now that we've been in the tent so long – I have turned eleven and my little brother is nearly three although he is so small, only his head is big, he's not come right in it yet – some people have dug up the bare ground around the tent and planted beans and mealies and cabbage. The old men weave branches to put up fences round their gardens. No one is allowed to look for work in the towns but some of the women have found work in the village and can buy things. Our grandmother, because she's still strong, found work where people are building houses – in this village the people build nice houses with bricks and cement, not mud like we used to have at our home. Our grandmother carries bricks for these people and fetches buckets of stones on her head. And so she has money to buy sugar and tea and milk and soap. The store gave her a calendar she has hung up on our flap of the tent. I am clever at school and she collected advertising paper people throw away outside the store and covered my school-books with it. She makes my first-born brother and me do our homework every afternoon before it gets dark because there is no room except to lie down, close together, just as we did in the Kruger Park, in our place in the tent, and candles are expensive. Our grandmother hasn't been able to buy herself a pair of shoes for church yet, but she has bought black school shoes and polish to clean them with for my first-born brother and me. Every morning, when people are getting up in the tent, the babies are crying, people are pushing each other at the taps outside and some children are already pulling the crusts of porridge off the pots we ate from last night, my first-born brother and I clean our shoes. Our grandmother makes us sit on our mats with our legs straight out so she can look carefully at our shoes to make sure we have done it properly. No other children in the tent have real school shoes. When we three look at them it's as if we are in a real house again, with no war, no away.

Some white people came to take photographs of our people living in the tent – they said they were making a film. I've never seen what that is though I know about it. A white woman squeezed into our space and asked our grandmother questions which were told to us in our language by someone who understands the white woman's.

How long have you been living like this?

She means here? our grandmother said. In this tent, two years and one month.

And what do you hope for the future?

Nothing. I'm here.

But for your children?

I want them to learn so that they can get good jobs and money.

Do you hope to go back to Mozambique – to your own country?

I will not go back.

But when the war is over – you won't be allowed to stay here? Don't you want to go home?

I didn't think our grandmother wanted to speak again. I didn't think she was going to answer the white woman. The white woman put her head on one side and smiled at us.

Our grandmother looked away from her and spoke – There is nothing. No home.

Why does our grandmother say that? Why? I'll go back. I'll go back through the Kruger Park. After the war, if there are no bandits any more, our mother may be waiting for us. And maybe when we left our grandfather, he was only left behind, he found his way somehow, slowly, through the Kruger Park, and he'll be there. They'll be home, and I'll remember them.

SINDIWE MAGONA

Stella, Sheila and Sophie

STELLA

'Saw your medem's car drive off. Guess she's off to her Self Defence Class? Thought I'd pop over. Put the kettle on, girl. You know my Goat Food Woman, the fridge is full of leaves, seeds, growing things, and smelly rotting things. The milk is from beans, she tells me. Beans. I wasn't raised by people who milk beans. Beans have teats? Hey, if we're not careful, one of these days these strange women we work for will feed us snakes and frogs I tell you.

'There, the kettle is boiling. We have no tea or coffee in that house. "Those are drugs, Stella," my medem tells me. But my head tells me something else.

'Thank you, sure smells good. Thank you. If I had the money, I'd buy myself at least coffee and put it in my room.

'I don't know why I go on working for such a sour *suurlemoen* of a woman, you know? Believe me, I know we say a lot of bad things about stork legs, your medem, but at least with her, you know where you stand. Not that change-face so-and-so I work for.

'I'm sure you've seen her with her always-mouth-open-face: she could win a Mrs Sunshine Sweetest Smile Competition; couldn't she? Always cheerful she looks, hey? Don't be fooled. I could tell you things about that woman – things you would never believe.

'Gets me downright mad to think of the way she has used me over the years. But, I get her back; and then some more.

'She wipes her sunshine smile away when she talks to me and she wants to tell me something she knows is not nice.

' "Stella," she will say Thursday lunchtime, "can you please be back for dinner? I'm having visitors tonight".

'Now, tell me that is not cruel. Here's a woman who has seven days a week like everybody else. When does she choose to entertain? On the one evening a week she knows her maid is off. And her smile is there for everyone to see how kind she is.

'From the word go, I knew there was something not nice about this woman I work for. First day here, what do I find? There's her bath tub full of water. The same water she's just had a bath in. Her dirty water. Dirty from her own body. It is too dirty for her to put her hand in and pull the plug out. Can you believe that? This woman would leave her bath water for me to let it out?

'I'm not saying she should wash the tub. Hey, she's paying me to do that – O.K. But, you mean she can't let out her own, own water?

'And, if you think that's all I found in that tub you're wrong. There, swimming, afloat in that water of hers, was her panty … she'd left it in there for me to wash.

'What! Me? I taught her a lesson, that very first day. I took something, a peg, I think, and lifted that panty of hers and put it dripping wet, to the side of the bath which I then cleaned until it was shiny-shiny.

'You think she got my message? Wrong. Doesn't she leave me a note: "Stella, wash the panty when you wash the bath."

'What do you mean what did I do? I did not go to school for nothing. I found a pen in her bookshelf and found a piece of paper and wrote her a note too:

' "Medem," I said in the note, "please excuse me but I did not think anyone can ask another person to wash their panty. I was taught that a panty is the most intimate thing … my mother told me no one else should even see my panty. I really don't see how I can be asked to wash someone else's panty."

'That was the end of that panty nonsense. You see, she leaves the house very early. And at that time I worked sleep-out for her so we used to write a lot of messages for each other.

'And then every Sunday she's off to Church. Hypocrites, these white people are. Real hypocrites. Never practise what they preach.

'She goes to Church every Sunday, but when Master isn't here, you should see what goes on in this place. Then, she comes home early from work: "Stella, you can take the rest of the day off."

'What am I supposed to do with a half day off I didn't know I was getting? You think I have money to be running up and down for nothing? But, that doesn't worry Sunshine Smile. All she wants is that there's no maid to see her business. Hypocrite and *skelm* on top of it too.

'But me, I take the cheek out of her. I take the half day off she gives me. But I stay right here in my room and give myself a rest.

'And she doesn't know I need to rest. She thinks I am a donkey that can go on and on working. When I'm off, do you know she can think nothing of giving me a whole suitcase full of clothes. Don't think she's like other medems who give their girls their old clothes. Not this one, my friend. She wants me to sell those clothes for her.

' "Here Stella," the smile is bigger than the whole sky, "I'm sure your friends in Langa would like these clothes. Almost new."

'That's the woman I work for. It is not enough I work for her six to six, six days a week. On my half day off I must be working for her. Selling her second-hand clothes. She even pins the price on each one.

'Now don't think these almost new clothes have been dry-cleaned. You think she'd spend her money like that? There, I must carry clothes smelling her smell, carry them home and sell them to my friends. Of course, the one's the donkey can wash, those she sees to it that they *are* washed and ironed. She's not stingy with my strength, oh no!

'Then she'll take one of these clothes, look at it like it was a child going away, and say – "Take this one for yourself." That is how she pays me for carrying a heavy suitcase, making my friends laugh at me selling her silly clothes. You know, some-times I just save myself the trouble, take the clothes and pay her the money - bit by bit - until I've paid all of it. Then, when I find someone going back to the village, I send the clothes to my rela-tives there.

'You don't think you would be sick working for someone like this – making you work like a donkey and feeding you goat food? She really gets on my nerves. But I must be careful. If there's one thing that makes her out and out mad at me – it's when I'm sick.

'My sickness she never understands. She thinks I'm made of stone. She can be sick and when she's sick I must run all over the

place making her feel good: "Turn the TV on. Turn the TV off.
Make me black tea. Warm me some milk. I want dry toast. Give
me margarine. Go get me the newspaper. I forgot, *Cosmopolitan* is
out. Take all calls and write down the messages. Is that Joan? I'll
take the call."

'But I must never get sick. "You think I run a clinic here, my
girl?" That's what she says the first day I'm sick. Day number
two: "Maybe you should go home and send one of your
daughters to help."

'You know this woman has children the same ages as mine. I
must send my children here to help her and her children while
I'm sick. My children must miss school to come and make sure
their goat food is made, the beds are made, their shoes are
polished, their clothes are washed.

'I also discovered she doesn't like me to be sick and stay here.
I think she believes my sickness will jump onto them and kill
them all. It's all right for me to catch their germs when they are
sick. But my germs – that's a different story.

'Ho! White people! You slave for them. Slave for their
children. Slave for their friends. Even slave for their cats and
dogs. And they thank you with a kick in the back.

'Anyway, I must go. I'm making yoghurt bread over there,
the dough must be ready by now. Hey, thanks for the coffee –
now, I'm really awake.'

SHEILA

'Did I wake you up? You weren't already asleep, surely? A
young woman like you, you should go out a bit you know. Then
again, what nonsense am I talking … when would you go out
since this woman you work for keeps you in her kitchen so late.
What time did you knock off tonight?

'Let me tell you something – this *mlungu* woman of yours,
she's a real she-dog, this one. Can't keep a maid; changes maids
faster than other medems change their stockings. Every day you
look, there's a new girl hanging up the washing in this yard.
Sometimes a girl's gone before the maids from around here have
even had a chance to get to know her name. How long have you
been here now? A month?

'Whaaat! More? My God, she should throw a party. I don't know how many girls, except the last one ... that one stayed with her a long time ... I don't know how many girls leave her by the end of the first month. And some have left even before that; many leaving their money behind too.

'You laugh? I'm serious as the back of pyjamas. Ask her for a raise. You should. A month with a woman like the one you're working for is like a year in another kitchen. The woman really eats up maids.

'Tell me, how much is she paying you? No, tell me. I can tell you if that's what she paid the last girl she had. She's funny that way; her wage jumps up and down all the time. I think she looks at a girl first and thinks to herself – "Aha! this is a *plaasjapie*! ... straight from the bundus. Knows nothing about money. She's never seen more than one ten rand note at a time." If that's what she thinks of the girl, 'strue's God, that *arme* girl will not get more than two hundred rands a month from her.

'That's what she's paying you, isn't it? I'm sure it is. Since you're so shy and you're young, she'll say you have no experience; and then start to rob you, paying you peanuts.

'That's something else, hey? *Blerry* cheek! What do these white women think they mean – no experience. Do they suppose we eat our food raw?

'You know, these women really take themselves a bit seriously, don't you say?

'So, she'll say you've no experience and pay you chicken feed. Is she going to send you to school to get experience for washing her dirty clothes? Does she teach you how to iron her husband's shirts? Can she show you how to cook?

'They're so *lekker* useless with their big mouths you know, they make me laugh. And then they have the cheek to *nogal* say we are dirty. Where would they be without us forever cleaning after them so they can be clean? Pray to God up high, my dear, you never have the bad luck to get a job where there was no maid for more than a week. You'll see then who is clean or not. One day, two days without a maid, and they start to stink. The whole place stinks inside a week; even if they buy those tins of air freshener stuff. That has no hands like the maid. All it can do is just dye the air; and the smells just laugh HA HA HA; like, what the hell's going on? Who you think is frightened of your silly air freshener stuff? No, my dear, nothing can make the white people clean like the maid does. But of course, they can't say we are the ones responsible for them being clean. They never give us our due; but never mind, we know what's what. And that's what is important.

'Mine knows all the complaints: I'm sure she reads them from a book. She's always reading. That's how she got her eyes condemned, you know. Without her thick glasses she can't see her own finger if she holds it up right in front of her own face. But my mistakes, ooh, *that* she sees very, very clearly, my friend. She is always complaining about everything:

' "You didn't fold the carpet back to sweep underneath it."

' "You left the washing outside too long; you'll have to damp it now before you iron it."

' "Did you rinse these glasses? You must always rinse dishes otherwise we are eating soap with our food, And, another thing, you didn't get the eyes out of the potatoes you cooked last night. Use the back of the potato peeler, the pointed end, you know? That's why it's there."

'One *shushu* day, when I'm nice and well-done fed up, I'm going to tell her to her face. "Do it and let me see how you want it done. Show me."

'And watch her burn her hands or cut a finger off – if it's my lucky day. She doesn't know the front side of the iron. That will shut her big mouth and give my hot ears a rest.

'But, at least, she pays me decent, more or less, for this area, I mean. The women in this area don't pay that much. If you want good wages, you should go and work in Cape Town, in Constantia or Camps Bay or Llandudno. And then you will not see another maid until you are on the bus on your off days. But the women there pay a lot because they knows it's too far and their maids see only the baboons. So you get paid for living with *mlungus* and baboons, six days a week.

'Have you heard about how maids should not let the white women call them girls or servants anymore? And we should join a group to fight for our rights? Do you think that can happen? White women can learn not to call us girl? After all these years they're used to calling us anything they like – never mind if the girl likes it or not; never mind if it's her name or not? Do you really think they'll learn that? Me, myself, I don't think so. I really don't think so.

'Of course, I think it's a great idea. We should have maids' groups. The women we work for *must* have their groups too. Otherwise, if they don't have groups all over the place, how do they know how much they pay us? They talk about these things, the white women. They tell each other what to do about maids. Only we're too dumb to see they do this and control us. You can't even change your job because the next medem is just like the one you're running away from. They treat us the same because they know what that same is.

' "You can ask around if you want, ask any girl around here, you won't get higher wages." How can the woman say that if she is not sure? If she is sure, ask yourself, how can she know so much what the other medems in the area pay their girls? They talk about us, about how much to pay us, what food to give us, I tell you, we are their number one problem. If they talked so much about their children, they would not have the spoilt wild animals we have to look after. But no, they must talk about our pay.

'You want to laugh? Let me tell you how much the woman I work for pays me. After eight years. Eight years. And when I complain she tells me, "Go ask the girl next door how much Mrs Van Niekerk pays her. Go. And she's been with them twenty years." How does she know ... since these white women don't visit and chat to one another as we do?

'But yours, yours, my dear, is something else. Her stingy is not the everyday kind of stingy. Her stingy is a sickness. You know something? She even sells her old clothes to her maid. Be careful if she gives you anything. Make sure she is giving it to you not selling it. One of the maids before you ended up in jail. Three months' wages she owed your medem. Three months of her sweat. And she is quick to call the police, that woman of yours. Watch your step with her.

'If you refuse to pay for something – clothing you didn't even know you were buying or a plate you broke by mistake: one-two-three, the police van will be at that house. Four-five-six you'll be in the police cell.

'You know the police won't even let you open your dirty mouth. You think they'll let a kaffir maid say the white medem is lying? Anyone who thinks that is mad or blind. Be careful of her. Careful. She's a real snake in the grass.

'She also goes to the maid's room when you are not here: off.
She wants to see if you've stolen her things. Listen to that, hey!
Isn't she full of nonsense? Don't think she'll come to your room
because something is missing from her house. Oh, no. She'll
come to your room to see if she can find something there that she
thinks shouldn't be there; something too expensive for you to
buy. Then, of course, she knows you stole it since she knows she
pays you only so much and you can't pay for things that cost
that much more than she pays you. Her suspicion was right. She
finds a nice thing in your room – except, it is not hers. You have
nothing of hers in your room.

'Don't think that is the end of the story.

'Now, she has to think about where you stole the thing from.
If not from her, then from whom? She can't worry herself thinking since she was wrong when she came to your room to see
what you stole from her maybe you didn't steal anything from
anyone. No. She isn't going to say to herself: "*Ag, here God,*
maybe I'm wrong, maybe my *arme* girl's not a common thief,
maybe she's a decent girl and I am wrong." No. She'll say:
"Okay, this is not mine. But, this girl didn't buy it. Now, where
did she steal it from?"

'All these women we work for, they all think we are thieves,
finish *en klaar*. Nothing but thieves. All of us. All of them think
like that. But yours goes right into your room behind your back
and she *kraps* around there while you're away visiting your
people in Duncan Village.

'Did you say you have a little one? *Ag tog*, what is it? Oo,
foeitog, die arme skepsel, mus' miss you a lot, hey? Cries when you
go away on your off-days, neh? *Ja!* It's a shame they made a law
so now you can't bring your baby to stay with you where you
work. Used to be like that when I had little ones. Mind you, it
was a lot of work. You were like working two jobs at the same
time; minding your own and the medem's and then all the other
work also, hey. But I think it was still better that way. Now, you
have to pay someone else to look after your baby. And you can't
always be sure they're doing a good job either, hey? It's a shame.

'I was telling you how much I get after eight years with this
woman, mmh? And only January this year, too, she tell me …
"Oh, master say yes, we can afford to give you a little extra, my

girl."

'Big thing. She talk about it from New Year's Day already. Talk. Talk. Talk. Until I can't wait to see what this "extra" looks like. I'm like a child waiting for a Christmas box. I wait for this January end of the month, all excited. I wait and wait and wait. Well, let me tell you something, two month-ends are slower than a blind, cripple, fat old man: end December and end January. Those two are always trouble end of the months. You know why? 'Cos, you're *mos platsak* broke from buying all the Christmas *lekker goed* and then come the school fees and the *blerry* school uniforms. You see how one dress never lasts for more than a year? These uniforms! They make them like that, you know, from the factory. They don't want them to last 'cos if they last, where're they going to get their money from? *Skelms*, the whole shoot: teachers, principals, inspectors; they all get a share from the factory. The school buys so many uniforms this year, they get so much from the money the factory or wholesale make. Who pays for their "scrub my back, I'll scrub yours"? We poor domestic servants … Listen to me; here I'm the first to forget I'm not a servant anymore. I am a worker, I must remember that. I'm just as bad as these white women, hey? Can't teach an old dog new tricks, as they say: heh?

'Juslike! Look at the time. You know what I came here to tell you? Tomorrow night, we're all meeting at Sophie's kitchen. You know Sophie? Down by the Greek Café at the corner of this street and Lover's Walk. Her medem is the crazy one who lets us use her house for our meetings. No wonder she is always in trouble with the government.

'Anyway, that is where we are meeting tomorrow night. Nine-thirty sharp. And don't let this woman keep you away from the meeting. Tell her early in the morning, before she comes with her own nonsense about what she wants you to do for her in the evening, tell her you have to take food money to your baby as soon as you've done the dishes.

'In fact, let me phone you in the morning, mine goes bowling at ten. After I put the phone down she will ask, "Who was that?" They always want to know who was that when you get a phone. Then, you can tell her it was the woman who looks after the baby telling you she has run out of baby food.

'She'll let you knock off early then, maybe eight or half-past eight. Don't waste time then, rush over to my place and you can wait there till it's time to go to the meeting. If you wait here, she'll suspect something. And then she'll find something you didn't finish or didn't do well. That's the trick they always use to get a girl back into the kitchen in the middle of the night.

'My dear, I must go and let you go back to sleep. Can you imagine what we'll feel like tomorrow morning when our alarms go?

'One last thing – and then I really must leave you. Let me give you a tip. Friend, don't listen to anything the other maids tell you about the woman you work for. Or her husband. Sometimes people tell you things and it's because they're jealous, that's all. These maids here are full of rubbish. You just go on doing your work – keep your mouth shut. And when they tell you things – listen with one ear only. Many will be wanting the same – the very same thing they will tell you: "Don't do that." You listen to me.

'Hey, if you don't let me go, your alarm will start to ring and I'll still be here. Let me run.'

SOPHIE

'*Wethu!* Why didn't you come to the meeting last night? My *mlungu* woman has been asking me about that the whole morning. You know how she is – for her, whether she's at the Advice Office or back here in the house, it is all the same. She must be putting her nose in everybody's business.

'I told her you said you were coming and I didn't know why you hadn't showed up. "Are you going to find out? Or shall I?" she asks, knowing I don't like her talking to all the maids and their medems. That is how she ends up asking me things I don't want to talk to her about; and she gets me into trouble with the medems of these women. You would think a *mlungu* woman wouldn't worry herself about maid gossip: not the one I work for, *hay' mntakwethu.*

'How is legs of a bird these days? I hope she's sick and tired of changing girls. We are sick and tired of seeing new faces from her kitchen every day. But I think you use your head; I think you're going to stay with her, never mind her nonsense. That's good. You must think of your children.

'You know something? I think medem is worried your *mlungu* woman will mess you up the same way she messed up Imelda. You know Imelda can't take? That is why that nice young man who works at Groote Schuur Hospital changed his mind about marrying her. He had already sent his people to her people and they were talking *lobola* business.

'But he was worried. They had been trying to have a child. A long time they tried and tried. But no, she would not take. Witchdoctor after witchdoctor couldn't help Imelda. And you see, seeing she'd been pregnant before (that was before this man) she knew she could take. And the man has a child already. So he knew he was well. They tried and tried and tried. But no, Imelda couldn't take.

'A white doctor finally told them what's what:

' "When were you last pregnant?" he asks her.

' "*Hanana-hanana; hanana-hanana* ..., " Imelda is all over the place. Remember, the boyfriend-nearly-husband has not heard anything about – "Hey, by the way, once I was nearly a mother." Mmh? But only then did Imelda see the truth; see what had been done to her by her medem's doctor.

'That doctor her medem had taken her to when she had stopped, that doctor cleaned up Imelda. Cleaned her up not only for what was inside her then – but for all those that would have lain inside her in time to come.

'What could the poor man do after hearing that? What else did he want her for? If he'd wanted a bull he'd have bought himself one.

'My medem believes your medem is the worst medem because of that. Mind you, the woman I work for sees little good in medems – in white people generally. I tell you, that woman is a person, a human being although she is white. She feels for another person.

'You know she bought me the house I live in in Mdantsane? Mmhh? Do you know that? And this is not my mother's child I'm talking about. She is not my sister but a *mlungu* woman I just work for, that's all. But she buys a house for me. How many medems would do a thing like that for their girls? How many?

'Of course I pay for her being so nice to me. Oo, my friend, do I pay. You think a person who walks on two feet can do so much for you for nothing? Didn't the Indian man at the shop tell us: "Naasing for naasing and very littel forahh siiling"?

'I have a beautiful house with electric and hot water; but my shoulders and my knees are always burning: Work. Work. Work. I work until I drop each day.. *Whuwoo!* Get her money right out of my shoulders and my knees? That, she does. Oh, yes, that she does.

'Hey, I haven't seen Nombini for a while. How is she? What do you mean you don't know? I thought you two were cousins. No?

'I'm surprised she doesn't come here to your room every day. Nombini is a born manager, you know. She should have been a teacher or had twelve children of her own and a husband who earned enough so she could be with the children all the time bossing them.

'You didn't let her push you around, I see. That must be why she is not in and out of your room telling you what to do and what not to do. Right?

'Actually, now I remember someone, Stella I think it was, telling me only last week that Nombini had told her she had learned her lesson; she would never help anybody again because here she'd harboured you and now you were choosing other maids as friends.

'You know what I said to Stella? I said, "I bet my fish and chips on Saturday, Tiny didn't let Nombini treat her like her first born."

'I know Nombini by now. If you don't say yes to everything she wants you to do – you are no good, she'll say. To her, friend means "my sheep that follows me everywhere I go, does my bidding, and asks no questions".

'For a long time she used to bully me too. Not any more. Medem called her and scolded her. She told her to leave me alone or there'd be big trouble.

'How are your children? Did you manage to bring the younger ones you say you are worried about? Shame.

'Good news: Sylvia has found a Saturday afternoon char. And it pays well. That she-dog she works for pays her pocket money, as you know. But the good thing is that because she doesn't want to be feeding her over the weekend she gives Sylvia Saturday afternoon and all of Sunday off.

'Now, Sylvia has a job, Saturday afternoons. Fifteen rand, just for the afternoon. I told her not to take the money until month end. Sixty rand for four Saturdays. Isn't that good money? Really, students pay better and fuss less. These women we work for treat us like dogs, worse than their dogs, in fact. That is, most of them.

'I feel so bad when I complain about mine because she really is a good, good person. All the other girls complain about real things – real problems which are big. Their medems pay them little. They don't give them enough rest; one hour every day, half a day each week, and only two weeks of holiday for the year. I get all those things.

'Am I not the one all the other girls envy? "Oh, Sophie, God loves you, my dear. How did you get a *mlungu* woman who is so-oo good?" I listen to those words and my heart tells me there is truth in them.

'I can't complain like the other girls: I get good wages. When I have trouble at home, if she knows about it, she does something to help. She's cross if I don't tell her my troubles. So, you see, I really shouldn't complain.

'I tell myself I should understand her side when she's cross – like if I'm late. I can be late if she's not going anywhere or if she's not having people over. But if my lateness makes her look bad, then she could boil me alive.

'I have a good medem; that is the truth. But when she brings the whole Duncan Village here to dinner – and I must cook and wash dishes up to nine at night, then I complain in my heart.

'I complain very much although I say nothing to her. I complain because I don't know why she has to make me serve people who are black just like me. It is a punishment, I feel.

'I am a maid and they are teachers, and nurses, and social workers, and so forth. So what! I leave the location and its people and I come to work in a white woman's kitchen. And there she takes her kombi; takes it and goes to the location to bring it right back here to her kitchen. Is she going to serve this whole location she brings here? No. The maid is there. Now, I am a maid to serve black people.

'I am not saying she shouldn't like all people. But, really, it's not fair to make me sweat for people who are just as poor as I am. Not one of these people has ever given me a tip. Not a single

one. White people tip. Black people just sit there and eat and eat
and eat. I'm lucky if *one* says "thank you" to the cook. No manners, even if they are educated.

'I sometimes get so angry I think of leaving this woman. But
she bought me a house, a beautiful house in Mdantsane. It has
carpet on the floor. It has a real bathroom; a bathroom I can use.
How do you leave a *mlungu* woman who has bought a house for
you?

'I feel the house is cement; because of it I can never leave this
woman. Cement is like that. Never put your feet deep into wet
cement. If you do, make sure you get it out before the cement
dries. My cement has dried and both my feet are in this woman's
house. I am stuck – for the rest of my life. But, I shouldn't complain.

'I have a house; my very own house. How many of us can say
that; including the educated ones? Even after a long life of hard
work every day – how many of us can say: I have a house and it
is mine?

'When I think of just that, I am ashamed I complain in my
heart. Even if medem doesn't hear me complain, I shouldn't
complain: it is not right that I do. This woman is too good to me.

'I feel sorry not more white people are like medem. But there
are so few good white people that the bad ones swallow them
and we don't see the good ones. And then we forget they are
there.'

BHEKI MASEKO

The Prophets

The Durban-bound train was due on Johannesburg station at any time. The 'black' side of the platform was crowded while whites, accompanied by trolley-wheeling porters, moved freely at the other end of the platform.

MaNgubane and her grandson Nhlanhla waited anxiously keeping a close watch on the luggage that was clustered around their feet. At frequent intervals she put her hand between her breasts to feel if the knotted handkerchief in which she had put four hundred rand was still there. She knew that it was during a stampede that pickpockets turned pockets inside out.

She was on her way to Ladysmith to visit her late brother's children. She was also going to slaughter a goat and brew some beer to cleanse her brother's children as custom demanded.

On the station to see MaNgubane off were her grandsons Nhlanhla and Sipho. They were also there to help with the luggage and secure their grandmother a seat on the train. Amid the crowd that stood at the edge of the platform awaiting the arrival of the train was Sipho.

The train lights winked at the dark end of the platform causing the crowd to surge forward. Before it came to a halt people had already jumped in through the windows and doorways. And by the time it stopped most of the cubicles were occupied and bolted from within.

'Gogo, Gogo! Woza ngapha!' (Grandmother, Grandmother! Come this way!) Sipho called, waving from one of the train windows. MaNgubane and Nhlanhla grabbed the luggage and rushed to the window where they squeezed suitcases and bags through to Sipho.

Then the old woman squeezed her way through the congested corridor where her enterprising grandson had 'booked' her a seat.

Before long the final whistle blew and the train screeched out of Johannesburg station and on its long journey.

Sitting next to MaNgubane was a fat young man dressed in a white overcoat. He wore his beard very long, which gave him a somewhat priestly look. MaNgubane felt uneasy when he squeezed his fat body between her and another old woman.

'Sorry, my people,' he said, smiling apologetically. 'I don't mean to make you uncomfortable. You can see for yourselves that things are bad.'

Before the train reached Germiston the young man had set the cubicle into a lively discussion. He was a prophet from Evaton where he was born 32 years ago. His father was a priest of the Roman Catholic Church, but he himself decided to join the Zion Church because he had the holy spirit that gave him the power to prophesy.

'Right now I'm on a mission to Newcastle to kick out a tokoloshe that is giving the Khambule family sleepless nights. I want to give him a whipping that he will never forget. He'll never set his foot in that house again.' For emphasis he tapped his lap with his forefinger.

The train rambled on. Vendors forced their way in and out of the compartments to sell their snacks. The friendly prophet joked good naturedly with the vendors. And he proved to be generous too; he bought apples for everyone in the compartment. And helpful; each time someone alighted at some or other station, he would help take the passenger's luggage on to the platform.

'I once went to Koloni to get rid of a mpundula. This is an evil spirit sent by a person to someone to kill or frustrate another person by kicking him. This mpundula appears to the victim as a bird or a well-dressed gentleman but it is invisible to anyone else. The mpundula had already killed many members of the Majola family.'

The prophet paused awhile to munch a banana.

'That was one of the most difficult tasks God had assigned me,' he continued. 'That man who came to ask me to undertake the task said he was told by his late father to consult me because many prophets and traditional doctors had failed.

'I knew the undertaking was a risk. My own life would be in danger. But what could I do?' The prophet looked at each of his listeners in turn and wiped his sweating hands on a huge hand-kerchief. 'God had chosen me to do the job.'

'What happened then, my child?' asked an old woman clad in

a church uniform. She had been sitting in a corner listening attentively. 'Did you manage to stop the mpundulu?'

'Mama,' the fat man assured her 'nothing will stand in your way if you really believe in your God. I knew I would have to take precautions because what I was going to face was not child's play. I took all my herbs, called on all my ancestors and prayed to God to give me strength.'

'Mmm mm,' the old woman murmured in awe. The train trundled on.

MaNgubane and the woman clad in church uniform were so enthralled that they related their own experiences of faith. MaNgubane saw this as an appropriate time to tell the purpose of her journey.

The next stop was Newcastle. Some passengers gathered their luggage, others were already making their way down the corridors towards the exits.

Slowly the train crawled into Newcastle station until it finally came to a halt.

The prophet alighted and joined the throng of people on the platform. He waved cheerfully to his companions in the compartment who had further to travel.

Two hours later the train pulled into Ladysmith. MaNgubane joined the crowds of people hurrying to catch buses or taxis to various destinations.

She was struggling with her heavy luggage down the platform when someone touched her shoulder and called her by her name. When she turned around she came face to face with a neatly dressed man wearing a clerical collar. He was a total stranger to MaNgubane.

'Don't be surprised to hear me call you by your name, mama, the man said. 'I am a messenger of God. I have something very important to tell you, but can we move out of the way of these people?' Gently he took MaNgubane aside.

MaNgubane was in a state of confusion. Many things went through the woman's mind as she complied with the man's request. The man seemed harmless and looked every inch a priest.

'I am sorry to tell you that I have bad news for you, MaNgubane,' the man began. 'I had a vision for you for the greater part of the journey ... I did not expect to meet you so soon.'

'What bad news do you have, my son?' MaNgubane gasped, laying her hands on her enormous chest.

'Don't be afraid, mama,' the priest reassured her. 'Nothing on earth can defeat God who helps all those who believe in Him. First I must tell you that Isithunywa, God's messenger, has told me that you are MaNgubane from Senaoane in Soweto.'

'Hawu, hawu, hawu, my child! How did you know that?'

'Wait, mama, I still have more to tell you. You are going to KwaNomlebhelele to see your late brother's children. Your brother died in a car accident a year ago.'

MaNgubane was dumbfounded. She tried to say something.

'Quiet, mama,' the man raised his hands to silence her. 'The most important thing I want to tell you is that you will not reach your destination. The person who caused the death of your brother is after you. You will die the same way as your brother.'

'Oh my God,' moaned the old woman, shaking with fright. 'What have I done in this world?' Her knees felt weak. 'Please tell me what to do, my child. Help me, help me!'

'I can help if you really want me to, mama. But you are free to seek help elsewhere if you wish. I have done what God has assigned me to do.'

At that moment a woman approached them.

'Excuse me, mama,' she broke in, 'may I please have a word with the mfundisi?'

Before MaNgubane could say anything the woman turned to the priest.

'Mfundisi, I need your help,' she said desperately. 'Everything you told me on the train is true. If you don't help, I'll be in trouble.'

'Okay, my child,' the man assented, 'I shall help you.' He turned to MaNgubane. 'Mama, I'll need your co-operation to solve this child's problem. She will have to leave her luggage as well as everything that is metal or paper with you while I say a little prayer for her in the change-room.'

The young woman fished out some paper money from her bosom. She put it into a purse and handed it to MaNgubane. She also pushed her luggage nearer to the old woman before disappearing into a change-room with the priest.

MaNgubane waited anxiously, still thinking about what the priest had told her. Before long the young woman appeared looking relieved and contented.

'The priest says you can come, mama,' she said. 'He is waiting for you. I'm happy that I met this man of God. I don't know what I would've done without him.' She smiled.

'I wish he can help me too,' MaNgubane said, a note of despair in her voice. Trembling, she took a purse from her pocket. She removed the knotted handkerchief from her bosom and unclasped the pin that held it to her dress. She handed the handkerchief to the young woman and asked her to take care of her luggage.

'So you've come, mama,' said the priest as MaNgubane entered the change-room. 'Let's not waste time.'

He produced a bottle of water, uncorked it and ordered the old woman to open her hands. He sprinkled some water on her palms.

'Close your eyes now and pray silently to your ancestors to brighten your path.'

With her hands clasped before her, MaNgubane mumbled softly while the priest placed one hand on her forehead, the other on her chest, appealing to God to have mercy upon her.

'You may go now, mama,' the priest said presently, shaking her hand. 'God will surely be with you.'

MaNgubane left the change-room with a mixture of confidence and anxiety. She walked for some time before realising that something was amiss: where was the young woman with her belongings? She looked around to make sure that she had not passed the young woman. But the platform was almost deserted after the rush earlier and the woman was nowhere to be seen.

The money! The luggage! MaNgubane's heart was pumping fast. Her knees felt lame. Quickly she ran to the change-room. The priest was gone!

'Hawu Nkosi yami, imali yabantwana!' Her voice echoed on the station platform. She slumped to the ground, sitting flat on her buttocks, and sobbed.

A crowd gathered instantly.

'Kwenzenjani, mama?' someone asked.

'My children's money,' was all she could say.

Every now and then, through her tears, MaNgubane thought she saw the priest, the young woman. But every time she was mistaken.

JOEL MATLOU

Carelessman was a Madman

He used to chew his pillow until 3.30 a.m. The grass-eater who escaped mysteriously from a tribal cell in Winterveldt is still mad. I tell you, he used to chew his pillow until 3.30 a.m.

A man believed to be Mr David Letshwene, about 36, was found in Soutpan in the Moretele district on Sunday morning, near a tap, drinking water from the dirty furrows. When people saw him they became scared. After drinking some water he crawled on his hands and knees to nearby shrubs, where he started eating grass. The people realised something was wrong with him and caught him. His speech was unintelligible, but at some points he spoke sense. When they gave him food he refused it and said he was not allowed to eat anything that was cooked. They then put him in a cell, hoping to take him to the Temba Police Station the following morning. But when the time came he was nowhere to be found.

The man was not aggressive. He gave people no trouble. He spoke clean English. He was wearing Florsheim shoes, black socks, grey trousers and jacket, a Scotch tie, white shirt and brown hat. He was clean-shaven. Most people, when they saw him, said, 'This man is not mad, but he is careless and lazy.' But the man was a 'madman'.

The story of the carelessman-become-a-madman spread as far afield as Johannesburg, Cape Town, Messina, Botswana and Windhoek. Many people on the streets, in taxis, trains and buses, in newspapers, at home in towns and farms claimed that Satan had fallen in Hammanskraal. 'Satane o wele kwa Hammanskraal,' as they said in Setswana.

The carelessman lived in a two-roomed mud house with the top made of grass. Next to his huts was a big marula tree. His huts faced the bush next to Moretele stream, where he used to wash his clothes. His wife had deserted him long years ago because of his manners. No child was born from them, and no one knew his family.

The self-styled madman did no work. Many villagers hung around his place like a dark blanket to see what he would do next. When he was among people he was normal and he spoke clearly like any normal person. He was not a danger in public, like small children. His favourite meal was grass and water. People thought he was mad, but he was really facing up to his future. Even people who passed on the main road near where he lived stopped to have a look.

His house was full of self-made furniture, made from wood and planks. At night when he slept he chewed his pillow until 3.30 a.m. Then he got up and made a big fire outside his hut with big pieces of wood and he sang songs of winter using his two big teeth. He never walked with his feet, he used his hands and knees. To make fire and to clean the house, the furniture and his small yard he used his knees. He never smoked or drank. He was a gentleman without problems. But his future rested on only one thing: he was mad.

His doors were painted in six colours to attract people, mostly young children. Black, yellow, blue, green, brown and red were the colours. At the gates were fourteen red lights which used a car's battery and flashed at night. The place was like a hotel, except that inside it was the same as outside.

Because of his big morning fires people called him Satan. His hairstyle was like a Rastaman in Zimbabwe. At the back of his huts he had dug himself a grave. In one of his rooms was a self-styled coffin made of wood.

The man never stopped chewing his pillow. And each morning he walked for six kilometres without stopping or looking back where he had come from. He walked under the strong sun. For his journey he carried a 20-litre bucket full of water. He ate grass and drank water to the end of his lonely trip. Some people called him 'Cowman'.

He never took his trip down the road, he took his trip in the bush. He crossed rocky mountains and hills. Something was shaking trees in the bush, and when he looked nearer he saw a brown cow mooing because it wanted to be milked. Instead of milking the cow nicely the careless madman milked it on the ground. All the fresh milk from the cow went on the ground. And the man just chased the cow away and took on his trip again.

When he saw people he crawled like an animal, but when no person was near he walked on foot like an ordinary man. He uprooted grass and small weak trees and threw them anywhere he liked. When he was unhappy he walked backwards, not looking where he was going.

One day the old man known only as 'New Year' visited the carelessman. This old man was a priest, a Moruti. It was in the early morning when he approached the madman at his common hut. The madman was sitting on his stoep facing his gate, and he saw the visitor coming.

New Year greeted the man and said, 'Dumela Madala.'

The madman said, 'Also to you.'

They talked for a few hours without funny words.

The door of the one hut was wide open and everything in the hut was visible. When the priest looked inside he saw a dirty double bed and a few blankets. Under the bed was a 'nightpot' or 'passport' as it is known nowadays. (Many South Africans also call it 'serua'.) The nightpot was a 10-litre tin. On the floor were plenty of pieces of cloth, which looked as if the rats had been busy chewing them. The priest looked at the man and said, 'Why are these pieces on the floor?'

The man replied, 'At night when I sleep I chew my pillow until 3.30 a.m.'

Priest: 'Why do you chew?'

Madman: 'This is my best "night chappies".'

The priest never asked more questions than answers. He started to talk about the Sunday Church. He opened the Bible for the man at Mark, chapter 7, verse 7. When the priest read the first verse the man stood up, and jumped high, and screamed the Word of God. His eyes were wide open. Time and again, as the priest read, the man shouted, 'Hallelujah! Amen!' He sat down and started to concentrate on the priest. Everything was going correctly and he was giving the priest no problems. When the priest spoke he wrote down the verses on a piece of paper.

At 11 a.m. the priest invited the man to the church. The man prepared himself and they left. When they entered the church-yard the people were already inside the church singing slowly. The priest opened the wooden door and they entered. In the church there were many people; adults, children and babies were there. The man never gave people any problems. He spoke

sense like any other person. During the singing he never said a
word. He was a gentleman among gentlemen.

But his stay in church made him change his mind. He stood
up nicely and walked to the door and opened it. People thought
he was just going to the toilet, but the truth was far from that.
The madman kneeled down at the back of the church and started
eating grass faster than ever. After a while somebody came out
of the church to drink water. When he approached the tap he
saw the new member of the congregation crawling out of the
churchyard. He called to the man, but no answer was heard.
This church member then went inside and spoke to the priest
quietly in his ear, and the priest sang a song and came out to
investigate what was going wrong. When he checked outside the
yard, the man had already eaten the ground. He had disappeared. The priest became worried, because he had told the
members of his church that the new gentleman would be bap-
tized today.

The madman was far away from the church and he was never
seen there again. Back at his huts he lit his candle during the
day, at twelve o'clock on a Sunday. He started to read his Bible
loudly as if he was fighting with a woman, but the madman was
alone. After reading two verses he started chewing his Bible into
pieces, until his jaw became tired. The candle was still burning
and he did not care. In the house the candle's heat was very
strong, so he chose to stay outside on his rocky stoep, where the
snakes were living. Outside he started talking with his hands,
and he took off his shirt and jacket and threw them on top of the
hut, and started dancing slowly.

People were watching him, some were using their cameras.
The carelessman didn't care.

When he entered his hut again he found that the burning
candle was finished and there were no candles left. He started to
hit the wall of the hut and throw all the furniture outside. People
were laughing at the madman, and no one helped him. No one
called the police, or the fire-fighter, or even the strongest men
from the village. No one helped the lonely man, although they
could see that he was mad.

He broke down his furniture and burned down his one hut.
No one helped.

'Ag shame, arme skepsel,' said an old Ndebele woman standing next to the unburned hut. 'Ag toggie tog tog.' This woman was so old she even had an artificial third leg, which we call 'stick'. She wanted to help, but she did not know how to start helping, because the madman was very strong and wild enough.

While the people were looking at the damaged hut the man crawled into the bush and entered into the river fully clothed. People were screaming and some were laughing when the man swam and moved with the river. The man just disappeared with the water and was never seen again. He had left everything behind. The grass-eater was buried by Moretele River.

VUSI BHENGU, GOODMAN KIVAN, NESTER LUTHULI, GLADMAN 'MVUKUZANE' NGUBO and NOVEMBER MARASTA SHABALALA

The Man Who Could Fly

This story was written during a creative-writing workshop run by Astrid von Kotze. The authors were students of a course run by the Culture and Working Life Project at Natal University. Von Kotze provided a skeletal outline of the plot and the authors wrote different 'versions', as if by different narrators, which were later combined.

I want to tell you the story about a man who could fly. No, don't laugh! I have not eaten the *ntsomi* root, nor am I insane.

After leaving school I decided to visit my uncle down at Umtanvuma river to assist him with looking after his cattle and to lend him a hand in the mealie-fields, before going to the mines.

Indeed, I strode the hills and valleys until I reached my destination at dusk. Mind you, the countryside where my uncle lives has its own history. No, don't worry, I won't tell you the history of my uncle's countryside, I will get to the man who could fly.

When I was about to enter my uncle's yard what an extraordinary thing happened! The wild dogs were yelling and barking at me in such a strange rhythm I had never experienced before. What frightened me most was how the dogs were let loose and that no one dared to come out of the hut to rescue me from those savages.

Faced with that horrible dilemma, I forcefully entered the yard and what a tussle I had with the dogs! I was pounding, kicking and doing whatever I could to quell the fury of the dogs. Yes, you may laugh! The tussle for power between me and the dogs continued for quite a while. I finally forced my way to the door of the big hut while the dogs were pulling me with their big jaws.

Eventually I yelled for help and was rescued. I asked my uncle why it had taken such a long time and he explained that his country had been enveloped by a cloud of fear because of the vigilantes who were rampaging and killing innocent people. Therefore no one had had the courage to come out into the darkness to look at what the dogs were barking at.

The following day I was in strength to go to the field to hoe. The day was cool and calm. The vultures were gliding high in the sky. Small birds sang sweet melodies.

I began with my job of hoeing and while I was sweating I heard a strange rhythmic noise like the galloping of horses. As I turned my head to look I saw a man running as if he was fleeing the anger of pharaoh's warriors. As I was about to ask who he was and where he was heading to, a horde of heavily armed men emerged, in a violent mood, hunting him down.

'How can this man escape from these savages?' I asked myself coldly. 'Why do they want to kill him?' Seeing that the victim was about to be mauled, I felt a cold chill running down my spine. At that moment the man was no longer running, but just wobbling as if he was drunk.

There was no mercy in the eyes of the vigilantes, as there was no hope in the eyes of the prey. But just as the attackers were assured of getting the victim a miracle happened. The man flew like a bird up to the sky.

You laugh, my friends – but the vigilantes asked their feet to carry them away in different directions. They, too, ran as if they had wings, their weapons scattered all over the ground.

I myself tried to run as fast as I could but I was just wobbling and paddling as if I was wearing gumboots in a mudpuddle. When at last I managed to reach the nearby bush I had to relieve myself.

When I regained my strength I decided not to look and see what had happened to the man who flew to the sky but to go straight to my uncle's house. But when I related the story to them they just laughed and thought I was telling lies. Even the dogs rattled outside as if they laughed at me.

The next day my uncle decided to go with me because he thought that I was lazy or bewitched. Indeed we undertook the journey to the mealie-fields and we saw a group of people yonder the river at the extreme end of the bush. But the man who flew we could not see.

* * * * *

On that sunny day, I decided to park my car along the side of the road. Taking my camera, I jumped out. My aim was to take some pictures of that area which was looking more green in that summer season.

I was still looking around when suddenly I heard the sound of voices shouting somewhere in the fields. I took a sharp focus on the spot where the voices were coming from. Not very far from me a terrible thing was taking place. I quickly put two twos together, and realised the situation.

A certain black man was running like a springbok away from a group of men who were chasing him with axes, assegais and pangas.

'Oh, this violence is still continuing. I don't know what's wrong with these black people. Killing each other every day. Just look at those weapons, absolutely dangerous, but all the time they are claiming them as traditional ones. Or probably it's their tradition to use them in killing each other. Just look, they are even shouting, showing that they are enjoying what they are doing. Let me take some pictures. But nonsense! Everybody has seen pictures of this thing all the time in newspapers,' I thought to myself.

When I looked again the men were right on his heels. But then I suddenly saw a wonderful thing which I had never before witnessed in my life. I saw the victim lifting up his body, leaving the ground and flying into space.

'Hey, what's happening now?' I asked myself with amazement. But then I remembered that our garden boy, James, was always telling us unbelievable stories about incidents which occurred during their faction fights. He said that they were using some herbs, which they call *muti*, which was preventing them from getting injured by bullets.

'Maybe this is one of those magics!' I wondered shaking my head. I watched him until he was beyond the hill. 'But why are these fools still running and following him?'

I didn't take pictures of that area after all. I just went to my car and drove off, thinking about what I had seen.

* * * * *

'Earth, make me a hole to disappear into.
Things are bad outside!
Holediggers that never sleep, come!
Elephants that grind everything, come!

What is happening in this world?
What is happening in this country?

Ancestors, when are you going to remember us?
Because we trust in you,
Do you still visit the Lord?
Aren't you close to Him?
Here we are dying of violence!

My children are finished!
My sisters are finished!
My brothers are finished!
The same thing goes for my wife.

What is happening in this world?
What is happening in this country?

Earth make me a hole to disappear into.
Things are bad outside!
Holediggers that never sleep, come!
Elephants that grind everything, come!

Please help!
The spring winds are blowing me away.
Ancestors, are you the same as Noah's pigeon?
Do you still visit the Lord?

Please run and tell Him the story:
Your grandchildren are dying!
Hawu! Do you still remember me?
I thought you had long forgotten me!

Please pass my greatest gratitude
To that unseen man!

Now I've got wings!
I am a bird with wings!
Remain behind with your spears!
Remain behind with your assegais!
You satans with degrees!
You holediggers who never sleep!
You elephants who grind everything.'

* * * * *

I was walking through the fields when I heard a voice calling
me. It was my boyfriend, Mpo. I asked him why he was running
and he said that the vigilantes wanted to kill him.

I called him to come to me so that we could pray together. I
believe God is going to help us when we look in His face. And so
I started to pray and called His name: 'God please help me and
my boyfriend! You've got the power and no one can help me in
this case except you. Please enter my heart and my boyfriend's
heart and dwell.'

The next minute my boyfriend flew away to the sky and disappeared. The vigilantes came over to me and asked me what
had happened to the man who had been with me. And I
answered, 'He is in heaven. If you want to follow him you must
pray to God. He is the helper.' The vigilantes were too scared to
say they were trying to kill my boyfriend. So they started to ask
me how to pray to God and I explained to them that God said,
Thou shalt not kill. So they must not kill each other. They kept
calm and were so amazed about what had happened in front of
them and they also heard my preaching.

Then afterwards when I was still praying, and after the
vigilantes had gone into the bush, I saw my boyfriend coming
back. He came to me and he also became a born-again like me
because he saw the power of God. He explained that it happened
like he was dreaming. He praised the Lord and thanked him.

* * * * *

'I think everybody is ready for action as we are hiding here. As soon as we see him walking there along the road, we immediately attack him,' I said with anger, reminding my group.

Mpungose whispered that he wished the man had already approached because he wanted to stab him several times on that big mouth he's always shouting with, boasting around.

'O.K., let's wait and see,' I responded. A few minutes passed by and on the road we saw him walking.

'There he is,' nearly all of us said simultaneously and jumped off, running towards him. He glanced behind and saw us. No one told him what to do.

Dube, an old athlete even during our youth days, was running closer and closer to him.

'You catch him until we arrive!' someone shouted among my group. 'Hhewuuuu ... today is today!' some of us were shouting.

Dube knocked a stone and fell down. I cursed him inside my heart but he quickly stood up and tried to run again. But he suddenly stopped and looked at his weapons to make sure that they were all still with him. Not taking any care of him we passed by. But very soon he was amongst us again.

Our victim was now getting tired and he was shouting, asking the animals of the field for help. We also shouted, calling him to stop. But he never did.

We were just really close to him, when he suddenly did a wonderful thing. He lifted off his body and flew into space.

'*Habe*, what is he doing now?' I asked loudly and we all watched him flying higher and higher.

We were still confused, when Ngcobo, a short coal-black bald-headed man whom we had left some distance away, reached us. With great anger he shouted to us, 'Hey, *madoda*, this donkey thinks that he knows, let us follow him!' He said that and took a small bottle of *muti* from his pocket. He shook it and poured some of its contents on the ground. 'He is going to come down here again, I'm telling you. Let's follow him.'

We didn't say a word but started running after that bird-like man. He flew beyond the hill. We ran also towards his direction. Beyond that hill we found him hanging on telephone wires.

'I've told you. You see where he is now? Not very long and he will be on the ground again,' Ngcobo said with satisfaction.

We shouted, calling him and swearing at him. Then a man

with tools arrived and stood at a distance. We didn't bother him.
But when we saw the police van approaching we dispersed.

* * * * *

When I was a child, here in this place, people used to fight and
kill each other. These wars were caused by arguments or fights
between people who believed different things.

One day the war was on in our area and people were dying
like ants. My family and I decided to leave the house that night
and go for hiding in the forest. At sunset we started our walk to
the forest where we were going to spend the night in order to
survive. On our way I got lost from my family. This was a hard
time for me because I couldn't call their names as my shout
would fall into the wrong ears, that is my enemies' ears. They
would catch me and kill me like an ant.

I was so tired of walking and I ended up being fast asleep in
the middle of the forest. My first night in this place was so bad,
as I had never slept in the forest before.

By the time I woke up, the sun was high up in the sky. I was
so frightened when I thought of those killers that if they saw me
sleeping there they would have killed me. But my only worry
was the separation of myself and my family.

I started looking for my family. I looked and looked but
couldn't find them, even when I went to look for them at home
there was no sign of them. I felt very bad because I didn't know
what had happened to them. I left my home to carry on searching for them in other places. When I was a long distance from
my home, I saw a group of people making a circle like a kraal.

I realised that they were part of my enemies, and I prayed as I
was sure that that was my last day. That day it wasn't a sunny
day but I felt hot and sweaty like I couldn't believe. I saw the
earth becoming small like a fish can, that time I just thought of
death and nothing else. While I was still in that state of confusion I heard a voice from the sky, it said to me that I mustn't be
frightened. Even though I heard that promise, I didn't believe
that I was going to survive as I was facing death. These people
were coming closer and closer to me and I knew very well that I
was going to die.

When they were only metres away from me something

unbelievable happened. A strong wind blew all over the place and these people were blown backwards, their weapons were thrown down. I felt as if something lifted me up to the sky.

After that I can't tell you what happened because I was like a corpse or a fainted person. Yes, I flew like a bird that day. But I did not enjoy myself because I was not conscious.

Slowly, slowly my memory returned as I was still flying up in the sky. When I looked at myself I realised that my head was facing downwards and my feet upwards, I was going down to the ground. When I arrived on earth I felt that someone was catching me and placing my feet on the ground. As I came down I realised that I was at home. I saw a lot of changes, like trees and grass, and it was clear to me that I had been away for a long time. I had long forgotten my brothers, sisters and my parents.

When I got home, my whole family was shocked, they all ran away from me except my mom who just came to me, touched me and realised I was not a ghost, I was still alive. They only believed that I was their brother when they heard me talking to them. My family was so excited and surprised when I explained what had really happened to me, about my flying. They gave me a warm welcome by organising a big party for me where they slaughtered a cow. They invited all the relatives and we had a nice day together.

* * * * *

One day I was called for a faulty telephone wire in the township. As usual I took my record book and toolbox together with my mobile receiver and left in my bakkie.

When I arrived I found that up on pole number 2234 a man with wings was hanging. Down near the pole was a group of men with dangerous weapons like pangas, axes and spears. I was frightened but I also felt irritated by the extra work: the man with wings was destroying telephone wires with his weight.

I felt cold all over and my feet and hands would hardly move to stop the bakkie. I stopped the bakkie quite close to the group and with eyes wide open from fear I asked, 'What happened to that half bird and half man?'

One of the vigilantes answered in a harsh voice. 'We don't know. Go and ask Unyoko, you blerrie fool.'

Looking fearful at the assegais made me keep on praying for my stomach which I considered as a first and soft target.

Suddenly the man hanging above us shouted in a crying voice: 'Hey, I am better off here. I'd rather be killed by telephone wires than by cowards or fools.'

I was confused and frustrated but managed to drive a little further on to the telephone booth. I took out my mobile receiver and phoned the manager. I took my time explaining the situation and problem to him but he just said, 'I know it is a Friday today but it is too early that you are so badly controlled by alcohol, the way you behave, man. Vusi, I have no time to be wasted by you. Get up and fix the lines before it is too late. There is no man with wings and there are no vigilantes there! Start your work and all the vigilantes will run away and the man with the wings will fly away. Good luck Vusi!'

I was very frustrated. When the manager put down his receiver on the other side I sat down, with tears hot in my eyes. He was so free that he could not understand my problem.

Three children came around. I heard them loudly saying, 'Hoo, what happened to the big bird up there?' One child screamed and said, 'What kind of bird is that, it looks like a human being.' Another said, 'Hey forget about the bird, what about those *impis* with pangas and axes, let us run away.' They ran away quickly.

One of the vigilantes said harshly, 'Zakewu, Zakewu, drop down from the tree.' The joke was quoted from the Holy Bible but by a vigilante, it was another case.

I thought to myself that maybe I was asleep and dreaming.

Suddenly, a police van came fast in our direction with dust from the street flying up. I do not know who called the police. The weapons were scattered all over the streets as the vigilantes were running away as fast as they could.

A white policeman asked me, 'What is taking place here?' I answered, 'I do not know. I came here to fix a faulty line! When I arrived I saw a group of men with weapons and that man up there with wings.'

Another white police directed his question to the man up on the lines. '*Wat makeer met jou? Wat is jou naam? Is jy 'n man of 'n dier? Praat, jou donner.*' He then took out his gun and pointing it at the man shouted, '*Praat man, of ek maak jou vrek.*'

I came to my sober senses and went out of the bakkie to listen to the story. The man on the wires looked down and cried loudly. He pleaded, 'Help me down and I shall tell you the whole story.'

After some argument, one of the policemen, a short fat white man, came out fast from the van with a saw and angrily began to saw at the pole. When it fell over he said, '*Kom hier, the job is klaar.*' The man fell down with a thud, and feathers from the wings scattered all over. The policeman took out sjamboks and gave the man a thrashing.

The weather changed suddenly, and it became cloudy but with some rainbows.

For 'Points for Discussion', see page 211.

BIOGRAPHICAL NOTES AND POINTS FOR DISCUSSION

MIA COUTO

Born in 1955 in Beira, Mozambique. In the early 1970s he moved to Maputo to begin medical studies but did not continue because of his involvement in the independence struggle. He became a journalist; he has been the director of the Mozambique Information Agency, and editor of the magazine *Tempo* and the newspaper *Noticias*. He has had collections of poetry and short stories published in Portuguese.

THE BARBER'S MOST FAMOUS CUSTOMER

1. Here's a 'people's story', coming straight out of a village community in Portuguese colonial Mozambique. The colonial oppressors are represented by the PIDE, Salazar's political police; they refer disparagingly to 'the one called Mondlane' (Eduardo Mondlane was the leader of the Frelimo movement in the years before Independence; he died in 1969). Yet the atmosphere of the story is bright, sunny, peopled by gentle characters who do no harm to anyone. What is this saying about the storyteller?

2. The people enjoy the barber's boasting. When he shows them the postcard of Sidney Poitier, the writer tells us, 'the customers cultivated their disbelief'. What does this mean? What do you think of the fine distinction they draw when one of them says: '... this one isn't even a lie. It's propaganda.'?

3. The pleasure in this kind of comedy comes from the fact that the barber's boastfulness and lies are what finally land him in trouble. It's the 'chickens coming home to roost' situation. Is the writer suggesting that it would have been better for everyone if the barber hadn't behaved in the way he did?

4. Look at the end of the story. Does it have a happy ending? Or do things turn sour? Why is Firipe Beruberu described as treading the sandy path of Maquinino 'for the last time'? In the final sentence, everything was 'waiting for the return of Firipe Beruberu' – but does he return?

Born 1948 Johannesburg. Between 1973 and 1978 he was a banned person in South Africa. In 1980 he won the Mofolo–Plomer Prize for his collection of short stories, including the brilliant novella *Waiting for Leila*. He has also published a novel, a play and two collections of poems. He was a manager for an international company in Johannesburg, and is the chief executive officer of the Kagiso Trust.

THE HOMECOMING

1. The references to Troy and Ithaca relate to one of the most famous journeys in all literature, that which Homer related in *The Odyssey*. Can you track down the significance of the two place-names? Do they serve a particular purpose here in this story?

2. The Newclare in which most of the story is set contained a mixture of people, separated, Dangor tells us, by means of a 'demarcation ... not one of race, but one of class ... The African bus-owner lived alongside the Indian shopkeeper and the Coloured artisan who ran his own business.' In the old days of apartheid, such areas were rich in the stuff of life which literature is made of. Look at Ahmed Essop's stories set in Vrededorp, Don Mattera's set in Sophiatown, and Richard Rive's and Alex la Guma's set in District Six in Cape Town. Why do you think such areas served as the backdrops for so many stories, novels, plays, poems? And why does Dangor make the point in this story of the separation based on class?

3. Did the ending come as a surprise to you? What might have led you to anticipate it? Why do you think Nicholas makes this decision? What will be the effect on his parents?

4. Look at the structure of the story:

* It covers less than 24 hours in the 'present', from his arrival at lunchtime to his buying his train-ticket the next morning.

* But it keeps flashing back to the past. Or, rather, to three different 'past's: Nicholas's travels in Europe (where he parts from his newfound friend Simon), the forced removal of people from Dikies Diek (when his friend Aaron leaves), and the weekend of the police-raid (when his friend Daniel is drowned).

* Inside that weekend, there are three distinct recountings: the sangoma-smelling-out (presumably on the Saturday), the

cricket-game and police-raid, and then the search for Daniel (these events on the Sunday).

How easy did you find it to move backwards and forwards in these time-segments and still know where you were? Why do you think Achmat Dangor has chosen not to tell this particular story chronologically?

5. What effect have the the two major events in his boyhood had on Nicholas's personality as we get to know it on his return to his home?

6. Would you guess there is a strong element of the autobiographical in this story? Why or why not?

AHMED ESSOP

Born 1931 in India. With a BA Honours in English from the University of South Africa, he has taught in various schools in Fordsburg and Lenasia. In 1979 he won the Olive Schreiner Prize, awarded by the English Academy of Southern Africa, for his short stories. He has published two collections of these, *The Hajji* and *Noorjehan*; as well as two novels, *The Visitation* and *The Emperor*.

GERTY'S BROTHER

1. Think how remarkable it is that the young man who narrates the story should say: 'You must understand that this was the first time I had ever picked up a white child.' What must he have felt at that moment? Do you think it's plausible, or somewhat far-fetched, that a young man, probably in his twenties and living in a city, should say this?

2. There is a kind of interplay in this story between something quite romantic, on the one hand, and a pretty squalid reality, on the other. Can you identify and define each of these two elements?

3. What lies behind the final words of the story: ' ... with the hackles of revolt rising within me'?

4. What do you imagine were the thoughts running through little Riekie's mind as he stood clutching the bars of the gate and hearing the old man shouting at him to go away?

5. The narrator of the story does not take a particularly active role in the events described. He's more of an observer than a participant. But one does get an idea of the kind of young man

he is. Sometimes this is just from the kind of language he uses. Think of a sentence like: 'The party got going and we danced, ate the refreshments provided and talked some euphonious nonsense.' How does he come across to you?

6. The South African critic and writer Lionel Abrahams has described 'Gerty's Brother' as 'astringently poignant'. Try to find out and decide exactly what he meant by that. Do you agree with him?

7. Some readers feel that Essop's stories never really 'end', they don't have a 'punch-line', or anything that 'clinches' things. Was that something that worried you in reading this story? Did it seem to end in an unresolved way? You can ask the same questions about any short story, of course.

NADINE GORDIMER

She was born in 1923 in what was then the small mining town of Springs, where she attended a convent school. She studied at the University of the Witwatersrand. She is South Africa's most distinguished and honoured novelist and short story writer. Her work has on occasion been banned in South Africa and then been unbanned. She has always lived in South Africa, rejecting exile. Among the many literary prizes Nadine Gordimer has won are: the CNA Prize (3 times), the Booker McConnell Prize 1974, the WH Smith Award 1960, the James Tait Back Memorial Prize 1972, the Modern Languages Association International Award 1981, the French award the Grand Aigle d'Or. In 1981 she was awarded the Scottish Arts Council's Neil Gunn Fellowship. In 1991 her long and distinguished writing career was crowned by the award of the Nobel Prize for Literature. She has been Visiting Professor at Columbia University, and has taught and been honoured by many universities worldwide. Among her ten novels are *A Guest of Honour*, *Burger's Daughter* and *July's People*. Her most recent collection of short stories is *Jump and other stories*. A book on her work is Stephen Clingman's *The Novels of Nadine Gordimer: History from the Inside*.

THE BRIDEGROOM

1. How do you imagine everyone (young man, Piet, new wife, work gang) will react and adjust to the arrival of the new person in their small community? The word 'community' seems oddly

appropriate. What in the story suggests it?

2. Gordimer takes her time in building the character of the young man: we gradually develop a full picture of him. What elements do the following details contribute to his characterization?

* 'Suddenly he gave a smothered giggle, to himself, of excitement.'

* '… he at once became occupied with the pure happiness of eating, as a child is fully occupied with a bag of sweets.'

* 'The young man gave a loud, ugly, animal yawn, the sort of unashamed personal noise a man can make when he lives alone.'

3. Gordimer's main character has oddly contradictory attitudes to people. He refers to his prospective wife as 'the girl'. He clearly has a certain respect and liking for Piet, but he refers to him as 'my boy' and 'that kaffir'. He enjoys the company and the music of the work-gang, but they become 'a raw bunch of kaffirs'. Can you understand and resolve these mixed attitudes?

4. In this story plot is clearly not of any great importance. Nothing much can be said to 'happen' in the course of the story. It's the setting up of the relationship between the characters that is important, and the establishment of the 'milieu' into which the new person is going to come. If I were to use the words 'warm, intimate, exclusive' to describe these things, and to suggest there's a potential danger here, would you see what I was getting at?

5. Perhaps the moment that carries some sense of foreboding is when we learn that the young man 'simply did not think at all about what the girl would do while he was out on the road'. It appears that she, too, has not thought about this. What could happen? And why has Gordimer not gone on to tell that part of the story? Why does she end the story the night before, with the young man 'ready for the journey'?

6. The young man's life could be said to be pretty empty and routine: would you say he was happy and contented? Do you think he will be in, say, six weeks' time?

THE ULTIMATE SAFARI

1. Now that you've read the story, look back at the travel advertisement that Nadine Gordimer has placed at the head of the story and from which she has taken the title. Why has she

used this particular advertisement to introduce this particular story? Try to find out the meaning of the word 'irony' as a literary term, and examine the terrible irony in the title.

2. It's obvious that Nadine Gordimer felt that this story needed to be told, that the world needed to know what was happening to thousands of Mozambicans in the late-80s early-90s. Why do you think she chose to write it as a short story, as a piece of fiction, with characters and a plot? Why not write it, in the way a journalist might, as a piece of documentary reportage? (She has written non-fictional pieces about Africa.) What's the difference in forcefulness, power, impact? How does all of this relate to Gordimer's own statement that: 'in a certain sense a writer is 'selected' by his subject – his subject being *the consciousness* of his own era.'

3. How can a woman almost 70 at the time of writing get inside the head and heart of a young girl of 9 at the start of the story, 11 at its end? Do you think Nadine Gordimer has found the right 'voice' for the girl, the right language, the right set of values, reference-points and interests?

4. There is 'away' and there is 'home'. The white female interviewer in the refugee camp asks for reactions to both. How differently are those two places (states of mind?) viewed by the grandmother and the girl?

5. Do you find it amazing that at the end of so terrible a journey, so devastating an experience, there is still a place for hope, for optimism, for a belief in a good future? What is the ending of this story saying about the young girl? And – a somewhat different and more dodgy question – what is this ending saying about the *writer*, who could have chosen a very different ending for her story?

XOLILE GUMA

Born in Swaziland. After taking his 'A'-levels at Waterford Kamhlaba School in Swaziland, he did a BA degree in Economics at the then University of Botswana, Lesotho and Swaziland, followed by an MA at the University of Toronto, and a Doctorate at the University of Manchester. He is now a Senior Lecturer in Economics in the Faculty of Social Science at the University of Swaziland. He is married to Lindiwe Sisulu, daughter of Albertina and Walter Sisulu.

AFRICAN TROMBONE

1. Try to determine exactly what the 'point' of this story is. Is it contained in the final paragraph of the story? Or is it framed in the second-last paragraph, in 'what he said to me with that trombone'? Is it the unfeeling superiority of the colonizer, as seen in the priest and the British ambassador's daughter? Are there still other possibilities?

2. Examine the use made of the pregnant young woman. She's clearly pivotal in the plot of the story: she provides the focus for the old man's clumsy compassion and his confrontation with the priest. But do we know enough about her to care? Do we need to know any more? Is it enough that she is there to serve as the life-death (or is it birth-death?) juxtaposition?

3. As an insight into immediately-post-Independence Southern Africa, this piece is somewhat unnerving. Who is to blame? With whom do you sympathize? How is one ever going to give rightful place and position to all these different and disparate influences in what now makes up modern Southern Africa?

4. Let's look at the role of the narrator:

* Is he the author? You can't know that, so you can't assume it. The author may be speaking through some sort of mask, or 'persona'.

* Is the narrator even male? In this particular story, the moment of encountering the pregnant woman seems to give sufficient clue. But don't necessarily assume that, if the author is male, the narrator will be male, or vice versa.

* Is the narrator a character in the story? He certainly moves through the action, but his involvement is pretty passive: 'I stood, pensive.'

* Christopher Isherwood once described his role as storyteller in these words: 'I am a camera.' That implies not only being the observer, but also directing the focus.

* Does the narrator have a personality? or is he a bland faceless 'camera'? What sort of personality comes across, for instance, in a sentence like this: 'The bus stop was opposite a church whose wares, not being amenable to advertisement by neon lights, were surreptitiously implicit in the mystical darkness which it exuded'? Can you draw up an 'identikit' of this young man by assembling small aspects of his character?

BESSIE HEAD

(1937 – 1986) She was born in the Pietermaritzburg mental hospital, her white mother having been admitted there by her wealthy family after a liaison with an unknown black man. She had a very difficult childhood, first returned by a white foster-family, then with a 'Coloured' foster-mother (whom she took to be her own mother), and then in a mission-orphanage. She trained as a teacher, and also worked for a time as a journalist (for *Drum* publications). After a failed marriage in Cape Town and some contact with political affairs, she was refused a passport and so left South Africa on an exit permit in 1964, and she and her son settled in Botswana. She was twice refused Botswanan citizenship and lived for some years as a refugee in Francistown. Eventually granted citizenship, she remained in exile in Serowe village until her death. She died of hepatitis at the age of 49. Her three major novels are all set in Botswana: *When Rain Clouds Gather*, *Maru*, and *A Question of Power*.

THE WIND AND A BOY

1. The title and the opening of the story show a preoccupation with the wind. The writer makes good use of it. How does she relate it to the boy's death? She doesn't say a word about the wind in describing the death, yet we feel its 'presence', as it were. You could say she uses the wind as a symbol – of what?

2. Bessie Head clearly eliminates the element of suspense from her story by telling us, well before the end, that Friedman is going to die. What do you think of that? Does it in any way weaken the story, or do you find it good in that she is not artificially 'manufacturing' an ending or manipulating our response to it?

3. Does the way Bessie Head has written the story prepare you for the last paragraph? Is the story a good fictional illustration of the sociological point she is making? Or does the sociological comment sound 'tagged on' to you?

4. The mix of African and Western cultures is put in a nutshell when Friedman asks: 'Is that a special praise-poem song for Robinson Crusoe, grandmother?' Is Bessie Head successful in her blending of the two cultural traditions? Is Friedman himself an instance of it – in name, with his bicycle, and in the manner of his death?

   5. Read other of the Botswana village stories of Bessie Head in her collections *The Collector of Treasures* and *Tales of Tenderness and Power*. Would you say that she treats the interaction between cultures as a major theme? In what ways would you say that her having lived first in South Africa and then living in exile in Botswana contributed towards this?

                                    LUIS BERNARDO HONWANA
Born in 1942 in Maputo, Mozambique. His political involvement with Frelimo in the years before Independence led to his imprisonment and subsequent exile in Portugal, Switzerland, Algeria and Tanzania. He returned to Mozambique to work in the cabinet of the Prime Minister of the transitional government. He has served the Frelimo Government as Chief of Staff, and then as Minister of Culture until 1992; he now devotes himself to writing and various cultural enterprises in Mozambique. His younger brother, Fernando, was Special Adviser to President Samora Machel and was killed in the same air-crash as the President.

THE HANDS OF THE BLACKS
   1. How do you react to the various notions and explanations offered to the boy? Are they offered as entertaining fancies? Is the child simply being fobbed off? Are they part of a fabric of prejudice which becomes the 'accepted wisdom' of a community?
   2. What colour is the boy: is he a black native Mozambican, or a white expatriate Portuguese colonial, or is he a native village peasant of mixed-race? What evidence can you find in the story to support your answer? Does it matter what race he is?
   3. What about his mother? Is her race of any significance? What impressions of her personality do you form as you read about her encounter with her son? How are you affected by the explanation she offers her son?
   4. What do you make of the last sentence? Why is she crying? Is it still – or only – the 'laugh-until-you-cry' that the boy first told of? Do you think the author wanted this last sentence to be somewhat ambiguous? If so, why?

ALEX LA GUMA

(1925 – 1985) He was born in Cape Town, educated at Trafalgar
High School and the Cape Technical College. He worked as a
clerk, factory-hand, bookkeeper and journalist. He was a member of the South African Communist Party until it was banned in
1950; he helped to organize the Kliptown Congress of the People
in 1955 and to formulate the Freedom Charter. Between 1956 and
1960 he was one of the 156 accused in the Treason Trial. In the
1960 State of Emergency he was detained for 5 months; in 1962
he was banned and placed under house arrest for 5 years; during
this time he was again detained under the 90-day and later the
180-day regulations. In 1966 he left South Africa, lived in the
United Kingdom for some years, and then settled in Cuba,
where he was the ANC's Chief Representative for the Caribbean
and Latin America until his death. In 1969 he was awarded the
Afro-Asian Prize for Literature. His novels and short stories have
earned him a secure place as one of South Africa's foremost
writers; among his major works are *A Walk in the Night*, *The Stone
Country* and *Time of the Butcherbird*.

NOCTURNE

1. Two worlds meet: Alex la Guma's tough world of gangsters
and petty criminals leading more or less derelict lives, on the one
hand, and the refined sophisticated gentility of classical music,
on the other. Stated that way, it sounds pretty corny. Did it strike
you that way as you read the story? Or has La Guma interested
you sufficiently in the personalities involved to see it in less
obvious and simplistic terms than that?

2. Writing in the late-50s and early-60s, La Guma – or his
publishers – did not print expletives and violent language.
Hence the odd-looking 'Where the — you been?' and the even
odder ' "—", Moos said.' In his novella *A Walk in the Night* La
Guma takes the route of using the words 'muck' and 'mucking'.
Ernest Hemingway actually printed the word 'unprintable' in
place of the expletives. It is difficult now for these techniques not
to be funny, used as they often are in situations anything but
comic. Today, where violent language is required and is
authentic, it is printed, even though it may offend some readers.
What do you think is best? In reading aloud in a classroom situation, some people do not like speaking the expletives, and so it is

accepted that they simply omit them. You should discuss all of this together in an attempt to reach an agreed settlement that tolerates different views and sensitivities.

3. La Guma's stories are all strongly structured – he liked 'beginnings' and 'endings'. This one uses a witty verbal punch-line to clinch the story. Were you happy with it? Did it give the story a satisfying conclusion? Perhaps most important, was it fitting, apt, authentic, and not contrived, clever, inappropriate?

DORIS LESSING

She was born Doris May Tayler in 1919 in Iran (then Persia), and grew up in Zimbabwe (then Rhodesia) from 1924. Twice married and divorced (her second husband was a communist German exile Gottfried Lessing), she and her son left Rhodesia, first for Cape Town and then for the United Kingdom in 1949. She arrived in London with her now-legendary 'twenty pounds and the manuscript of her first novel'. This was *The Grass is Singing*, a great critical and sales success. She re-visited Rhodesia (then the Federation) in 1956 (her account was published as *Going Home*); she was barred entry into South Africa, and then declared a prohibited immigrant in both Rhodesia and South Africa. She is a welcome and frequent visitor to present-day Zimbabwe (these visits are recounted in her most recent book, *African Laughter*). She has had a most distinguished career in Europe as a novelist and short story writer. She has been awarded the Society of Authors' Somerset Maugham Award, and also the Prix Medici. Her African novels include the 'Martha Quest' novels, and her African short stories are collected in two volumes, *This Was the Old Chief's Country* and *The Sun Between Their Feet*.

TRAITORS

1. What are the elements in this story that make it unmistakably 'African'? See if you can identify an atmosphere, an 'ambience', that could only be African.

2. What do you make of the small episode with the old woman? Lessing only hints at things: 'wheedling voice', 'She sauntered off, swinging her hips', 'that taunting laugh'. As she is working through the personae of the two small girls, the nearest she can take us is: 'That laugh, that slow, insulting stare had meant something outside our knowledge and experience.' Fill

out the hints and insinuations.

3. The play-acting the girls do when they take turns to be Mr Thompson staggering about and 'shouting abusive gibberish' has a point, a significance, in the story's structure. It becomes important later – when, and why? Could Lessing have left it out?

4. The story has in it childish excitement, it has the elements of mystery, danger, fear of the unknown, and the youthful confidence in conquering and taking over the unknown. But perhaps the main interest in the story lies in the fine threads of inter-relationships it so subtly examines. What do I mean by this? The relationship between mother and father? between mother and daughters? between father and daughters? between Mr and Mrs Thompson? and, finally, between each of them and the girls?

5. Do the final paragraphs – sectioned off as they are – help to clarify why Lessing has called the story 'Traitors'? Who are the traitors? Who is being betrayed? In what way?

6. Lessing says about this story: 'It is about two little girls. Why? It should have been a boy and girl: the children were my brother and myself. I remember there was a short period when I longed for a sister: perhaps this tale records that time.' Can you answer Lessing's question? How would the story have been different if it had been about a boy and a girl? As you read the story, did you have any sense that it was autobiographical?

SINDIWE MAGONA

Born 1945 in Gungululu, a village 18 km from Umtata. As a small child, she moved to Blaauvlei, near Retreat in Cape Town, and later to Guguletu. She worked as a domestic worker, studied to be a teacher, and was granted a bursary to study at Columbia University in the United States. She has degrees from the University of South Africa and Columbia University, and has been awarded an Honorary Doctorate from Hartwick College, New York. She works at the United Nations. Her stories are published as *Living, Loving and Lying Awake at Night*.

STELLA, SHEILA AND SOPHIE from WOMEN AT WORK

1. It's a famous cliché about white South African women that all they can talk about when they meet one another is their maids. What has Sindiwe Magona done with this truism? Does it

come off, does it work? Can these three recountings be said to make up a short story? (They were not written as such; there are another six sections to what Magona called 'Women at Work'.)

2. The three different women are very carefully characterized and differentiated – so, too, are the 'medems'. Can you give a quick thumbnail sketch of each of them?

3. This characterization is particularly interesting in Magona's use of language. Each has a quite distinctive tone of voice and conversational manner. Can you pinpoint some of the verbal characteristics each woman has?

4. Sheila is good at manipulating situations as well as language. She starts off saying, 'Did I wake you up?' She acknowledges later, 'My dear, I must go and let you go back to sleep.' But by the last paragaph, how has she succeeded in re-interpreting this? Does she do something similar in the second-last paragraph?

5. The vocabulary of 'Maids and Madams': all three women call the women they work for 'medem', though it's interesting to see that Sophie uses 'the mlungu woman' as often as 'medem'. What about Stella's and Sheila's and Sophie's use of 'girl' or 'maid' or 'servant' or 'domestic worker'? To what extent have they themselves been 'conscientized' about the appropriate or inappropriate, acceptable or unacceptable labels?

DAMBUDZO MARECHERA

Born 1952 in Vengere Township in Rusape, Zimbabwe. He went to St Augustine's Mission School, and then to the University of Rhodesia, from which he was expelled for political activity. He was awarded a scholarship to Oxford University, and was sent down before completing his studies. He was awarded the Guardian Fiction Prize for his collection of short stories *The House of Hunger*. Between 1976 and 1982 he was a writer with no fixed employment or abode in Oxford, London, Wales, Sheffield, West Berlin. In 1982 he returned to Zimbabwe, where he found himself equally at odds with the new government and with society. He lived more or less as a vagrant for some years, and died of AIDS in Harare in 1987. In 1988 the Dambudzo Marechera Trust was founded, to collect his unpublished work and promote its publication, and to honour his memory by encouraging young writers. His published works include *Black Sunlight*, *Mindblast*,

The Black Insider and *Cemetery of Mind*.

THE CHRISTMAS REUNION

1. This is Marechera in a bright, sparky mood. He was often a lot more abrasive – and weird – than this! He always loved language, turning it inside out, making it slide about on the page and do exactly what he wanted it to. Can you offer some indications of this enjoyment of language that he had? And any hints of the abrasiveness and weirdness I mentioned?

2. Can this piece be seen as an illustration of an argument chasing its own tail in ever-increasing circles – and finally managing to bite it? Could it have gone on any longer, or has he successfully judged how much we could take?

3. Why is seven-eighths of the story one continuous paragraph? Was Marechera right in separating off the final paragraph?

4. The tensions and the interplay between being a Southern African and being part of a cosmopolitan Western world were never far from Marechera's mind. Has he worked things out in a satisfying way in this piece?

5. In the last paragraph he says: 'Then – god help me – I'll ...' Those three dots represent the closest the goat comes to having its throat cut. (They could also represent the first time the narrator pauses for breath!) How is it possible that three dots can come to hold this much significance? Has the writer led you, guided and directed you, to this suggestion? In the event, it's probable that some other action altogether takes place inside the space of those three dots: what might that be?

BHEKI MASEKO

Born in 1951 in Newcastle. He has worked as a truck driver, and in the laboratory of the Chamber of Mines. He now lives in Soweto, and is currently studying for a BA degree by correspondence. His stories were frequently published in *Staffrider* magazine, and have now been collected as *Mamlambo and other stories*.

THE PROPHETS

1. This very direct and straightforward story has the great strength of authenticity. Do you doubt that what Maseko des-

cribes here happens every day to some unfortunate trusting person? What's interesting is the extraordinary lengths the con-artists go to to effect their trick. Or do you think that this was an unplanned spur-of-the-moment opportunity?

2. Analyse the victim and the means of the deception: do they make the theft worse than if the victim had been a young, more sophisticated person and the means something other than religion? If so, why? Isn't theft theft, fullstop?

3. Is there something lurking inside you that secretly admires the con-artists? Or do they not display enough charm or cleverness or audacity to overcome your disapproval?

4. Look at the final picture Bheki Maseko gives of the old woman: 'She slumped to the ground, sitting flat on her buttocks and sobbed.' Is it possible to do it any better than that? What is it that is so right about the verb 'slumped'? What is introduced with the participial phrase 'sitting flat on her buttocks' that is exactly appropriate here? Can you dispense with the word 'flat'? Try re-writing that sentence five different times, changing whatever elements you can think of, and see if any of your versions is better than Maseko's.

JOEL MATLOU

Born in 1953 on a farm in the Magaliesberg mountains. He now lives in Mabopane. His stories were originally published in *Staffrider* magazine, and published as *Life at Home*.

CARELESSMAN WAS A MADMAN

1. Joel Matlou is one of the writers to whom Njabulo Ndebele refers in his essay 'The Rediscovery of the Ordinary'. He says: 'What is common to these writers (Joel Matlou and Bheki Maseko) is that they are storytellers, not just case makers. They give African readers the opportunity to experience themselves as makers of culture. They make it possible for people to realise that in the making of culture, even those elements of life that are seen not to be *explicitly* oriented to resistance, are valid.'

2. In this story, Joel Matlou is certainly describing someone who could be thought of as quite extraordinary and whose behaviour is extraordinary. Yet, in what tone of voice does Matlou tell of these things? Is this a part of what Ndebele is getting at – the stories of the ordinary people, which perhaps a more sophisti-

cated writer might not tell? Treating the extraordinary as ordinary – is that part of the secret of this kind of storytelling?

3. Rumour, pretty far-flung by the sounds of it, made out of the carelessman a 'Satan fallen in Hammanskraal'. However, Matlou seems to be at pains to draw a prtrait of a harmless person, with no guile or craft in him: 'He gave people no trouble', 'He was a gentleman without problems', he even painted his doors in different colours 'to attract people, mostly young children'. What causes people to spread rumours, to call a man 'Satan'? Could one reason be that 'his hairstyle was like a Rastaman in Zimbabwe'? (Incidentally, a *Staffrider* article of the time, about Bob Marley's visit to Harare, was titled 'A Rastaman in Zimbabwe'.)

4. 'People thought he was mad, but he was really facing up to his future.' What does Joel Matlou mean by this? And how does the sentence relate to the sad end of Carelessman, from his slow dance to his disappearing 'with the water' and not being seen again?

DON MATTERA

Born 1935 in Western Native Township, he spent some of his childhood years in Durban and in Sophiatown. He played football for the Sophiatown African Morning Stars, became a gang leader, then adopted the Islamic faith, and has become deeply involved in many community projects. Between 1973 and 1982 he was a banned person; and for three of those years was under house arrest. He lives in Eldorado Park with his wife and their eight children. He has published a collection of poems *Azanian Love Song*, an autobiography *Memory is the Weapon*, a collection of short stories *The Storyteller*, and a children's book *The Five Magic Pebbles*.

DIE BUSHIE IS DOOD …

1. This story comes out of the dark days of the mid-80s to late-80s, and, sadly, in one guise or another, can be replicated many many times. What elements in the story place it so specifically in this small segment of time?

2. As Johnny lies dying he says something. Someone in the crowd says: 'I think the Bushie wants to be taken to his own people.' Then Johnny is able to say to his friend Mandla: 'Comrade, take me home. I want to go to my mother's house.' Is

there a subtle difference between these two things? They may mean more or less the same thing; do they signify something different? Can you account for the assumption the man in the crowd makes?

3. The writer has constructed a tragic irony to carry the unhappy message of the story. And that is the family row that erupts that morning before Johnny leaves home. Do the arguments Joe and the boys' mother put forward carry any weight? Should Johnny have listened to them? What prevents him from hearing what they are saying?

4. Don Mattera has left it to you to imagine how Johnny's mother and brother would react to the news – or, worse, the sight – of Johnny's death. Can you think and feel yourself into the personalities of each of them, and give an account of your response? What part would be played by the last thing you said to Johnny?

5. How much of the story's power comes from the fact that the author has written it so simply, directly and briefly? Would a longer, more complex treatment, offering more contradictory viewpoints and positions have made a stronger or weaker story? A truer story?

GCINA MHLOPHE

Born in 1960 in Hammarsdale near Durban. She attended high school in Transkei and began writing poems and stories in Xhosa. She has achieved success as an actor, theatre director, author, and, above all, as South Africa's finest storyteller. Her published play *Have You Seen Zandile?* was an international success, having toured and been staged on all five continents. She has also published a number of books of stories for children. Her poems and stories have appeared in two collections of writing by South African women: *Sometimes When It Rains* and *Lip*.

THE TOILET

1. The experiences of this young woman deserve thinking about. How extraordinary do you find it that she has to 'hide' in her sister's room? How humbling or distasteful does it seem to you to have to spend hours sitting in a public toilet? Your responses will clearly be affected by your own life situations and experiences and those of members of your family or friends. Are

you pleased that Gcina Mhlophe decided to share these things in this story, or would you rather not have to confront and think about such issues?

2. The growing, developing spirit of the young woman is evident. Do you think she was fortunate to have had an interest in acting and in reading as well as a talent for writing? How different would her life have been had she not had these interests and talents? This raises the whole issue of consciousness and sensitivity in situations of oppression – is it 'better' to know and feel and suffer your oppression, or to be uninformed and 'unaware' of it and so perhaps less sensitive to it?

3. This is an autobiographical piece. It's good to know that Gcina Mhlophe has become internationally successful in both the areas of the theatre and of literature. Would she have been able to write this story, in this way, if she hadn't achieved renown and fulfilment?

4. What about the attitude of the writer in recounting this time of her life and development? Do you detect bitterness and resentment? Acceptance and a shrugging off? Even an affectionate recollection and acknowledgement that there were good things in these situations?

5. How did the small thumbnail sketch of the white 'Madam' strike you? When you heard her calling for 'Irene', did you predict that she would be this kind of person? Is this what one calls a caricature, a cartoon version of the real thing, a character written only two-dimensionally and not viewed 'in the round' as a complex being? Have a look at the priest in Xolile Guma's story 'African Trombone', and ask if he's a caricature, despite there being nothing funny about his actions and behaviour? What's the danger in drawing caricatures?

CHARLES MUNGOSHI

Born 1947 in Manyene near Chivhu, Zimbabwe. He was educated at All Saints School, Daramombe School and St Augustine's Mission School. He has worked for the Forestry Commission as a research assistant; as a clerk in a bookshop; as an editor at the Literature Bureau. Some of his works were banned in Rhodesia, but have now been printed in Zimbabwe. He has won several awards, including PEN awards in 1976 and 1981. He was a literary director of Zimbabwe Publishing House for some time; and is now writer-in-residence at the University of Zimbabwe. His published works include the novel *Waiting for the Rain*, the short story collections *Coming of the Dry Season* and *Some Kinds of Wounds*, and two books of Shona stories for children.

SHADOWS ON THE WALL

1. The writer does not give us anyone's name: we never know who the boy is, and he refers only to 'father', 'mother' and 'this other woman'. What is the effect of not individualizing the people involved? What would be different if they all had names given to them?

2. A static story, it does not require us to be overly concerned with any particular sequence of events, but rather with states of mind and the hidden consequences of family interactions. Does it still qualify as 'a story'? Does it find a place in your own definition of what 'a short story' is?

3. The story is full of images, doubtless because of its preoccupation with shadows. In just the first two paragraphs there are four different similes, all images of the shadows the boy sees ('like a black scarecrow ...', 'like a ghost ...', 'like the presence of a tired old woman ...', 'like that creepy nameless feeling ...'). Read the rest of the story, watching out for the succession of images. What is the cumulative effect of these images?

4. Focus now on one image, that of the two dove nestlings. Apart from its being a boyhood recollection that made a strong impact, the writer uses it again in another way in the story. Examine it carefully and decide how he uses it. Can it stand up to the function the writer wants it to serve? Does it fit the other circumstance closely enough?

5. This story is unrelieved in its oppressiveness and sadness. What has the writer managed to inject into it that makes us interested to go on reading it? (That assumes, of course, that we did go on reading it!) What part does its shortness play in this regard?

NJABULO NDEBELE

Born in 1947 in Western Native Township, he grew up in Charterston Location in Nigel. He holds a Master's degree from Cambridge University and a Doctorate from the University of

Denver in the United States. He was known initially for his poetry, and then became one of South Africa's most influential short story writers. His book of short stories, *Fools and other stories*, won the Noma Award for the best book published in Africa in 1984. He was Professor of English and Pro Vice Chancellor at the National University of Lesotho; then Professor in the Department of African Literature at the University of the Witwatersrand; in 1991-92 he was Deputy Vice Chancellor at the University of the Western Cape; in 1993 he became Rector and Vice Chancellor of the University of the North. He is the national President of the Congress of South African Writers. He has published a collection of essays on literature, *Rediscovery of the Ordinary*, and a number of children's books, including *Bonolo and the Peach Tree* and *Sarah, Rings and I*.

THE MUSIC OF THE VIOLIN

1. What are the different pressures acting upon Vukani? Is he coping with them? As a result of the events of this particular evening, will he cope better in the future?

2. Vukani's mother is clearly very preoccupied with – not to say obsessed by – white 'standards' and white 'culture' and pretty well everything 'white', even white recipes! Why do you think this is? Does it connect with Vukani's father's seeing government policy as a means of 'uplifting the Black nation'? Are these parents living proof of the success of apartheid? Or are they battling desperately against apartheid, are they trying hard not to fit the stereotype that official policy projects?

3. What did you feel about the extraordinary moment when Vukani's mother berates her own children as: 'Kaffir children! That's what. Always ungrateful!' Is that believable?

4. There seems to be little point in asking 'Who's to blame?' for the unhappy situation in Vukani's home. Ask, rather, who earns your sympathy and understanding? And then ask, further, who *deserves* your sympathy and understanding? You may come up with some surprising names.

5. Why does Doksi not seem to have the sort of problems Vukani has?

6. Njabulo Ndebele has managed a small miracle in the final paragraph in precisely pinpointing, with great economy, the momentous emotions succeeding one another within Vukani's

mother. Can you trace these emotional upheavals, as her focus moves from Vukani and Teboho to Vukani's father to the visitors until she retreats into her bedroom and then into herself? Do you understand the full import of the last sentence?

RICHARD RIVE

(1931 – 1989) He was born in District Six in Cape Town, and was educated at Trafalgar High School. He held a Bachelor's degree from the University of Cape Town, a Master's degree from Columbia University, and a Doctorate from Oxford University for his thesis on Olive Schreiner. He spanned the whole of South African literature from the mid-50s to the 90s, from 'Protest' literature through 'Black Consciousness' to the present. His short stories are among those South African stories most anthologised in overseas collections and have been translated into many languages. He was for many years the Head of the English Department at Hewat Teacher Training College in Cape Town. He was murdered in his home in 1989, just two weeks after completing his last novel and less than two weeks before the opening of his dramatization of *'Buckingham Palace', District Six*. His short story collection is *Advance, Retreat*, and his three novels are *Emergency, Emergency Continued* and *'Buckingham Palace', District Six*.

RAIN

1. There are several ways of building atmosphere. You can see one technique at work here: the writer selects, sifts, narrows down to those sights, sounds, smells, human types, activities, that will all add up to the atmosphere-mosaic she or he wants. Take any one of those elements (sights, sounds, smells etc.) and read this story again, noting how Richard Rive has made use of it as a technique in putting his story together.

2. Look at the way Rive has built the character of Solly. If you make an 'inventory' of his physical and apparent social attributes under 'plus' and 'minus' column-headings, he appears to be a thoroughly unpleasant and unfriendly personality. Yet – is that really so? What may suggest otherwise? What part is played by his refrain of 'Close 'e blarry door!'?

3. Have a technical look at the first paragraph. Apart from the first sentence, it is made up of what are, grammatically, 'non-

sentences'. There may be a subject but there is no main verb, only a succession of participles (eg reflecting ... overflowing ... squelching). Why has Rive done this? Can you find other instances in the story where he does the same thing, and to what effect?

4. In this story people address one another in a very abrupt, rather insulting way. This is seen in the dialogue of the characters, and so cannot be taken to reflect attitudes held by the author. What does this tell you about the sort of people who use words so unthinkingly? Now look at the way individual people in the story treat one another (rather than what they say to one another) – what force is there behind the way they address one another, in fact? Does it play any part in the actual intercourse between the people?

5. Why has Rive chosen to call Solly's shop the 'Grand Fish and Chips Palace'? Is it the right kind of name?

NORMAN RUSH

Born in 1933 in San Francisco in the United States. He was educated at Swarthmore College, Pennsylvania, and started writing stories while working as a dealer in antiquarian books. From 1978 to 1983 he lived and worked in Botswana as the Co-director of the Peace Corps operation. He now lives near New York City. His collection of stories about aid-workers in Botswana is titled *Whites*, and he has recently published a novel.

BRUNS

(The writer is American; the narrator is an American aid-worker in Botswana. For the story to be authentic, the conventional North American spelling has been retained.)

1. This is a good story through which to examine attitudes and prejudices:
  * The Boers towards the Bakorwa and towards Botswana
  * The Bakorwa towards the Boers
  * The Boers towards the chiefs
  * The chiefs towards the Boers
  * The Boers towards Bruns
  * Bruns towards the Boers.

2. Above all else, there is the viewpoint of the narrator, as representative of the volunteer American aid-workers. All of the

attitudes and prejudices enumerated above are seen through the filter of her own attitudes and prejudices. Can you identify her views on each of the groups of people involved?

3. Using this sort of narration means the writer does not need to pretend to any objectivity, and can assume a particular 'tone of voice' for added effect. How would you define the narrator's tone of voice? The last section of the story – perhaps even the last five words – may be your strongest clue.

4. Look at the last section, starting with the words 'The ruin is absolute'. Is it feasible that all of these consequences could result from this one incident? Is the writer 'piling it on' for effect? Is the effect comic?

5. This is the only story in this collection by someone who does not come from Southern Africa (although Doris Lessing was born elsewhere she spent all her formative years in Southern Africa; Ahmed Essop, also born elsewhere, has lived all of his life in Southern Africa). So Norman Rush can give us 'the outsider's view'. But, to do that in a way that is authentic, that rings true, he has to know Southern Africa really well. What sorts of things in this story suggest that Rush has observed, seen, heard, listened carefully, accurately and sensitively so that he knows his Southern Africa thoroughly and truly?

ZOË WICOMB

Born in 1948 in the Cape. She completed an Arts degree at the University of the Western Cape and then studied English Literature at Reading University. She lectured in English at Nottingham, and was writer in residence at Glasgow and Strathclyde University in 1990. She now lectures in the Department of English at the University of the Western Cape, specialising in feminist and cultural theory.

ASH ON MY SLEEVE

1. Old friends meet over a distance of years and continents. Can you feel the awkwardness between them? And yet the way familiar phrases and privacies slide their way into the conversation? This story could be described as an exercise in imaging the fine threads of tension that run between people in any relationship of some intimacy. How accurately, and acutely, has

the writer captured the tensions between, for instance, Frieda and Desmond?

2. As also a study of newly affluent middle-class suburbia, what is this story saying about the effect, the influence, that settled success can be said to have? You will notice that Moira refers to the 'estate' they live in as against the 'townships' such as Manenberg.

3. Moira is very clear-thinking in her analysis of where the so-called 'Coloured' people fit into the scheme of things. Because of this analytical tidiness, are you surprised by her inability to cope in the kitchen, for instance, or by her forgetting her children's bedtime?

4. What do you make of the episode with the people out in the back garden? What element does Zoë Wicomb introduce into the estate-household here? What is Moira's involvement, and why does she keep it from Desmond?

5. This story comes from a collection called *You Can't Get Lost in Cape Town*. Zoë Wicomb uses an interesting structural technique: the whole can be read as a continuous novel (doubtless strongly autobiographical?) with differently titled chapters; or, equally satisfyingly, each 'chapter' can be read as a separate short story, able to stand on its own without the support of the others. In theme, it connects with Achmat Dangor's story 'The Homecoming'; in structure, it pre-dates Joel Matlou's collection *Life at Home* (see the story 'Carelessman was a Madman').

6. Why the title?

VUSI BHENGU, GOODMAN KIVAN,
NESTER LUTHULI, GLADMAN 'MVUKUZANE' NGUBO and
NOVEMBER MARASTA SHABALALA

THE STORY ABOUT THE MAN WHO COULD FLY

1. This becomes an interesting experiment in changing perspectives: the same basic story-line, the same basic facts, but treated in very different ways. Identify what kind of person the narrator might be in each case, and see in what ways the narrator's identity affects what she or he sees and experiences.

2. What differences in structure, form and plot are also noticeable?

3. Of course, you (in the plural – or in the singular?) can also write such a story …

ACKNOWLEDGMENTS

The compiler and the publishers are grateful for permission for use in Southern Africa of copyright material in this book as follows:

Vusi Bhengu, Goodman Kivan, Nester Luthuli, Gladman 'Mvukuzane' Ngubo and November Marasta Shabalala: 'The Man Who Could Fly' from *Soho Square V* (Bloomsbury 1992), reprinted by permission of The Writers' Culture and Working Life Project Course, University of Natal. Mia Couto: 'The Barber's Most Famous Customer' translated by David Bradshaw in *Voices Made Night* (Heinemann 1986), reprinted by permission of David Bradshaw. Achmat Dangor: 'The Homecoming' from *Waiting for Leila* (Ravan 1981). Ahmed Essop: 'Gerty's Brother' from *The Hajji* (Ravan 1978). Nadine Gordimer: 'The Bridegroom' first published in *Friday's Footprint* (Gollancz 1960) and then *Selected Stories* (Penguin), reprinted by permission of the author; 'The Ultimate Safari' from *Jump* (David Philip 1991) and then *Crimes of Conscience* (Heinemann 1991), reprinted by permission of the author. Xolile Guma: 'African Trombone' from *Forced Landing* (Ravan 1980), reprinted by permission of the author. Bessie Head: 'The Wind and a Boy' from *The Collector of Treasures* first published in South Africa by David Philip 1977; and then Heinemann 1977, reprinted by permission from Heinemann Publishers (Oxford) Ltd. Luis Bernardo Honwana: 'The Hands of the Blacks' translated by Dorothy Guedes in *We Killed Mangy-Dog and Other Mozambique Stories* (Heinemann 1969), reprinted by permission of A.P. Watt Ltd. Alex la Guma: 'Nocturne' from *Quartet* (Heinemann 1963) © Blanche la Guma. Doris Lessing: 'Traitors' from *African Stories* © 1954 Doris Lessing, reprinted by permission of Jonathan Clowes (London) Ltd on behalf of Doris Lessing. Sindiwe Magona: 'Stella, Sheila and Sophie' from *Living, Loving and Lying Awake at Night* (David Philip 1991). Dambudzo Marechera: 'The Christmas Reunion' from *The House of Hunger* (Heinemann 1978). Bheki Maseko: 'The Prophets' from *Mamlambo and Other Stories* (COSAW Publishing

1991). Joel Matlou: 'Carelessman Was a Madman' from *Life At Home and Other Stories* (COSAW Publishing 1991). Don Mattera: 'Die Bushie is Dood ...' from *The Storyteller* (Justified Press 1991), reprinted by permission of the author. Gcina Mhlophe: 'The Toilet' from *Sometimes When It Rains* (Pandora 1987), reprinted by permission of the author. Charles Mungoshi: 'Shadows On the Wall' from *Coming of the Dry Season* (Zimbabwe Publishing House 1972). Njabulo Ndebele: 'The Music of the Violin' from *Fools and Other Stories* (Ravan 1983), reprinted by permission of the author, and Ravan and, for rights for Zimbabwe, by Shelley Power Literary Agency Ltd. Richard Rive: 'Rain' first published in *Quartet* (Heinemann 1963) then in *Advance, Retreat* (David Philip 1989), reprinted by permission of David Philip Publishers. Norman Rush: 'Bruns' from *Whites* (Paladin Grafton 1983). Zoë Wicomb: 'Ash On My Sleeve' from *You Can't Get Lost in Cape Town* (Virago 1987), reprinted by permission of the author.

Every effort has been made to trace and acknowledge copyright holders. Should any mistake have been made, the publishers apologise and will correct it in the next impression.

AFRICASOUTH PAPERBACKS PUBLISHED BY DAVID PHILIP

Africasouth Paperbacks was launched in 1983 with the aim of making available previously banned or neglected southern African writing. This series includes works of southern African literature that are otherwise available only in hardback or are out of print or not readily accessible.

'... a notable success story of contemporary publishing and deservedly so ... striking cover designs superbly produced series ...' (Gerald Shaw *Cape Times*)

Peter Abrahams **The Path of Thunder**
John Howland Beaumont **The Great Karoo**
Jillian Becker **The Virgins**
Douglas Blackburn **A Burgher Quixote**
Harry Bloom **Transvaal Episode**
Guy Butler **Karoo Morning: An Autobiography 1918-35**
Jack Cope **Selected Stories**
CJ Driver **Elegy for a Revolutionary**
Perceval Gibbon **Margaret Harding**
Gerald Gordon **Four People**
Charles Hooper **Brief Authority**
Dan Jacobson **The Trap** and **A Dance in the Sun**
Alex la Guma **A Walk in the Night**
Alex la Guma **The Stone Country**
Peter Lanham/AS Mopeli-Paulus **Blanket Boy's Moon**
Hugh Lewin **Bandiet**
Ethelreda Lewis **Wild Deer**
Todd Matshikiza **Chocolates for My Wife**
Z K Matthews **Freedom for My People**
Es'kia Mphahlele **The Wanderers**
Alan Paton/Krishna Shah **Sponono: A Play in Three Acts**
William Plomer **Cecil Rhodes**
William Plomer **Selected Stories**
William Plomer **The South African Autobiography**
Richard Rive **Emergency**
W C Scully **Transkei Stories**
Pauline Smith **The Little Karoo**
Wole Soyinka **AKÉ: The Years of Childhood**
Sylvester Stein **Second-Class Taxi**
Can Themba **The Will to Die**
Ngugi wa Thiong'o **Petals of Blood**
Elizabeth Marshall Thomas **The Harmless People**

AFRICASOUTH NEW WRITING PUBLISHED BY DAVID PHILIP

The Africasouth New Writing series aims to introduce new authors who have not yet established a following, and also includes works published for the first time by well-known writers.

Michael Cope **Spiral of Fire**
Menán du Plessis **A State of Fear**
Menán du Plessis **Longlive!**
Bessie Head **The Cardinals With Meditations and Stories**
Denis Hirson **The House Next Door to Africa**
Ellen Kuzwayo **Sit Down and Listen**
Sindiwe Magona **To My Children's Children**
Sindiwe Magona **Forced to Grow**
Sindiwe Magona **Living, Loving and Lying Awake at Night**
David Medalie **The Shooting of the Christmas Cows**
Sembene Ousmane **Niiwam** and **Taaw**
Mewa Ramgobin **Waiting to Live**
Richard Rive **'Buckingham Palace', District Six**
Richard Rive **Emergency Continued**
Hjalmar Thesen **The Way Back**
Miriam Tlali **Footprints in the Quag: Stories and Dialogues from Soweto**
Etienne van Heerden **Mad Dog and Other Stories**
Ivan Vladislavić **Missing Persons**
Ivan Vladislavić **The Folly**

ALSO COMPILED BY ROBIN MALAN AND PUBLISHED BY DAVID PHILIP:

EXPLORINGS

A Collection of Poems for The Young People of Southern Africa
Poems to introduce young people of southern Africa not only to the world out there but also to one another. As Robin Malan writes, 'Perhaps nowhere is the sense of Who am I? and Where do I fit in? more urgent and complicated than in southern Africa now.' Poets as varied as Sipho Sepamla, Seamus Heaney, Musaemura Zimunya, Douglas Livingstone, e e cummings, Sylvia Plath, Achmat Dangor, explore such questions so that their readers can see from different angles, perceive, contrast, compare …